HORRORS

EERIE TALES OF SUPERNATURAL HORROR!

WITCHES TALES

HARVEY HORRORS

C O L L E C T E D   W O R K S
WITCHES TALES
V O L U M E   F O U R

December 1953 - December 1954

Issues 22 - 28

Foreword by
James Lovegrove

PS
Artbooks

HARVEY HORRORS
Collected Works
WITCHES TALES
Volume FOUR

FIRST EDITION
FEBRUARY 2013

Bookshop ISBN 978-1-84863-518-0
Slipcase ISBN 978-1-84863-519-7
Traycase ISBN 978-1-84863-533-3

Published by
PS Artbooks Ltd.

A subsidary of PS Publishing Ltd.
www.pspublishing.co.uk
award-winning, UK-based, independent publisher of SF, fantasy, horror, crime & more...

Copyright © PS Artbooks 2012

Originally published in magazine form by Harvey Publications, Inc.

Foreword © James Lovegrove 2012
Painting of James Lovegrove © Adam Brockbank 2012
Article on Tom Hickey © Peter Normanton 2012

Printed in China

design communique

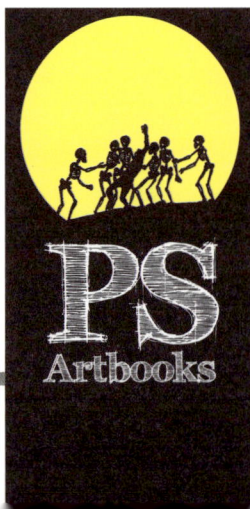

PS
Artbooks

ACKNOWLEDGEMENTS

As much as the Publishers would like to take
all of the credit for this wonderful volume,
they had some help along the way.
Thus we would like to express our warmest thanks
to the following for efforts above and beyond the call of decomposition.

James Lovegrove
http://www.jameslovegrove.com.

Adam Brockbank
http://www.adambrockbank.com

Peter Normanton
http://fromthetomb.blogspot.com/

Heritage Auction Galleries
http://www.ha.com/c/index.zx

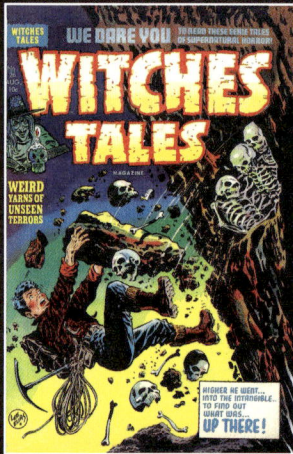

James Lovegrove - Original illustration by Adam Brockbank

Tomb Of The Unknown Writer

Foreword by
James Lovegrove

It's crazy to wish you were older, but whenever I read 1950s horror comics, I do.

I wish I had been born twenty years earlier and had stumbled across copies of **Chamber Of Chills**, **Tomb Of Terror**, **Adventures Into The Unknown** and the like at the age of nine, ten, eleven. The sweet-spot age. The impressionable age. The golden age.

I would have lapped them up. I would have devoured them. I would happily have allowed my pliant, still developing brain to be warped by the feverish dementia of the strips they contained. I would have applauded and appreciated them in the way that only a kid can – unthinkingly, unquestioningly, uninhibitedly. I wouldn't even have minded the sleepless nights they doubtless would have caused. Braving unseen fears in the bedroom dark is one of the true heroic feats of childhood, and the victory is incalculably gratifying.

Not that I'm complaining, I hasten to add. My 1970s upbringing had its share of decent horror comics. Weaned on the Marvel reprints of the old, milkily sanitised Atlas-era horror anthologies, I soon graduated to stronger, spicier stuff. "Monster superhero" series such as **Tomb Of Dracula**, **Werewolf By Night** and **The Living Mummy** were my gateway to the black-and-white Marvel/Curtis magazines – **Vampire Tales**, **Monsters Unleashed**, **Tales Of The Zombie**, **Dracula Lives!**. These boasted great artwork from Marvel's stable of Filipino talent – Tony DeZuniga, Sonny Trinidad, Alfredo Alcala, Rudy Nebres – and sometimes great stories to match.

Then came the discovery of the Warren titles which the Marvel mags were trying so desperately to ape: **Creepy** and **Eerie**. This was the motherlode, the throbbing jugular, the atom-bomb epiphany. They showed explicitly the gore which the Marvel magazines, for all that they were liberated from the constraints of the Comics Code by their size and format, still only hinted at. They had truly twisted twist endings. They were vile and violent and giddyingly, exhilaratingly **wrong** – and therefore just right.

One tale continues to linger with me. It was from an issue of **Creepy**. Unaided, I do not recall which number, but internet research tells me it was #85. The story was called "Orem Ain't Got No Head Cheese", and it was about a family of cannibal hillbillies – you know, **those** guys – who get more than they bargain for when their latest victim turns out to have terminal brain cancer. The tumour somehow takes over all the bits of offcut and offal that the hillbillies have tossed into a slops pit. It assembles a crude, squamous body which slithers out to exact awful vengeance.

Icky, nasty, perverted, sick. Brilliant. I was maybe twelve when I read it. The copy of **Creepy**, with its spectacular Abominable Snowman cover by Ken Kelly, had been doing the rounds at school, but I honestly felt I was the only person on the premises who genuinely relished it, understood it, needed it. Thirty-four years on, "Orem Ain't Got No Head Cheese" remains an indelible part of the makeup of my own head cheese. It was a classic horror-comic squib as good as any in these PS Artbook collections – as transgressive, as weirdly moralistic, as unforgettably skin-crawling.

Something else about it that I cannot recall unaided is who wrote and drew it. Again, the internet comes galloping to the rescue: the script was by Bill DuBay, the art by José Ortiz.

Warren titles at least credited their creators. That courtesy was denied the people who purveyed the majority of the content of Harvey and ACG horror comics.

Which brings me to my sort-of point.

As a diehard, old-school Marvelite, I grew up taking the splash-page credits box for granted. I had no reason not to assume that everyone involved in the making of a comic, even the letterer, automatically received acknowledgement in print for his or her contribution. Nowadays we're used to seeing the entire editorial staff, the publisher, even the publisher's dog name-checked on the frontispiece or at the back of every issue and reprint collection. It was not ever thus. In the good old bad old days, comics creators were low-waged, deadline-doomed hacks who were treated like slaves and, like slaves, were deemed unworthy of the dignity of a name. They toiled in obscurity, paid by the page, receiving a dismal flat-rate fee for the sweat of their brow. We know now who they were largely thanks to the diligent efforts of comics historians who have trained themselves to recognise this particular person's style, that particular person's quirks.

The artists – pencillers **and** inkers – are almost invariably identifiable. But the writers? Not so the writers. Seldom are they remembered and named. Look at the credits in these volumes. How often is the writer of a strip listed as "Unknown"? Peruse the Grand Comics Database. See how many times the poor, lowly scribe of a Harvey or ACG strip is recorded only as a mere plaintive question mark.

It's generally accepted that most of the stories were penned by the anthologies' editors, men such as Sid Jacobson and Richard E. Hughes, along with the occasional slumming-it prose author such as Frank Belknap Long. The assumption must be that the remainder were banged out by jobbing nonentities who perhaps had once had an ambition to write the Great American Novel, only to see their dream founder on the rocks of ineptitude – or possibly the rocks of a whisky-on-ice.

Yet what if – **what if** – all these wonderful, mad, depraved, irony-laden supernatural sting-in-the-tale jobs were the brainchildren of one single man? What if there was only ever one Unknown?

Picture him at work at his desk. I say "desk" but it could just as easily be "packing crate" or "park bench" or "bar". Behold how he hammers relentlessly at his portable typewriter, filling up page after page with reanimated corpses, revenging revenants, frightened superstitious wives, ancient curse-carrying tomes, crumbling castles, deadly dream homes, bewitching zombies and zombifying witches. All these tales of mystery and imagination – all these visions – spring fully-formed like Athena from his head. One lone man originates them all.

His eyes are so bloodshot, their sclera show hardly any white, only overlapping webs of red. His hair is wayward and torn from the number of times he runs an agitated hand through it. He sweats. Oh, how he sweats. Great globular beads of perspiration cling to his skin, pearling his face. His collar is askew and his tie, half-undone, dangles round his neck like a hangman's noose.

Something drives him, some satanic goading impulse that will never let him rest. The tales keep coming. They have to. The next batch of commissions appears, as does the next batch of bills and mortgage interest payments. He meets demand. Meagre dollars slip into and through his fingers. He cannot stop.

He is haunted by language, hounded by fiction. Exaggerated punctuation marches past his eyes in a staggering parade.

The exclamation mark! Oh God, the exclamation marks!!!

Not to mention -- the double dashes.

And the ellipses...

This book, like its companion volumes, stands as tribute to the tireless efforts of poor, penurious Unknown. It is the slab of headstone marking his final resting place. With its solid binding and its smooth glossy pages it celebrates and commemorates all that he achieved during his long, laborious, broken life.

But what's this?

The grave is unquiet. The soil stirs. A wormy hand bursts forth from the dirt, clutching a sheaf of rotting, tattered script pages...!

For, in truth, Unknown can never die. As long as you or I read his captions and speech bubbles, thrill at his sometimes surreal turns of phrase, and let the nightmare logic of his plotting beguile us, he is damned to live.

Anonymous, yet eternal, immortal.

James Lovegrove
2012

James Lovegrove is the author of more than forty books. His most recent novels are Age Of Aztec, *latest in his bestselling Pantheon series, and* Redlaw: Red Eye. *He has written extensively for teenagers and younger children, and his work has been translated into a dozen languages and shortlisted for numerous awards, including the Arthur C. Clarke Award, the John W. Campbell Memorial Award, the Bram Stoker Award, the British Fantasy Society Award and the Manchester Book Award. His "Carry The Moon In My Pocket" won the 2011 Seiun Award in Japan for Best Translated Short Story. James is a regular reviewer of fiction for the* Financial Times *and contributes frequently to the magazine* Comic Heroes. *He lives in Eastbourne with his wife, two sons and cat.*

Macabre Maestros

Featuring artist

Tom Hickey

(1910 - United States)

Many of the creators mentioned in the previous volumes of *The Harvey Horror Collection* could recant at will tales from their earliest days in the industry, a wealth of which date back to those halcyon years that have since been hailed the Golden Age of comics. These reminiscences would tell of a time when the superhero reigned supreme, and four-colour terror was merely a fleeting afterthought. Tom Hickey's tales go a little further back, to a period immediately prior to the dawn of this Golden Age; for he was amongst the vanguard, whose pioneering spirit would very soon precipitate the birth of the superhero.

The flair he displayed as a teenager brought him to the National Academy of Design in New York City, a body established in 1825 by a group of respected artists, amongst whom the names Samuel F. B. Morse, Asher B. Durand, and Thomas Cole could be found. Through this institution, they aspired to "promote the fine arts in America through instruction and exhibition." Their vision would bequeath the arts a seemingly endless succession of genius; and amongst their illuminati would come the esteemed Louis Comfort Tiffany and Frank Lloyd Wright. While Tom's legacy wasn't to radiate across the international art scene in quite the same way as these distinguished innovators, his endeavours would leave a lasting impression, one that would span the decades to come.

The early 1930s were a troubled time for anyone trying to find work in the United States, however soon after graduation, Tom was appointed as a teacher with the WPA's Federal Art Programme in Manhattan. Here, unemployed men and women were provided with the opportunity to enhance their skills under the careful guidance of a highly trained group of professionals. By day, he nurtured his collective of budding artists, and then in those hours away from the classroom he too worked to refine his technique, paying close attention to an artist by the name of Alex Raymond. The young Raymond

had been introduced to the syndicated newspaper strip in 1930, when he was but a lad 21 years of age. The confidence evident in his detailed line aroused Tom's artistic stirrings, and became a major influence on his work, particularly in his early years with DC. In this period of dour austerity, he recognized that the newspaper strip offered a chance to express his artistic leanings and could become a much-needed source of employment.

The spring and early summer months of 1936 proved to be an exhilarating time for this enthusiastic young man, with two of his episodic adventures, Wing Brady and Golden Dragon, seeing print in the pages of DC's *More Fun Comics* #11 (July 1936) and *New Comics* #6 (July 1936). Their design, initially portrayed as two-page episodes, each crediting Tom with the script, pencils and inks, suggests that they were intended for the more respected world of the syndicated newspaper strip. However, they only ever enjoyed publication in these early comic books and it would be many years before Tom ascended the ladder to assume a place on a prized newspaper strip. He refused to be deterred, and the thrilling exploits of Brad Hardy and Mark Marson soon followed in the contents of these same comics, with Bruce Nelson making it to the premiere of a rather exciting new title by the name of *Detective Comics* in March

Chamber of Chills #11 August 1952

Chamber of Chills #9 June 1952

GHOSTS of Famous Pirates

WHEREVER MEN MEET AND TALK, STORIES OF *ADVENTURE* AND *MYSTERY* ARE SURE TO BE TOLD, AND, THE MAN WHO IS LISTENED TO THE *HARDEST* IS THE MAN WHO CAN TELL A STORY ABOUT THE *GHOST* OF A *FAMOUS PIRATE!* PERHAPS, ONE LIKE *"THE GHOST OF THE PIRATE 'BLACK' BELLAMY!'*

ONE NIGHT, IN THE YEAR 1717, A "SNOW," A THREE-MASTED SAILING VESSEL, WAS BEING *PURSUED* BY THE *PIRATE FLEET* OF *BELLAMY,* THE *BLACKEST* PLUNDERER ON THE DEEP.

WHAT THE *PIRATES* DID NOT KNOW WAS THAT THE BOAT THEY WERE CHASING WAS A *DECOY* TO GET THEM INTO THE HARBOR AND *GROUND* THEIR LARGER SHIPS IN THE SHALLOW WATER.

AS THE *CHASE* REACHED THE HARBOR, A SUDDEN *SQUALL* RIPPED IN FROM THE NORTH AND, SOON, THE SHIPS WERE BEING *TOSSED* AROUND ON THE *RAGING WAVES* LIKE CORKS.

BUT, THE *PIRATES* HAVING ALREADY ENTERED THE HARBOR *GASPED* WITH *HORROR* AS THEY REALIZED THEY HAD BEEN *TRICKED.* THEY COULD DO NOTHING, HOWEVER, AS THE STORM *DRAGGED* THEM TOWARDS THE ROCKS SURROUNDING THE BAY!

AS HIS SHIP NEARED ITS *DOOM,* "*BLACK*" *BELLAMY* RAISED HIS ARMS TO THE *EXPLODING* SKIES AND SHOUTED THAT HE WOULD *NEVER DIE.* HE WOULD *GUARD* HIS TREASURE, BURIED SOME TIME BEFORE, *FOREVER!*

THE WHOLE *PIRATE* FLEET WAS *DESTROYED* AND ITS ENTIRE CREW *KILLED* EXCEPT "*BLACK*" BELLAMY! INHABITANTS OF THAT NEW ENGLAND HARBOR CITY, TO THIS VERY DAY, SAY THAT A MAN IN ANCIENT CLOTHES WALKS ITS STREETS, PAYS HIS BILLS IN GOLD AND AVOIDS ANYTHING HOLY!

IT IS ALSO SAID THAT EVERY YEAR, ON THE NIGHT OF THE FLEET'S DESTRUCTION, THERE IS *LOUD LAUGHING* AND *BOISTEROUS TALKING* IN THE ROOM OF THE MAN IN THE ANCIENT CLOTHES. ONCE, SOMEONE LOOKED INTO THE ROOM AFTER SUCH A NIGHT AND SAW THE *REMAINS* OF A *SUPPER* FOR AT LEAST *TWENTY MEN !!!*

Witches Tales #1 January 1951

1937. That same month Golden Dragon made a quick getaway to join the roster of **New Adventure Comics** with its 14th appearance, a move which came in the wake of the demise of **New Comics** #11 and its festive celebrations (December 1936). The adventures of Wing Brady and Mark Marson were later revived to enjoy welcome reprints in the pages of H.C. Blackerby's **Warrior Comics**, which saw release some years later in 1945.

Tom was now getting a real taste for this gripping new medium and it was also beginning to pay its way; his fastidious line work became a regular feature in the pages of DC's **Detective Comics** and **New Adventure Comics** along with **More Fun Comics**, until the early months of 1940. Although he was never offered the chance to collaborate on any of the adventures of DC's illustrious Golden Age costumed heroes, his six page entry that formed the first part of his Bruce Nelson adventure "The New Orleans Mardi Gras Murder" were included in the contents of the now legendary **Detective Comics** #27 (May 1939). The team of creators that DC assembled for this issue was akin to a comic book hall of fame, with contributions from Gardiner F. Fox, Charles Biro, Fred Guardineer, Jerry Siegel, Joe Shuster and, let's not forget, Bob Kane.

While engaged by several book publishers as an illustrator, Dell Comics began to ply Tom with an abundance of work, which would keep him in their service for the rest of the decade. Dell's line of comics had originated in 1929, and by the end of the 1940s, they were considered one of the most eminent comic book publishers in the United States. His debut for Dell came in Funnies #35 (September 1939), where Tom Beatty was swiftly ensnared by the Black Widow. Shortly afterwards his pencils were sharpened for an appearance in the company's prolific **Popular Comics**, which led to his appointment as the lead artist on The Sky Hawk for all of four issues of **War Comics**. This title endured a subtle transformation to become the pulp-styled **War Stories**, offering one more Sky Hawk tale, illustrated with Tom's aptitude for precision. The renditions presented in these pages were so typical of the era's more refined draughtsmen; coupling an attention for detail with the dynamics that pulsed to hold the attention of its thrill seeking audience. Sky Hawk would make guest appearances in **Key Ring Comics** and **Popular Comics**, where Tom continued in the illustration of his death defying escapades. During the mid 1940s, he was brought in to assist the team dedicated to Dell's popular line of funny animal comics, while resuming with a regular slot in the company's moral boosting War Heroes.

After a brief sortie in the short-lived D.S. Publishing's Underworld, an outfit whose output was unpredictable at best, varying from the lacuna of the bland to the extremes of unrelenting violence, Dell chose Tom as their artist for **The Lone Ranger**. He debuted with the 13th appearance, cover dated July 1949, before bowing out over eighteen months later with issue #29 in the November of 1950. For those with a fondness for Tom's brush strokes, these 17 issues were to elevate him to stand amongst the unsung paragons of the period; they also attracted rather favourable glances from the boys in the editorial offices of Harvey Comics.

When Tom went to work for Harvey, after an impromptu appearance in **Hi-School Romance** #5 (June 1950), he was considered by many to be a time served veteran, whose dexterity could be adapted to almost any genre. While in the employ of Dell, he had also worked for Fawcett, Lev Gleason and Quality, and was now handed a series of scripts that would lead him into the vagaries of comic book romance as well as the latest craze to sweep across the industry, those interminable horror comics. Having forged a worthy reputation as a true professional, the artwork on show in **Hi-School Romance** revealed an artist with yet another string to his bow, an eye for a pretty girl. For the next few years, he would charm his young female readership with the trials and tribulations of romance and heartbreak, even surviving the ravages of the intrusive Code, before turning to Harvey's celebrated range of children's comics.

Collectors of Tom's original artwork, which had been commissioned for Harvey's romance comics, remain astounded by his meticulous line, so much of which was inspired by the then developing Alex Raymond. There are very few corrections observed in these renditions, revealing an artist of considerable reliability, who could deliver as the whim of his editors demanded. Current research alludes to only two entries from his drawing board making it to Harvey's line of horror comics. The first of these came in **Witches Tales** #3 (May 1951) "The Forest of Skeletons," which isn't a particularly chilling yarn, but did present Tom with the prospect of pencilling a series of unusually detailed pages, in what looks to have been a well researched historical drama. **Chamber of Chills** #9's "The Captain's Return," went that one-step further in exposing this man as an artist who was genuinely at ease with the supernatural. This wasn't a gory addition to the Harvey catalogue of atrocities, but it was an unsettling offering, which revelled in the brutal strangulation of its victim.

As a freelance artist, Tom broadened his horizons finding a bounty of work with **Feature Comics**, which only dried up when the Comics Code insisted on its limiting seal of approval. However, along with Harvey, Gilberton managed to remain in operation throughout this desperate period, and he gladly accepted their invitation. While many of his colleagues fell by the wayside, Tom's reputation kept him in ready employment. Finally, in 1958, if only for a short time, he achieved his ambition to have his name appear on a syndicated newspaper strip, which was entitled **Slapsie**. It wasn't to last, but the American Comics Group, whose wholesome approach to supernatural adventure had acquired an appreciative readership, now called upon Tom's skills. He would work there until 1967, regularly contributing to their long running mystery titles **Adventures into the Unknown** and **Forbidden Worlds**, while making the occasional appearance in **Unknown Worlds** and **Gasp**.

His wealth of experience, particularly on the cartoon-styled comics for Dell and Harvey, put him in good stead for further openings, which led to a stint in the production of filmstrips for Bob Clarke and a position as a storyboard artist for television commercials. It was while working at home as a commercial artist he was introduced to the son of one of his neighbours, who had a similar aptitude for art and cartooning. Tom could see the potential in the young Roger Kastel, and succeeded in getting him work as an illustrator for a corporate handbook on the use of their machinery. The teenage Roger didn't disappoint and went on to become an artist in his own right. Amongst his many accomplishments would be the poster to **The Empire Strikes Back**.

Tom Hickey was one of the few comic book artists who could lay claim to having been there just as the comic book industry was beginning to take shape. He may not have been one of the architects of this dazzling phenomenon, but he was an artist, whose professionalism allowed him to adapt his style over a thirty-year period, responding to the ever-changing challenges set by his senior editors. His standing was such that he remained in gainful employment for a four-decade period, leaving behind a substantial volume of work, which would inspire a legion of artists to take up their pencils and follow in his wake.

Peter Normanton
2012

Witches Tales #3 May 1951

Witches Tales
December 1953 - Issue #22

Cover Art - Lee Elias

Day of Panic
Script - Howard Nostrand
Pencils - Howard Nostrand
Inks - Howard Nostrand

Chain Reaction
Script - Unknown
Pencils - Pete Riss
Inks - Unknown

The Hunter
Script - Bob Powell
Pencils - Bob Powell
Inks - Bob Powell

Double Crossed
Script - Unknown
Pencils - Jack Sparling
Inks - Jack Sparling

TCHES
ALES
WE DARE YOU
TO READ THESE EERIE TALES
OF SUPERNATURAL HORROR!
WITCHES
TALES
WEIRD
YARNS OF
UNSEEN
TERRORS
LIVE THROUGH...
A DAY OF PANIC!

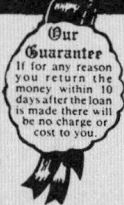

WITCHES TALES, DECEMBER, 1953, VOL. 1, NO. 22, IS PUBLISHED BI-MONTHLY
by WITCHES TALES, INC., 1860 Broadway, New York 23, N. Y. Entered as second class matter at the Post Office at New York, N. Y., under the Act of March, 3, 1879. Single copies, 10c. Subscription rates, 10 issues for $1.00 in the U. S. and possessions, elsewhere $1.50. All names in this periodical are entirely fictitious and no identification with actual persons is intended. Contents copyrighted, 1953, by Witches Tales, Inc., New York, City. Printed in the U.S.A. Title registered in U. S. Patent Office.

This is the season for horror...and WITCHES TALES is right in tune. Never behind the times, always two steps ahead of shock, this mag brings out the best in terror and adorns the cloak of suspense!

From the raging vacuum of horror's nether region comes the billowing clouds of tales told in a squeaky voice...and the door held by rusty hinges swings open to reveal the inner circle and the inhabitants enclosed within it!

Since the dawn of violence, there never has been a story like a DAY OF PANIC! Fury mounts as the hunt for a vampire increases in tempo...until there's no place to go.

Every link in CHAIN REACTION is forged from terror and branded in impact. Circumstance becomes mother of fate...whose child is death!

THE HUNTER follows the track of the cat...through the treacherous paths winding about a mountain...facing the elemental dangers... facing mental pitfalls!

Finally, a stab in the back is the theme behind DOUBLE-CROSSED...where the victim becomes the victor... where love becomes hate and a gun spouts flame!

22

23

THE OLD MAN REFRESHED HIMSELF WITH THE COLD WATER!

I THANK YOU VERY KINDLY!

OH, THAT'S ALL RIGHT! IT'S A PLEASURE TO TALK TO SOMEONE! YOU *COME* FROM *TWIN OAKS*, DON'T YOU? A RIGHT-PLEASANT TOWN!

IT *WAS* THAT! AIN'T NO MORE! *EVERYBODY'S LEFT IT!* TOWN'S DESERTED! PEOPLE CLEARED OUT IN *ONE* DAY... THAT DAY...

..."WHEN OLD DOLPH'S BOY CAME A-RUNNIN'"...

MA....*MA!* I SAW DEEK JACOBS...HE'S *DAID!* HE'S... STRANGELY DAID!

DAID! HUSTLE YOUR HIDE!... AND *FETCH* SHERIFF *DUNCAN!*

THE BOY GOT DUNCAN! ANYTIME THE SHERIFF IS CALLED THERE'S A TO-DO ABOUT IT! NOBODY, THOUGH, EXPECTED TO SEE WHAT *THEY SAW!* FOR, DOWN BY THE POND, BY OLD DEEK'S BODY...

HOT GOSH! HE'S DAID, ALL RIGHT! BUT ...LOOK...

HIS THROAT...THE *MARK* OF THE VAMPIRE...

VAMPIRE... VAMPIRE...

IT LOOKED AS THOUGH THE WORD--*VAMPIRE*-- SET THE GROUND TREMBLIN' AND ROCKIN'! TWIN OAKS WAS ASTIR! IT WAS A PROBLEM FOR BIG MEN...LIKE SHERIFF SETH DUNCAN AND MAYOR LEM HOOPER!

IT'S REAL *TROUBLE*, LEM! WE GOT TO *HUNT* OUT THIS VAMPIRE! *I'LL* LEAD A VIGILANTE COMMITTEE!

NOTHIN' DOIN', SETH. *I'LL* FORM A...*POSSE!*

CLEVER, AIN'T YA? YOU WANT *ALL* THE *GLORY* TO Y'SELF....JES' 'CAUSE IT'S *ELECTION* TIME! WELL, I SAY...*VIGILANTES'*

AND...YOU WANT *MY* JOB! NO SIREE! I SAY... *POSSE!*

24

THEN, THE FOLKS OF TWIN OAKS WANTED NO MORE PART OF THAT TOWN! THEY BEGAN TO HUSTLE OUT!

C'MON, PETEY... WE'RE LEAVIN'!

THEY DIDN'T LIKE TWIN OAKS NO MORE. THEY WAS *SCARED!*

STAY...STAY...

PRETTY SOON, THE TOWN WAS QUIET, IT WAS PLUMB *EMPTIED-OUT!*

I'M ALL... ALONE!

TWIN OAKS TO ME WAS MY *LIFE!* BUT THAT DAY OF PANIC WAS JES' LIKE A TYPHOON...IT CLEARED OUT EVERY-THIN' IN ITS PATH! AND...I WASN'T GOIN' TO STAY IN A TOWN WITH NOBODY LIVIN' IN IT!

GOT T'HAVE PEOPLE ...IF I WANT TO BE HAPPY!

A *SHAME*... THAT'S WHAT IT IS!

ALL 'CAUSE SOMEBODY HOLLERED *"VAMPIRE!"*

DID THEY EVER CATCH THAT CREATURE...THAT... THAT *VAMPIRE?*

TO TELL YOU THE TRUTH...

NO!

THE END

27

the BABY

"Don't feel that way," Dr. Little told his wife Lois. "Please, darling, don't feel that way."

"I can't help it, William," she said between tears. "I don't want to . . . but I can't control myself."

He held her tight, brought her close to him, tried to soothe her as best he could. But it was no use. Her crying wouldn't stop.

"Oh, William, it's not that I'm ashamed of our baby . . . it's just that I can't be proud! Friends, neighbors, everyone talks about any and every baby — but ours! There's always a good word, a compliment. But has anyone ever said anything about ours? No! We don't even have anything to say about him!"

"Darling, please . . . please don't hurt yourself. I realize it, too, sweetheart, but there's nothing we can do. We've just got to accept it!"

"Accept it!? Remain the laughing stock of the world! And the baby's own father is a doctor!"

Dr. Little became excited at the last remark.

"What would you have me do?" he shouted. "I'm a doctor, not a creator! I can only work with what has been given me! Do you think I enjoy this situation!"

Lois was sorry. She really hadn't meant it. "William," she said, "oh, forgive me, please. It just gets me down and I don't know what I'm saying."

He brushed her tears away and kissed her on the forehead. "Things will be all right," he told her. "You'll see."

Then he left her. He went into the baby's bedroom. He looked down at the boy, the poor boy who could do nothing. The poor boy who had never said a smart remark. The poor boy who hadn't a face you could talk about — not even an ugliness you could worry about. The poor boy who was nothing but an existence.

Dr. Little looked down at the baby and tears came into his eyes.

"If there was only something I could do," he murmured. "And perhaps there is!" he suddenly shouted.

His eyes were shining panic as he lifted the baby into his arms. He snuggled it close to him as he dashed through the rooms of the house.

"What are you doing?" Lois screamed.

Her only answer was the slam of the laboratory door.

There were screams from the laboratory now, and Lois ran to it and pounded her fists on the door.

"What are you doing? What are you doing?"

Then the door was opened. Lois shrieked. She felt as if a knife had cut her to bits.

"Isn't it wonderful," Dr. Little smiled. "Now everyone will talk about our baby — without a head!"

Mother Mongoose's NURSERY CRIMES

HECTOR PROTECTOR, A *TOUGH* PRIVATE *EYE*,

SILENTLY *FOLLOWED* A ROUGH-LOOKING *GUY!*

CRASH

HE *DREAMT* OF PUTTING HIS *TARGET* BEHIND *BARS...*

BUT *HECTOR* HAD *SPOTTED* A MAN FROM MARS!

Mother Mongoose's NURSERY CRIMES

HANDY SPANDY, JACK-A-DANDY,

COULD FIX FLEA'S EARS-- OR STALE CANDY!

HAPPY·HANDY, SMILING· ON THE JOB--

ACCIDENTALLY TURNED THE WRONG KNOB!

YAAAAH!

DEATH IN THE VILEST OF WAYS IS THE CONNECTING LINK IN THIS...
CHAIN REACTION
THE MAN WAS HURRIEDLY WALKING THROUGH THE ALLEYWAY LATE AT NIGHT WHEN HE HEARD IT!
FOOTSTEPS! SOMEONE'S FOLLOWING ME!
WHA----T?
BLAM

OUR PROBLEM IS SOLVED!

AND THIRTY MINUTES LATER, IN ANOTHER SECTION OF TOWN...

YOU'RE RIGHT ON TIME, DARLING! I MISSED YOU!

I'M ALWAYS ON TIME, HARRY! I FEEL GOOD TONIGHT -- *REALLY GOOD!*

I'M CRAZY ABOUT YOU, CAROL! THE *MORE I SEE* YOU, THE *MORE* I *WANT* YOU! IF ONLY *BILL WEREN'T* YOUR *HUSBAND* --!

THERE ARE WAYS TO PUT BILL OUT OF THE PICTURE, HARRY -- A *LOT* OF WAYS!

A *GUN!* WHERE DID YOU GET IT? IS -- IS IT *LOADED?*

OF COURSE IT IS! AND I'VE GOT THE PERFECT PLAN! *LISTEN!*

THEN SHE COAXED HIM, CAJOLED HIM, PLEADED, BEGGED AND SCHEMED...

I -- I DON'T KNOW... SUPPOSE SOMETHING GOES *WRONG?* SUPPOSE SOMEONE FINDS OUT? *IT'S CRAZY!*

THE PLAN'S *FOOL-PROOF! NOTHING* WILL GO WRONG! IT'S *NOT* OUR GUN! I FOUND IT! 'AFTER THE *MURDER* WE'LL GET *RID* OF IT! HARRY, DON'T YOU *WANT* ME?

I'LL *NEVER* LET YOU GO, CAROL -- NEVER! EVEN IF I HAVE TO -- GIVE ME THAT GUN!

I *KNEW* YOU'D DO IT! *I KNEW IT!*

SQQUEEAKK
NOW, HARRY! NOW!
BLAM BLAM BLAM
A FEW INCHES TO THE RIGHT--AND YOU'D HAVE KILLED ME! YOU'RE BOTH UNDER ARREST!
T-THE POLICE!
W-WE MADE A TERRIBLE MISTAKE, LIEUTENANT! CAROL--UH--MRS. HUGHES AND I THOUGHT YOU WERE A ROBBER. I--I'M A FAMILY FRIEND! WE WERE WAITING FOR BILL, HER HUSBAND. HE'S DUE HERE ANY MOMENT!
THAT'S RIGHT! UH--THIS IS BILL'S GUN--A WAR SOUVENIR! HE ALWAYS KEEPS IT IN HIS BUREAU...
PICK UP THE GUN, PETE!
WELL--THAT'S IT! THIS LOOKS LIKE THE MURDER GUN ALL RIGHT!
M-MURDER GUN? WHAT ARE YOU TALKING ABOUT? WE WERE JUST JUMPY, THAT'S ALL! SURELY, YOU CAN'T--
SAVE IT! WE WERE COMING HERE TO TELL YOU THAT YOUR HUSBAND WAS KILLED A FEW HOURS AGO BY A BULLET FIRED FROM A LUGER--AND THIS GUN'S A LUGER! BALLISTICS WILL DOUBLE-CHECK ON IT!
BUT IT'S NOT OUR GUN!
NO USE, CAROL! OUR FOOLPROOF PLAN BACKFIRED! HA, HA... WE'RE CAUGHT ON A MURDER WE DIDN'T DO! HA! HA!
THE END

35

36

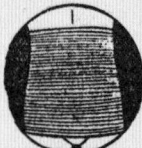

THE HUNTER

"I'LL GET YOU!!!"

THE BREAKING OF WINTER TO SPRING IN THE ROCKY MOUNTAINS IS A HARBINGER OF *DEATH!* THE MOUNTAIN LION...*THE BIG CAT*...PROWLS FOR FOOD,...AND SOMETIMES *FINDS* IT! IT'S THE TIME WHEN THE ORDINARY FARMER BECOMES THE *HUNTER!*

THAT ROTTEN CAT! I'LL *KILL* IT...IF IT'S THE *LAST THING* I DO!

THE HUNTER IS GRIM. DETERMINATION ETCHES STRONG LINES ACROSS HIS FACE. HE MUST PREPARE FOR THE TRACK...THE *TRACK OF THE CAT!*

NO-GOOD, LOW-DOWN CAT! PROBABLY IN THOSE DAD-BLAMED MOUNTAINS!

SO THE HUNTER SET OUT WITH PACK AND RIFLE -- FOR THE *HUNT*...

TREACHEROUS...THESE CRAZY MOUNTAINS. CAN GET HOG-WILD LOST IN 'EM!

THAT CAT'S SOMEWHERE NEAR! I CAN *FEEL* IT!

SO THE HUNTER CLIMBED HIGHER AND HIGHER... AND THEN...

WHA?!!

THE HUNTER HAD TO USE THE INSTINCT OF AN *ANIMAL* AGAINST THE ANIMAL'S INSTINCT! IT MEANT SWIFT ACTION! HE COULDN'T LOSE TIME!

BLAMED CAT'S... LEAPING...

2

THE HUNTER HAD SHOT. THE ACTION WAS TOO FAST. THINGS HAPPENED IN A BLUR. HE COULDN'T TELL WHETHER HE *HIT* THE BIG CAT, BUT... HE *HAD TO FIND OUT!*

ROTTEN CAT ...MOVED!

CAT'S GONE! I MISSED! I.... HOLD IT!

A CLOSER SEARCH INDICATED REWARD. DROPS OF RED LIQUID LOOKED DULL-BROWN AGAINST THE CRAG'S SURFACE. THEY FORMED A ROAD UPWARD, HIGHER INTO THE MOUNTAIN!

BLOOD! I *NICKED* IT, ALL RIGHT! THAT CRITTUR SNUCK UP INTO THE MOUNTAIN!

THE HUNTER WENT STILL HIGHER... NOW FOLLOWING THE *BLOOD* OF THE CAT!

NOW THE TRAIL'S GONNA BE MUCH EASIER!

SNOW BEGAN TO FALL! LITTLE FLURRIES FLOATED DOWN, SWIRLED BY THE MOUNTAIN WIND! IT BECAME HEAVIER AS THE HUNTER TRAVELED INTO THE ROCKY DEPTHS!

—GASH—DARNED SNOW! COVERING THE BLOOD! CAN'T SEE...

NO SENSE TRYIN' TO GET IT *NOW!* I'LL BED DOWN FER THE NIGHT AND START OUT AT DAWN.

3

THE SNOW PERSISTED. NIGHT CREPT INTO THE MOUNTAINS. THE HUNTER, COLD AND TIRED, PREPARED TO GET SOME SLEEP. HE WAS ALONE. HE *THOUGHT* HE WAS ALONE!

YOU! THERE HE IS!

BLAM

MISSED HIM! THUNDERATION! IT'S LURKIN' AROUND SOMEWHERE...JUST WAITIN' FER ME TO CLOSE MY EYES! BUT... IT AIN'T GONNA CATCH ME ASLEEP!

THE HUNTER WAS ONLY *HUMAN*. HE NEEDED SLEEP. BUT HE HAD TO WATCH FOR THE CAT. THE SNOW STOPPED. NIGHT FADED INTO DAWN. THE FIRE DIED DOWN, BUT... STILL THE HUNTER WAS *AWAKE!*

AND...THE HUNT STARTED AGAIN!

DEBUT!

"Leave me alone!" Greg Wilson shouted. "Can't you stop it?"

"I won't stop it," retorted his wife Celia, "till you let me do what I want!"

The scene was the Wilsons' living room where bitter conversation like this had been going on for weeks.

"Can't you get it through your head," said Greg, "that you're never going to make it . . . that you haven't got it in you to become a television star!"

"I do," insisted his wife angrily. "I could be on television if you only made enough money to give me proper schooling. Why, my school teachers always said I was a born actress . . ."

"Stop it! Stop it!" shouted Greg. "You've been through this a hundred times before. Forget your idiotic school teachers. They didn't know what they were talking about! I can't afford to give you any lessons, and that's final!"

Celia wasn't giving up. "You're just jealous, that's all," she said. "You're afraid that I'll become big and important! You dread the thought of being home in this living room, no one ever knowing of you, and looking into that television set and watching your famous wife sweep the country off its feet!"

Greg couldn't take any more. He had heard enough for the night. He went to the closet, took out his jacket and dashed out of the house.

"Good riddance," he heard as he slammed the door.

He walked the streets for awhile, not thinking of anything in particular, only trying to keep Celia out of his mixed-up mind. But his thoughts kept returning to her, almost as if she was a monstrous magnet. It was no use. He may as well go home, he thought.

He opened the front-door quietly. If she was asleep, there was no sense in waking her. But Celia wasn't asleep . . .

There was a light in their bedroom, and there were sounds of movement. Greg tiptoed his way to the door. His voice suddenly boomed:

"What are you doing in that drawer?"

She turned around shamefully. She tried to close the drawer of the dresser. Then she decided to admit it all.

"You know what I was doing!" she said. "I was looking for your money. Yes, I was going to use it for television lessons!"

A blind hatred was coming to a boil within Greg. He couldn't control it any longer; it was bursting forth!

"What are you going to do?" Celia stammered.

He came toward her, and she screamed. There was more and more screaming. Then there was silence. And soon Greg's voice could be heard.

"I hope you're satisfied now. You've finally had your wish!"

He spoke to Celia's bloody head that stared out from behind the television screen.

Mother Mongoose's NURSERY CRIMES

I SAW A SHIP A-SAILING, A-SAILING ON THE SEA!

DAYS AND DAYS I WAS ALL A-DRIFT, NOW THAT SHIP WAS A-SAILING TO ME!

FOR DAYS UPON THE SILVERY WAVES, A-BOBBING LIKE A CORK,

I SAW A SHIP A-SAILING THAT WASN'T BOUND FOR NEW YORK!

FLYING DUTCHMAN

Mother Mongoose's NURSERY CRIMES

RIDE A COCKHORSE TO BANBURY CROSS TO SEE A KNIGHT OF OLD,

MASKED IN BLACK FROM TIP TO TOE, AS MEAN AS HE IS BOLD!

CRY FOR THE KNIGHT TO SHOW HIS FACE... TO EASE UP ON HIS DREAD!

SO...RIDE A COCKHORSE TO BANBURY CROSS-- TO SEE A KNIGHT *WITHOUT A HEAD!*

WHAT WOULD YOU DO IF YOU WERE...
DOUBLE CROSSED
YEAH... THEY DESERVE TO DIE... BOTH OF THEM...
BLEARY WITH LACK OF SLEEP, HE SEES THE SILENTLY BLINKING TRAFFIC LIGHTS OF THE CITY WINK AT HIM LIKE SEDUCTIVE MONSTERS...
I... I'VE GOT TO DO SOMETHING TO STOP MYSELF! IF I GO BACK TO THE HOUSE, I KNOW I'LL USE THIS GUN! I DON'T WANT TO BE A MURDERER!
STOP! STOP! YOU'VE GOT TO HELP ME!
WATCH IT, JOE- THIS LOOKS LIKE SOMETHING PHONY!
POLICE
1

HERE—TAKE IT, *PLEASE*—BEFORE I *KILL* SOMEONE WITH IT.

OKAY— TAKE IT FROM HIM, JOE. I GOT HIM COVERED. IF HE MAKES ONE FALSE MOVE, HE'S MADE HIS LAST.

WE'D BETTER TAKE HIM DOWN TO THE STATION, MIKE!

YEAH, HE MIGHT BE A PSYCHO! WE CAN QUESTION HIM THERE!

THANKS, FELLAS—THANKS...

NOW JUST SIT TIGHT, MISTER! *RELAX!*

MAYBE I *WAS* A LITTLE CRAZY EARLIER— BUT I'M FEELING BETTER NOW! I JUST DIDN'T WANT TO KILL HIM!

BELIEVE ME— IT FEELS GOOD TO BE IN THE SAFE HANDS OF THE POLICE.

YEAH...YEAH...TELL IT TO THE SERGEANT! SAY, MAC— YOU GOT A *PERMIT* FOR THAT *GUN?*

SURE— I GOT A PERMIT. I'M A JEWELRY SALES-MAN. I CARRY IT FOR PROTECTION AGAINST ROBBERY. LOOK— DON'T YOU *UNDERSTAND?* I'M A *LAW-ABIDING CITIZEN!*

OKAY, MIKE— WHAT'S THE CHARGE? DRUNK DRIVING? DISTURBING THE PEACE? VAGRANCY?

WRONG THREE TIMES, SARGE! THIS ONE *ISN'T* EVEN *IN* THE *BOOKS!*

51

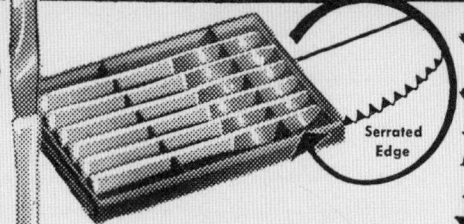

If You Like to Draw Sketch or Paint...

Make money with your brush and pen! Take the famous Talent Test. It has already helped thousands toward art careers. No fee. No obligation. Mail this coupon TODAY!

54

STRANGEST TALES OF FEAR AND TERROR!

BLACK CAT MYSTERY

Collect all 4 Volumes of Black Cat Mystery from PS Artbooks

Black Cat Mystery
Volume One

Black Cat Mystery
Volume Two

Black Cat Mystery
Volume Three

Black Cat Mystery
Volume Four

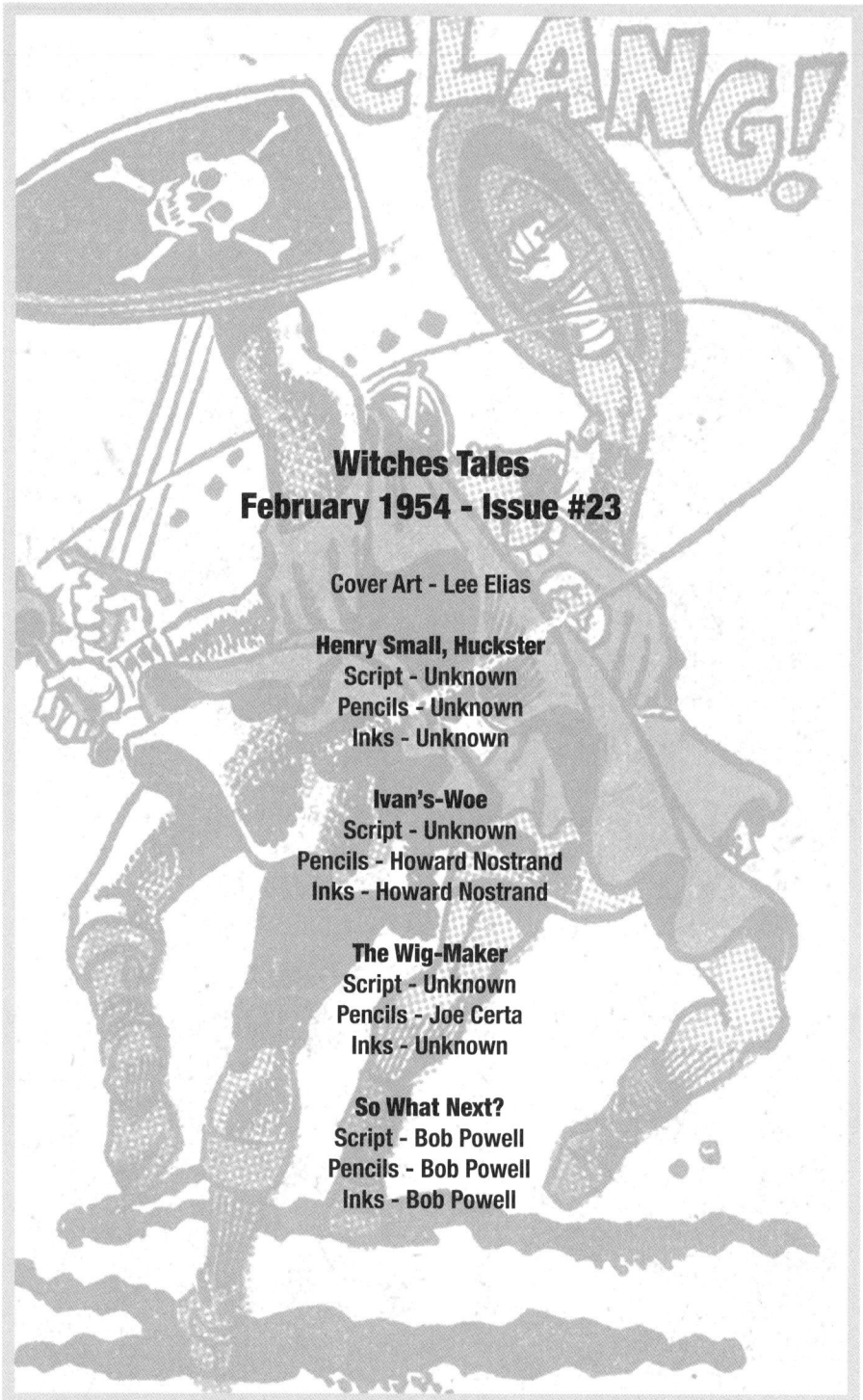

Witches Tales
February 1954 - Issue #23

Cover Art - Lee Elias

Henry Small, Huckster
Script - Unknown
Pencils - Unknown
Inks - Unknown

Ivan's-Woe
Script - Unknown
Pencils - Howard Nostrand
Inks - Howard Nostrand

The Wig-Maker
Script - Unknown
Pencils - Joe Certa
Inks - Unknown

So What Next?
Script - Bob Powell
Pencils - Bob Powell
Inks - Bob Powell

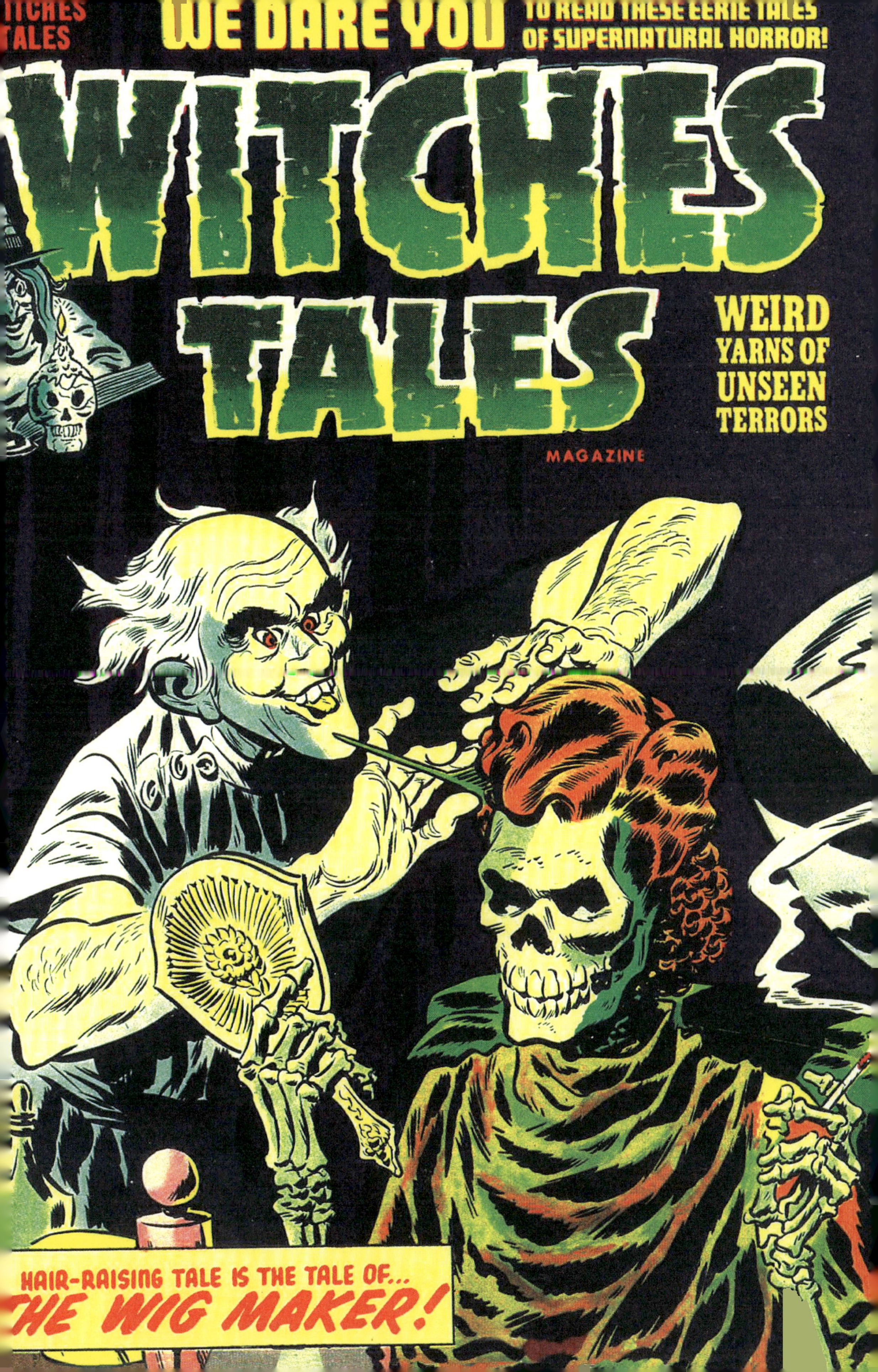

ITCHES
ALES
WE DARE YOU
TO READ THESE EERIE TALES OF SUPERNATURAL HORROR!
WITCHES TALES
WEIRD YARNS OF UNSEEN TERRORS
MAGAZINE
HAIR-RAISING TALE IS THE TALE OF...
HE WIG MAKER!

Draw This Car

Free $295.00 Art Course

6 PRIZES

1st: Complete $295.00 Art Course.

2nd to 6th: Complete Artist's Drawing sets.

Here's your big chance, if you want to become a commercial artist, designer, or illustrator! An easy way to win FREE training from the world's greatest home study art school.

If your drawing shows promise we give you professional comments on it free! Trained illustrators, artists and cartoonists are making big money. Find out now if YOU have profitable art talent. You've nothing to lose—*everything to gain.* Mail your drawing today.

AMATEURS ONLY! Our students not eligible. Make copy of car 8 ins. long. Pencil or pen only. Omit the lettering. All drawings must be received by Jan. 31, 1954. None returned. Winners notified

USE ONLY ONE COUPON... Leave the other coupons so your friends can also enter drawings. Pass this ad on to your friends. Maybe they'll win prizes, TOO!

Art Instruction, Inc., Dept. 11183-1
500 S. 4th., Minneapolis 15, Minn.

Please enter my attached drawing in your contest. **(PLEASE PRINT)**

Name_____ Age____

Address_____ Apt.____

City_____ Phone____

Zone____ County_____

State_____ Occupation._____

Art Instruction, Inc., Dept. 11183-2
500 S. 4th., Minneapolis 15, Minn.

Please enter my attached drawing in your contest. **(PLEASE PRINT)**

Name_____ Age___

Address_____ Apt.____

City_____ Phone____

Zone____ County_____

State_____ Occupation._____

Art Instruction, Inc., Dept. 11183-3
500 S. 4th., Minneapolis 15, Minn.

Please enter my attached drawing in your contest. **(PLEASE PRINT)**

Name_____ Age____

Address_____ Apt.____

City_____ Phone____

Zone____ County_____

State_____ Occupation._____

WITCHES TALES, FEBRUARY, 1953, VOL. 1, NO. 23, IS PUBLISHED BI-MONTHLY
by WITCHES TALES, INC., 1860 Broadway, New York 23, N. Y. Entered as second class matter at the Post Office at New York, N. Y., under the Act of March, 3, 1879. Single copies, 10c. Subscription rates, 10 issues for $1.00 in the U. S. and possessions, elsewhere $1.50. All names in this periodical are entirely fictitious and no identification with actual persons is intended. Contents copyrighted, 1953, by Witches Tales, Inc., New York, City. Printed in the U.S.A. Title registered in U. S. Patent Office.

Dear Readers

You wanted it! Now, you've got it -- a recipe of horror in two parts shock and one part fancy. This latest WITCHES TALES is really something to chill your spine -- and tickle your funny bone!

At first, these stories put a smile on your face -- and then fear in your heart. They butter you up with a feather, only to hammer you with terror! Chuckle in the night with them -- and scream in the shadows!

Let's hear your reaction to this fanciful, frightful brew of seering suspense and terrorific tales with that touch of the bizarre! Your opinions as expressed in your letters are what we want, so write as you think ...and don't spare the horses!

And here's something else. There is a surprise coming to you in next month's issue of WITCHES TALES.

It's, once again, that extra something you've gotten in the past. But, all that can be said now is that it's a blue-ribbon package of terror all prepared for you. So watch for it... watch out for shock!

So, from here to hysteria, it's WITCHES TALES ...and don't forget to write! The address of this prince of shock is....

WITCHES TALES
1860 Broadway
New York 23, N. Y.

WITCHES TALES

Contents NO. 23

huckster

henry small....

Ivan's-Woe

WIG-MAKER

So What Next

60

henry small.... huckster
4D
camel
in
with BASIL G. UMBLOWER
THAT "REAL-GONE" GAL
GLASSES AND INHALERS
A SID J. KOBSON PRODUCTION CAST OF THREE
OPEN FOR SUGGES
EDITORIAL DEPT.
ART DEPT.
EAT BOOB LOOK HOW BAD U LOOK
CAFETERIA
KNOCK KNOCK
BECKY'S FISH AND CHOPS ENGLISH STYLE
SPECIAL THIS YEAR ONLY
DINE AND DANCE WARM BEER
NAT'S
CLOSED FOR BUSINESS MGR.
OUR FOOD CAN'T BE BEAT
FRIEND LOANS
MONEY LOANED MONEY BORROWED MONEY MONEY HOOO-HAAA
BUNDLES FO BROOKLYN
WE WILL NO OVERPRIC
2 WAY
INTERPLANET XPRESS
HELP RAISE TAXES TODAY
EAT IT'S GOOD FOR U BECKY
THE...MEN IN BLUE! THEY NEVER LET A GUY MAKE A *DISHONEST BUCK!* NO TIME TO DAWDLE. I GOTTA GO...
GOT A MATCH
ABC
WE WANT MORE TAXES

Panel 1: FOR THE MOST PART, THIS WAS THE STORY OF HENRY SMALL'S LIFE... RUNNING FROM THE POLICE! HENRY WAS A HUCKSTER...A PEDDLER...A CON-MAN! HIS PRIME ASSET WAS TALK--BACKED UP WITH A PAIR OF FAST FEET...AND HE PUT THE LATTER TO USE AS HE RAN INTO A TRAIN DEPOT!

A *SATISFACTORY* PLACE!...NOISE... CROWDS...PEOPLE...

Panel 2: *PEOPLE!* ZOWIE! LOOK WHAT'S THERE!

Panel 3: THERE, NOT MORE THAN FIFTY PACES FROM HENRY SMALL, WAS A MAN, TEN-GALLON HAT, HIGH-BUTTON SHOES, STARCHED COLLAR, PEARL-STUDDED VEST...A RURAL SORE-THUMB IN AN URBAN TRAIN STATION!

WELCOME TO THE BIG CITY

TOKENS 15¢

Panel 4: NO COPS... ...AROUND!

Panel 5: HENRY SIDLED UP TO THE MAN, WAITED A FEW SECONDS, AND THEN BEGAN.

MISTUH...PSS-T! DON'T SAY A WORD, NOT A SOLITARY SYLLABLE. I NEED HELP. YOU'VE GOT TO HELP ME, YOU SEE--SOMEBODY STOLE MY WALLET. I'M STUCK... WITHOUT A *PENNY*. PLEASE...*HELP ME!*

SUH, I DON'T KNOW...

Panel 6: LOOK! LOOK AT THIS RING, IT--IT'S AN HEIRLOOM, MY POOR SICK MOTHER BEQUEATHED IT TO ME ON HER DEATH BED. THIS SOLID RUBY IS ALL I HAVE LEFT TO MY NAME. WOULD YOU LIKE TO BUY IT?

Panel 7: HOPE TO DIE, IF IT'S NOT REAL! WOULD MY POOR SICK MOTHER GIVE ME A FAKE? NOT *MY* POOR SICK MOTHER! ...FOR FIFTY DOLLARS.

WELL, NOW...A MAN FROM BOONE COUNTY NEVER LEAVES A FELLOW HUMAN-BEIN' IN THE LURCH, NO SIR! SUH...I WILL BUY YOUR RING!

Panel 8: A DEAL CONSUMMATED! YOU WILL NEVER REGRET IT. YOU HAVE A HEART OF GOLD...SOMETHING THIS WORLD NEEDS MORE OF! THANK YOU, OH, THANK YOU!

SAY NUTHIN' MORE, CHILD! GLAD TO HELP OUT...RIGHT GLAD!

Panel 9: HENRY SMALL EXCHANGED THE RING FOR THE STRANGER'S FIFTY DOLLARS! IT WAS AN HONORABLE TRANSACTION ON A SMALL SCALE, OF COURSE...

2

SECONDS PASSED BEFORE...

IT'S... GLASS!

THE SHOUT COULD BE HEARD THROUGH THE TERMINAL'S MARBLE HALLS! ITS VIBRATIONS ENTERED SMALL'S EARS, RAN THROUGH HIS BODY, ACTIVATED HIS LEGS, PROPELLED HIS FEET, SO... SMALL RAN...

AH'VE... BEEN... TRICKED!

THAT WAS THE WAY HENRY SMALL MADE HIS MONEY! A SIMPLE RUSE... A FAST SWINDLE... A SMOOTH LINE, A GLIB TONGUE! A CON JOB HERE! ANYTHING AND EVERYTHING THAT LOOKED SURE BUT TURNED OUT TO BE 100% - 14 K GOLD-PLATED FAKE! HE WAS A HUCKSTER IN THE TRUE MACHIAVELLIAN FASHION!

PSS-T! HEY, BUDDIE... WOULD YOU LIKE TO PURCHASE A CIGARETTE CASE? SOLID GOLD... SHINES LIKE A MIRROR... HOLDS TWENTY CIGARETTES! LIGHTS UP EVERYTIME YOU USE IT! I GOT TO GET RID OF IT... VERY FAST! IT'S YOURS... FOR CHEAP... CHEAP... CHEAP!

IF YOU ARE TALKING TO ME, WISEACRE ... PLEASE UN-HAND DA GARMENT! THEN... WE WILL EXCHANGE GAB!

(GULP!) SURE--SURE THING! I LOST MY HEAD! I... UH... WOULD LIKE TO RID MYSELF OF THIS CASE! A BARGAIN IS NOT THE WORD FOR THIS TRANSACTION. IT'S A... STEAL... A REAL STEAL!

DA THING LOOKS GOOD T'ME! IT IS IMPRESSING ME! I SHALL PAY YOU A DOUBLE-SAW FOR IT,... AND NOT A PLUG NICKEL MORE! DIS IS MY LAST WORD!

TWENTY BUCKS! FOR THIS! I... UH... MEAN-- FOR THIS? WELL, I DON'T KNOW! OKAY! SOLD!

HERE IS DA LOOT! NOW, MY GOOD MAN ... I WOULD APPRECIATE IT IF YOU WILL BE OFF! COP... A... WALK!

SMALL DID AS HIS CUSTOMER BECKONED. HE LEFT IN A SLOW WALK... IN A MORE-THAN-ADEQUATE TROT... THEN IN A VERY FAST RUN! SECONDS LATER...

...DA GUY IS A CROOK!

CLICK

AGAIN, HENRY SMALL'S FAST TALK HAD NETTED HIM A GAIN. BUT THIS TIME IT WAS NOT TO GO UNDISTURBED. HIS LATEST VICTIM DID NOT STEP OFF THE TRAIN. HE WAS NOT BORN YESTERDAY. HE HAD BEEN AROUND... AROUND A LOT OF VERY "INFLUENTIAL" PEOPLE...

IN THE PAST I AM DOING SOMETHING FOR YOU! NOW... RECIPROCATE! I WANT FOR YOU T' DIG UP DIS MOUSEY CHARACTER... DAT I AM TELLING YOU ABOUT... AND KINDLY PUT DA SCREWS ON HIM. I WOULD GREATLY APPRECIATE IT... IF YOU WOULD RUB HIM OUT!

TO ME... DIS CHARACTER SOUNDS LIKE... HENRY SMALL.

I AGREE!

SO... THE HUNT FOR HENRY SMALL BEGAN!

THE WORD SPREAD! HENRY SMALL... THE HUCKSTER... WAS ON DEATH'S AGENDA! THE DRAGNET CLOSED IN... UNTIL...

HENRY! COME QUIETLY... OR I'LL BLOW YOUR BRAINS OUT!

I AGREE!

LATER! HENRY, THE MARK HAS BEEN PUT ON YOU! DIS IS A NICE PLACE TO PUT YOU AWAY... QUIET, OUT OF DA WAY, ETC. YOU WILL ROT HERE, HENRY!

I AGREE!

B-BUT YOU CAN'T DO THIS. WHAT'VE I DONE TO YOU BOYS? I HAVEN'T PUT ANYTHING OVER ON YOU! I'M CLEAN. LET ME GO, BOYS! LET... ME... GO!

I COULD MAKE YOU RICH, BOYS! RICH! RICH! RICH! I GOT SOME GOLD-MINING STOCK! IT-- IT'S YOURS. TAKE IT OFF MY HANDS! ONLY... LET ME GO!

NO CAN DO!

GOLD?!

I DON'T AGREE, ALPHA! HENRY'S GOT GOLD. WE GOT NOTHIN'! WE COULD BE RICH! ALL WE GOTTA DO IS... LET HENRY GO! WHA'D'YA SAY, ALPHA? COME ON! HUH, ALPHA?

WELL, NOW... I DON'T KNOW...

YOU'LL BE RICH! RICH... RICH...

IT'S A DEAL, HENRY! WE'LL LET YOU GO... FOR THE GOLD STOCK!
I AGREE!
(WHEW!) YOU BOYS WILL NEVER REGRET IT! I GOT THE STOCK...
...RIGHT HERE! NOW, OF COURSE ...THERE'S AN EXTRA-ADDED SOMETHING I GOT HERE... FOR A VERY SMALL NOMINAL FEE... HEH! HEH!... VERY SMALL, INDEED!
MOMENTS PASSED... THEN SECONDS, FINALLY MINUTES! THE HEAVY AIR OF SILENCE WAS BROKEN BY SOMEONE WHISTLING A LIGHT TUNE...
WHAT A CINCH! A FAIR EXCHANGE! FAKE STOCK... FOR MY LIFE... PLUS THESE WATCHES AND RINGS! OH, WELL! ANOTHER DAY... ANOTHER DOLLAR...
SUDDENLY...
NOW WHO'S NEXT? LET ME... YAAAA!
BLAM! BAM!
IT IS A GOOD THING... I AM KNOWING DIS JOKER WILL TALK HIS WAY OUT OF ANY PRE-DICT-A-MENT! BUT... I DO NOT LIKE THAT! HE WILL NOT TALK HIS WAY OUT OF NUTHIN' ...NO MORE!
OH, NO?
--WHY ARE YOU THINKING ABOUT IT? HERE... TAKE IT! IT'S YOURS! STOP THINKING! TAKE THE WATCH OFF MY HANDS! ALL I WANT IS A SOFT JOB! A JOB... FOR A WATCH! WHAT'S TO THINK ABOUT? COME ON, LUCY... BE A SPORT...
I--I--UH... WELL... YOU SEE...
UCIFER PROPRIETOR
THE END
5

MISTER MASTER

Larry Benson was taking his usual after-dinner walk. He was walking casually... slowly...

And then suddenly he saw this gnome-like figure walking towards him. "He sure is a funny one," he said to himself.

"Hello, Mr. Benson," the little man said to Larry.

"Huh?" Larry sounded. "Hello, sir, but how did you know my name? I don't think I know *you*."

"No, Mr. Benson, you don't know me, but I know you very well. I've been watching you closely for quite a while..."

"Watching me closely? What do you mean by that?" This all seemed so stupid and silly to Larry. "Why are you so interested in me, Mr....."

"Mr. Master is my name, sir. Well, you see I was a very good friend of your father's, and when he died I promised I'd look after you..."

"But, my father died in an asylum! Were you a doctor there?" Larry stared at the little man and wondered how his father could ever become friendly with a strange creature like that.

"No," the little man laughed. "No, I wasn't a doctor. But I *was* very close to him."

Suddenly there was a voice... "Hey, Larry, how have you been?" It was Joe Stewart, Larry's neighbor.

"Oh, hello, Joe. I'd like you to meet Mr. Master, a friend of my father's!"

"Huh?" said Joe Stewart. "What are you talking about?"

"I said I'd like you to meet Mr. Master!" Larry was reasonably annoyed.

"Who's Mr. Master?" Joe didn't know what hit him.

Mr. Master was a friend of my father's..."

"I heard that, but where is he?"

"Now stop being funny, Joe! I'm sorry about all this, Mr. Master." Larry turned to his little friend with a beg-pardon look on his face.

"It's all right, Larry," said Mr. Master. "That's the way your father's friends treated me!"

"I'm getting out of here," shouted Joe Stewart. And he did!

Minutes later, Larry Benson presented Mr. Master to his wife, Martha.

"But, Larry, what are you talking about? There's no man with you!"

"Martha! Stop talking like that! I don't think you're being fair to Mr. Master!"

"Don't get excited," interrupted Mr. Master, "they always talk like that about me!"

"But, why, Mr. Master? I don't understand all this! Do you think it's fair?"

"It's not for us to judge, Larry. If they don't want to accept me, then there's noth- we can do about it!" The little man just shook his head.

"Don't worry, Mr. Master, they're going to accept you — or else!"

Days later, the "or else" took place...

"Gee, thanks for sticking up for me, Larry! You're just like your father was!"

"That's all right, Mr. Master. You'd probably do the same for me. At least everyone *here* accepts you! Hey, Napoleon, come here and talk with us!"

Mother Mongoose's NURSERY CRIMES

"As I was going along, long, long....

Singing a comical song, song, song!

They all thought my singing was wrong, wrong, wrong,

BOINNNNG!

Then all I heard was bong, bong, bong!"

Mother Mongoose's NURSERY CRIMES

"Solomon Grundy saw her on a Monday

Joy supreme it was his fun day!

Change of plans it was his run day!

Boy, oh boy! Did he wish it was Sunday!"

67

SIR IVAN GWAINE HAS WON *AGAIN!* OUR FEARLESS KNIGHT HAS *MASTERED* THE *KING'S TOURNAMENT!*

I HAVE FARED WELL, AS HEAVEN ORDAINED, BUT FORSOOTH--'TIS MUCH TOO VALIANT A KNIGHT I HAVE FACED NOT TO GO UN-HERALDED! RISE SIR GERALD--THOU HAST BEEN A *WORTHY* OPPONENT!

I PAY HOMAGE TO YOUR *SKILL*, SIR IVAN! YOU HAVE MY PLEDGE OF ALLEGIANCE IN ANY UNDERTAKING THOU MAY TAKE!

MY *DEAREST* IVAN! HOW MY HEART *FLUTTERED* WHEN I SAW THEE BEFORE ME! YOU ARE THE BRAVEST KNIGHT OF THEM ALL!

ELIZABETH--IT IS FOR *THEE* THAT I RODE AND FOUGHT! LET ALL WHO WITNESSED THIS MEET KNOW THAT *I, SIR IVAN GWAINE* OF *HAMPSHIRE*-- HAVE GIVEN THEE MY *HEART!*

DO THEY NOT MAKE A CHARMING COUPLE, SIR HUGO? SIR GWAINE HAS INDEED DISTINGUISHED HIMSELF AS MOST CAPABLY AS THOU!

NOT SO, FITZHUGH! KNOW THEE THAT *I* AM THE *KING'S EXECUTIONER*--AND AS SUCH--I AM *THE BEST KNIGHT* OF ALL! MY BATTLE SCARS, MY *UGLINESS* ARE PROOF OF MY *SUPREMACY!*

KING JOHN OF BRITAIN HAD INDEED MANY VALIANT KNIGHTS -- BUT NONE SO POPULAR AS SIR IVAN GWAINE. INDEED-- ALL KNEW THAT HE AND ELIZABETH, THE KING'S DAUGHTER, HAD ANNOUNCED THEIR BETROTHAL. THUS--AT THE CASTLE AFTERWARDS.

RISE MY BROTHER KNIGHTS AND VASSALS! A TOAST TO *ELIZABETH*, MY DAUGHTER-- AND HER FEARLESS GENTLEMAN-- A TOAST TO *SIR GWAINE!*

HEAR! HEAR!

TO THE *BEST* KNIGHT OF THEM ALL!

Panel 1: HOLD! I, HUGO LAVON OF BLACKMORE-- THE KING'S EXECUTIONER...THE BLACK KNIGHT...SAY HOLD!

Panel 2: I HAVE TOO LONG LISTENED TO THE SLANDERS WHISPERED ABOUT ME BY KNIGHTS WHO THINK THIS BOY WITH THE GOLDEN HAIR--THIS BEARD-LESS PUPPY WITH HIS MAIDEN'S FACE--IS MORE SKILLED THAN I! I MUST SPEAK! I BEG OF THEE PROPER ACKNOWLEDGE-MENT, SIRE!

Panel 3: YAY, I AM THE UGLIEST MAN IN THE KINGDOM... MY BLOODY SCARS MAKE ME SO! BUT IT IS THIS UGLINESS WHICH HAS MADE ME THY EXECUTIONER, AND BEARS WITNESS TO MY MASTERY!

CALM THYSELF, SIR HUGO! WE HAVE MEANT THEE NO SHAME. INDEED--THERE IS NO ONE IN MY ENTIRE REALM TO MATCH THY ARMS AND CUNNING! MY DAUGHTER APOLO-GIZES FOR HER RASH WORDS!

Panel 4: NAY! I WILL NOT HAVE AN UGLY MONSTER BULLY US INTO COWED SUBMISSION! SIR GWAINE HAS PROVEN HIMSELF TODAY--AND NO ONE CAN DENY IT! NOT EVEN THEE, BLACK KNIGHT!

I AM HUMBLED...FOR I WILL NOT DEFY MY PROTECTOR, THY FATHER BUT...WERE THEE A KNIGHT WHO SPOKE THOSE VAIN-GLORIOUS WORDS, I WOULD SPEW THEE IN TWO UPON MY SWORD!

Panel 5: THEN HAVE AT IT, MY JEALOUS COCK! I CANNOT LET YOUR INSULT TO MY FAIR LADY GO UNANSWERED.

SIR GWAINE! STOP!

Panel 6: TOO LATE, MY LORD! I CHALLENGE THY EXECUTIONER TO A TRIAL BY MORTAL COMBAT!

Panel 7: SO BE IT! SIR HUGO-- SINCE YOU ARE THE CHALLENGED PARTY, YOU HAVE THE CHOICE OF WEAPONS!

MY CHOICE IS--THE COMPLETE COMBAT ARMS OF THE BATTLE KNIGHT!

AGREED!

THAT NEXT MORNING--THE TRIAL BY COMBAT BEGAN!
CRASHH!
CLANG!
CRACK!
CRAASHH!
KLONG!
KRANGGG!
4

ON AND ON THEY FOUGHT—RIPPING, TEARING, CUTTING MAIMING ONE ANOTHER, UNTIL—

THIS IS YOUR—FINISH—SIR GWAINE—YOUR *FINISH*—

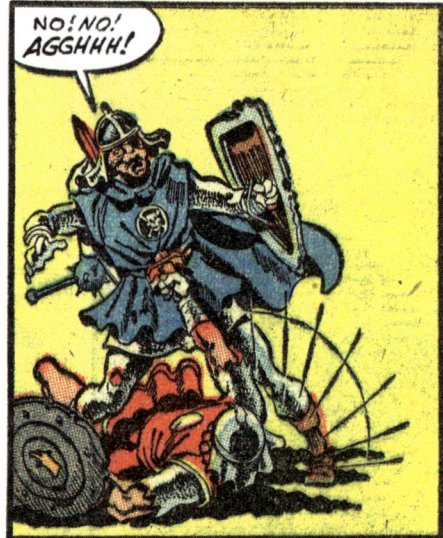

NO! NO! AGGHHH!

SIR GWAINE IS THE VICTOR! ALL HAIL THE VICTOR!

YOU HAVE DONE ADMIRABLY, SIR GWAINE! AND YOU SHALL HAVE YOUR REWARD—! THE *HIGHEST* REWARD OF THIS LAND! ALL MY NOBLES AND LADIES SHALL FOREVER ACKNOWLEDGE YOUR VICTORY OVER SIR HUGO!

AND TWO MONTHS AFTERWARDS—ON THE KING'S JOUSTING FIELDS...

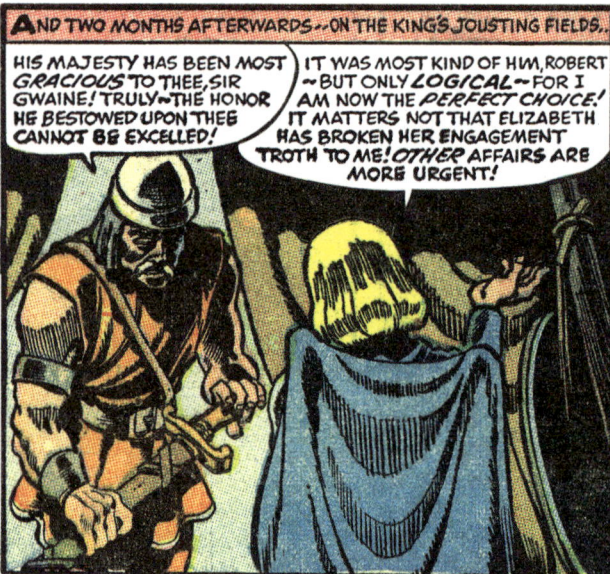

HIS MAJESTY HAS BEEN MOST *GRACIOUS* TO THEE, SIR GWAINE! TRULY—THE HONOR HE BESTOWED UPON THEE CANNOT BE EXCELLED!

IT WAS MOST KIND OF HIM, ROBERT—BUT ONLY *LOGICAL*—FOR I AM NOW THE *PERFECT CHOICE*! IT MATTERS NOT THAT ELIZABETH HAS BROKEN HER ENGAGEMENT TROTH TO ME! *OTHER* AFFAIRS ARE MORE URGENT!

SO SAYING, OUT STEPPED SIR IVAN GWAINE FROM HIS TENT THAT BRIGHT SUNNY DAY IN MERRY ENGLAND—CHANGED BY DAILY BATTLE AND COMBAT—TO THE *UGLIEST* MAN IN THE *KINGDOM*—THE *GREATEST* KNIGHT OF ALL—THE KING'S EXECUTIONER—THE *BLACK KNIGHT*!

The End

73

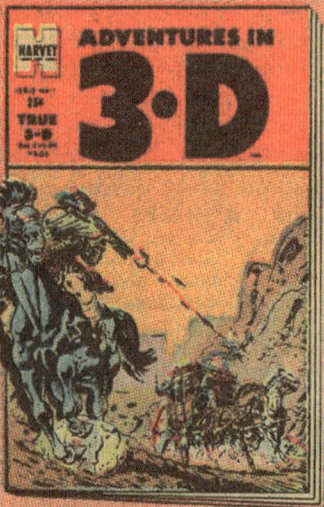

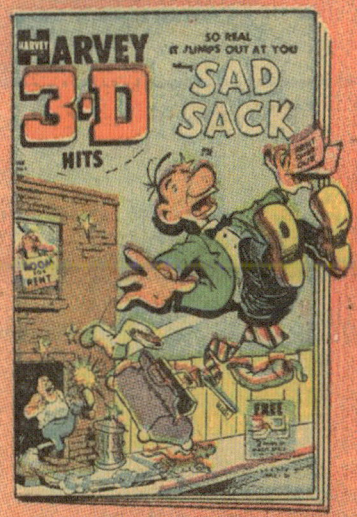

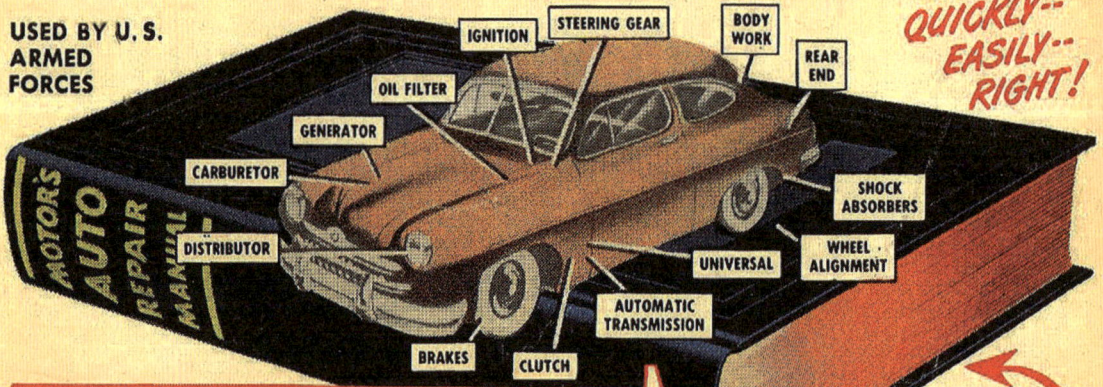

76

HERE IS A TALE TO MAKE YOUR HAIR STAND ON END! IT'S A REAL SHOCK SHAMPOO CALLED THE...

THE WIG-MAKER

J'MINY-HOSEPHAT! THIS SWEET LI'L OLE HAIR! SOFT 'N PURRIN' LIK' A BABY IN-FANT-ILE KITTY! I SUR' GIT GOOD STOCK!...WHEN I WANTA!

THE TOWN OF WEBSTER WAS SMALL IN 1890, BUT EVEN THEN IT HAD A MAIN STREET...A DIRT ROAD THAT WAS CAKED HOT IN THE SUMMER AND WHICH TURNED TO MUDDY SLUSH IN THE WINTER. ONE OF THE STORES ON THAT MAIN STREET WAS "LEMUEL BOONE'S RARIFIED WIG SALON"!

HOWDY DO, MR. AVERILL? NEVAH 'PECTED TA SEE YOU IN HEAH! COMES AS A RIGHT BIG SUH-PRISE TA ME! BUT...A PLEASANT ONE! YESIRREE!

I'VE BEEN HOLD-ING OFF THIS... UH...VISIT AS LONG AS POSSIBLE, LEM, YOU CAN UNDERSTAND WHY!

TING-A-LING!

YA DON'T HAVTA SAY IT TWIC'T, MR. AVERILL. I AM THE SPITTIN' IMAGE OF DEE-CORUM! 'COURSE T'AIN'T NUTHIN' TA BE ASHAMED OF...BALD-NESS, I MEAN!

NEVERTHELESS, I HAVE LOST MY HAIR! A MAN ...AHEM...IN MY POSITION...AHEM... WITH THE WOMEN CAN-NOT AFFORD SUCH A SLUR! YOU WILL MAKE ME A WIG! I STRESS EXACT DUPLICATION OF MY FORMER HAIR!

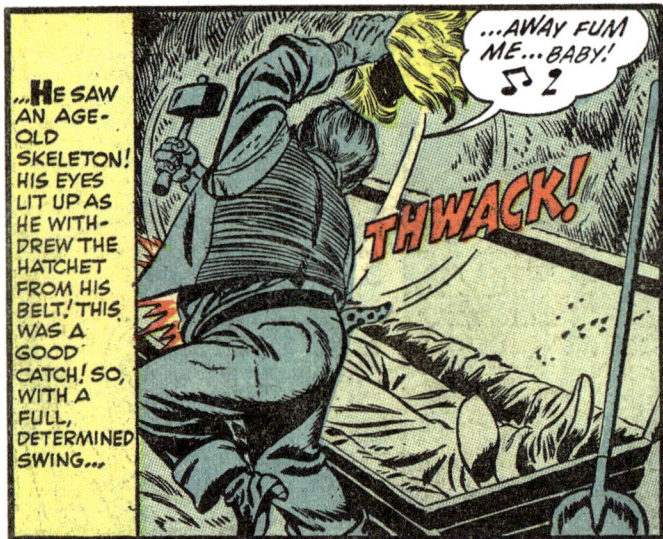

Panel 1: AFTER SOME MECHANICS, LEM HAD A FINISHED WIG! AND WHEN AVERILL CAME IN...

IT'S A...*MIRACLE*, LEM! I FEEL LIKE MY OLD SELF! A *STUPENDOUS* JOB!

THANK YA, MR. AVERILL! I KNEW YA'D *'PREC-I-ATE* IT! NOW... IF I CUD JES' *COLLECT* MY FEE...

Panel 2: THERE YOU ARE, LEM! YOU DESERVE EVERY PENNY OF IT! *YOU'LL GO PLACES!*

TWENNY...TWENNY-FIVE...SURE, MR. AVERILL...THERDDY...THERDDY-FIVE... GOODBYE, MR. AVERILL...FORTY...

Panel 3: SINCE WEBSTER WAS A SMALL TOWN, IT WAS VERY EASY FOR A MAN OF TALENT...SUCH AS LEM BOONE...TO RISE SWIFTLY! *DILIGENCE*...ONE OF HIS FORTÉS... HELPED GREATLY!

I DREAM O' JEANNIE...WITH THE...LI-I-I-GH-T BROWN HAIR...

THWACK!

Panel 4: WITH EACH SALE, LEM'S REPUTATION INCREASED! THE WORD SPREAD...EVEN TO NEIGHBORING TOWNS! LEM, PRESSED FOR SPACE, HAD TO MOVE TO BIGGER AND BETTER QUARTERS!

'MORNING, MR. BOONE!

LEM BOONE'S WIG EMPORIUM

HOWDY DO, MRS. MILLER!

Panel 5: WEBSTER WAS NO DIFFERENT THAN ANY OTHER TOWN! A TEMPORARY EPIDEMIC OF ROSE FEVER...BIRTHS...DEATHS! AND LEM TOOK MORE THAN A PASSING INTEREST IN FUNERALS!

POOR JUD IS...*DAID*! POOR JUD...

Panel 6: THWACK!

Panel 7: THERE WAS NO DOUBT THAT LEM WAS A MASTER TRADESMAN! MEN DOFFED THEIR HATS...NEVER KNOWING WHOSE HAIR WAS *REAL*...WHOSE HAIR WAS *LEM'S*! SUCH WAS THE CASE!

PLEASANT DAY, AIN'T IT, FRANK?

RIGHT PLEASANT, HORACE!

③

Panel 1: BUT...ONE DAY...A CUSTOMER ENTERED LEM'S WIG SALON! ONLY THIS ONE WAS DIFFERENT...*RADICALLY DIFFERENT!* IT HAD NEVER HAPPENED TO LEM BEFORE! IT WAS A...*WOMAN!*

UH...HOWDY...(*GULP*)...DO, MISS? YA AIN'T IN THE *WRONG* PLACE, ARE YA, MA'M? THIS IS LEM BOONE'S RARIFIED....!

YA CAN SETTLE DOWN, MR. BOONE! I *KNOW* WHERE I'M AT! AND...I KNOW WHAT I CAME FER! *A WIG!! FER...ME!*

Panel 2: YOU'VE GOT A HUGE REPUTATION, MR. BOONE! I CAN TRUST YA! I WANT A WIG OF...*STRAIGHT...LONG...BLACK...HAIR,* MR. BOONE! I WILL PAY ANYTHING FER IT...AS LONG AS I GETS WHAT I WANT! YA SEE...I'M WELL-TO-DO...*VERY WELL-TO-DO,* MR. BOONE!

YA FLATTER ME, MA'M! LEM BOONE'S ALWAYS PROUD TA SERVE THE *WELL-TO-DO!*

Panel 3: YA WON'T GET A PLUG NICKEL...IF YA DON'T SATISFY, MR. BOONE! DON'T FERGET...*STRAIGHT LONG BLACK HAIR!* GOOD-BYE, MR. BOONE!

NUFF SAID! YA'LL BE *DOO-LY* SAT-IS-FIED, MA'M! TAKE MY WORD FER IT!

Panel 4: HERE WAS A REAL CHOPPING GOOD CHANCE FOR LEM...AND HE HAD PLANNED TO EXECUTE IT IN THE USUAL WAY! HE WENT TO THE CEMETERY...FOUND THE SHOVEL...DUG...*BUT...*

OH, LOVELY TA LOOK...*HUH?!* THET...AIN'T LONG BLACK HAIR! GOT TA FIND IT....*IN ANUTHER PLACE!*

Panel 5: EXCITEDLY, LEM WIELDED HIS SPADE AGAIN, UNCOVERING ANOTHER GRAVE! BEADS OF SWEAT DOTTED HIS BROW! THERE WAS NOTHING! HE TRIED ONCE MORE! *NOTHING...*

WHAT'S GOIN' ON HEAH?!! I JES'...CAIN'T FIND THET STYLE HAIR!

REST IN PEACE

Panel 6: ONCE MORE HE DUG! *FAILURE!* AND AGAIN...*FAILURE!* HIS BACK ACHED...AND HE LEFT BEHIND HIM A TRAIL OF COFFINS AS HE LEFT THE CEMETERY AND ENTERED THE PRAIRIE!

Panel 7: THE MOONLIT PRAIRIE WAS WIDE AND EMPTY! LEM HAD USED UP HIS STORE OF GRAVES...NOTHING SEEMED TO BE LEFT! HE HAD JUST ABOUT GIVEN UP HOPE...WHEN...

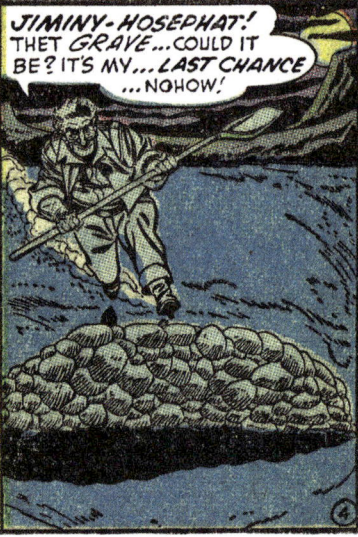

JIMINY-HOSEPHAT! THET *GRAVE*...COULD IT BE? IT'S MY...*LAST CHANCE* ...NOHOW!

DOOMSDAY

The night watchman at the Tower Art Gallery, elderly Thomas Gainor, turned the powerful beam of his flashlight up and down the corridor, revealing nothing but dignified emptiness. Gainor nodded, clicked the flash shut, and shuffled into the exhibition hall. His hand hovered at the light switch, then reluctantly moved away. No use antagonizing the boss.

The crowds had long since gone, and the gallery was dim and deserted. Even the echoes of the critics' excited, enthusiastic babble of acclaim for the artist were finally stilled. The mantle of midnight had fallen, shrouding in merciful darkness the walls of the Tower Art Gallery and the paintings by William Damon which hung upon them.

" . . . fiercely unconventional," the morning newspapers would say . . . "strange, darkly sinister subjects executed by a master hand" . . . "a great new talent, bringing something new and deeply disturbing to the American art scene . . ."

"But nobody ever said I couldn't shine my flash on the paintings!" the old man chortled silently. The harsh yellow beam played over the nearest one, a screaming study in scarlet, called simply "HELL." Gainor shuddered. Was this what modern art was coming to? The next one was even worse. A huge mottled blob of a face—undistinguishable as male or female — writhing and twisting in abject, consuming terror. Its name was "ECSTASY." It made the night watchman a little sick to his stomach.

By the time he reached the last one, the flashlight in Gainor's hand wavered noticeably. But it never occurred to him not to look. And this time he gasped aloud at what he saw. Against a background of roaring flames and toppling buildings, all the demons of eternity leered out at him from the canvas, their faces grinning monstrosities of joy at the total destruction around them. Only one face was not smiling — the face of a young, incredibly lovely girl who gazed up in horror at the demons from the pile of rubble on which she lay. The brass name-plate at the bottom of the painting read "DOOMSDAY."

. . . "it's pretty terrible, isn't it?" a girl's voice said quietly in the darkness . . . "to know that's what doomsday will be like . . ."

The old man spun around with surprising agility. "Who's there?" he croaked. The beam of his flashlight knifed through the dimness and encircled the slim figure of a girl who stood gazing pensively out the window. "What are you doing here, Miss?" he demanded shakily.

The girl didn't turn around, and when she spoke, her voice was dreamy. "I'm sorry if I startled you, sir," she said quietly. "I stayed after everyone else had gone this afternoon. I wanted to be alone with my face this one last time. You see, I was William Damon's model. It's my face he stole for that painting . . ."

"You make it sound as though he actually took your face off you and put it in the picture!" Gainor interrupted crossly.

. . . the girl turned around . . . "but that's exactly what I do mean," she said simply out of the empty space where her face should have been . . .

Mother Mongoose's NURSERY CRIMES

A FARMER WENT TROTTING ON HIS GRAY MARE, BUMPETY, BUMPETY, BUMP!

WITH HIS DAUGHTER BEHIND HIM, SO ROSY AND FAIR, NO RIGGETY-RAGGETY SHLUMP!

CLONK!

A SALESMAN CRIED "STOP!" AND BOTH LOOKED AROUND, STUMPETY, STUMPETY, STUMP!

FROM BEGINNING TO END, HE WAS VERY TIGHTLY BOUND, CLUMPETY, CLUMPETY, CLUMP!

Mother Mongoose's NURSERY CRIMES

"SEE A PIN AND PICK IT UP,

ALL THE DAY YOU'LL HAVE GOOD LUCK!

SEE A PIN AND LET IT LIE,

THUNK!

AGGSGH!

YOU'LL WISH YOU'D NEVER PASSED IT BY!"

83

AFTER SHOCK COMES THE QUESTION...

So What Next

YEAH, RACHEL~AIN'T THAT SOMETHING? WANTIN' TO GO OUT WITH *ME* AGAIN...AFTA HE TOOK ME TO A CRUMMY JOINT LIKE THAT? WHAT NERVE, I'LL SAY! I ASK YOU, ALREADY~~SO, WHAT NEXT?

"CADILLAC MISSY MODES" WAS A BUDDING TEXTILE FIRM! ITS FURNITURE WAS SECOND-HAND...ITS STYLES WERE YESTERDAY'S...AND ITS RECEPTIONIST WAS *DONA CHEPPER!*

DIDJA EVER SEE SUCH *CRUST?* WHAT? SURE I'LL SEE HIM! BUT, DON'T WORRY...I'LL PLAY *HARD-TA-GET!* THAT'LL TEACH 'M TA GET ON HIS HIGH-HORSE! YEAH...SURE...

MISS...CHEPPER! DON'T YOU EVER STOP TALKING?!!

AIN'T YOU THINKING OF THAT *LONG-DISTANCE CALL* I'M GONNA GET? HMMM? AIN'T YOU? IF YOU'RE GONNA WORK OVERTIME...DON'T BLOCK UP THE WIRES LIKE THAT! NOW~A FOND GOOD-BYE! I'LL BE BACK IN A LITTLE WHILE, MISS CHEPPER!

YES....MR. CRAVEN... YES!

MISS CHEPPER POLITELY WATCHED HER BOSS, MR. CRAVEN, TRUNDLE OUT THE OFFICE... ATTENTIVELY HEARD HIS FOOTSTEPS DIE OUT... THEN RETURNED TO THE SWITCHBOARD TELEPHONE!

HULLO, RACHEL? STILL THERE? YEAH, THAT WAS CRAVEN. WHAT? AW, WHO PAYS ATTENTION TA *HIM*? HE'S *NOTHIN'*! YEAH! I... UH... HOLD IT A SEC, WILL YA, RACHEL? THERE'S SOMETHING HERE...

DAILY NEW
MADMAN ON T... LOOSE AS THI... GIRL IS SLAI...
POLICE SEEK KILLE... ADMIT NO CLUES

RACHEL! I JUST READ THE NOOS- PAPER! YEAH! YOU, TOO? A GIRL AIN'T *SAFE* NO MORE, ALREADY! I'M TELLIN' YA -- SORT OF GIVES ME THE CREEPY- WEEPIES! WHAT? YA GOTTA HANG UP? OKAY, RACHEL-- DIG YA NOW... CALL YA LATER! TA-TAAA!

AFTER DONA TURNED THE LEVER KEY ON THE SWITCHBOARD ENDING HER CALL, THE SILENCE SEEMED TO BE DEAFENING! SHE QUICKLY READ THE STORY... RAVENOUSLY DEVOURING ALL THE SORDID DETAILS!

SHE FINISHED THE ACCOUNT... LEANED BACK IN HER CHAIR... AND BEGAN TO THINK! THE OFFICE WAS EMPTY! SHE WAS ALONE... AND IT WAS NIGHT! THEN... SHE FINGERED THE SWITCH- BOARD DIAL!

GOTTA TAWK TA SOMEBODY! I'LL GO OUTTA MY HEAD... IF I DON'! MAYBE... EMMA'S HOME?

HULLO, EMMA! MAN O' MAN... AM I GLAD TO TAWK TA YOU! YOU'LL NEVER KNOW HOW MUCH! SO, SPEAK TA ME, ALREADY! I'M ALL *ALONE* IN THE OFFICE... AND...

DONA CHEPPER BEGAN TO TALK AGAIN... NOT ABOUT ANY- THING IN PARTICULAR... BUT ABOUT THIS AND THAT! ANY- THING TO HEAR HERSELF! SUDDENLY, SHE SWIRLED TO A HARD KNOCKING ON THE DOOR...

YEAH... YEAH! OOOO! HOLD IT, EMMA... *SOMEBODY'S AT THE DOOR! DON'T HANG UP!* STAY... WHERE YA ARE! IF YA HEAR ME SCREAM... *RUN FOR THE NEAREST COP!* I'LL BE... DEAD!

KNOCK KNOCK

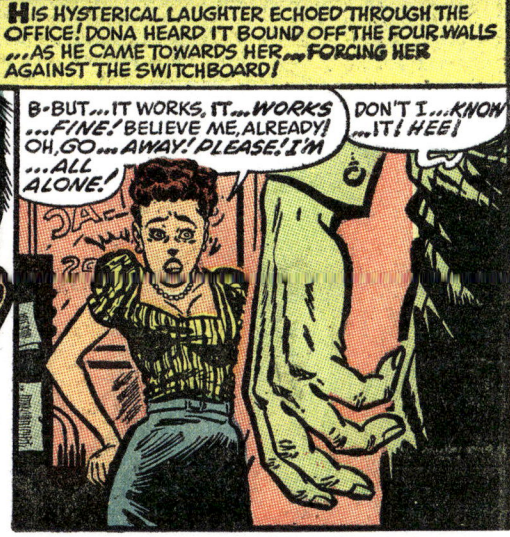

90

Men! Send for This Money-Making Outfit FREE!

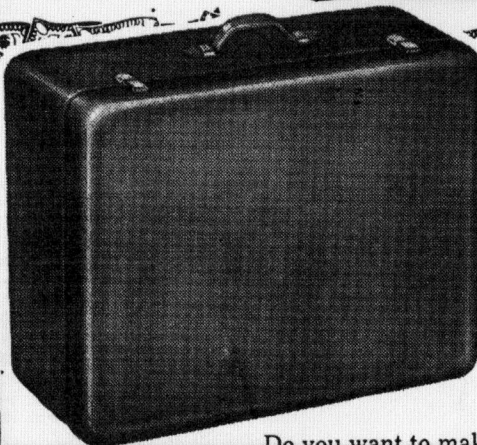

See How Easy It Is to Make UP TO $15.00 IN A DAY!

Do you want to make more money in full or spare time . . . as much as $15.00 in a day? Then mail the coupon below for this BIG OUTFIT, sent you FREE, containing more than 150 fine quality fabrics, sensational values in made-to-measure suits, topcoats, and overcoats. Take orders from friends, neighbors, fellow-workers. Every man prefers better-fitting, better-looking made-to-measure clothes, and when you show the many beautiful, high quality fabrics—mention the low prices for made-to-measure fit and style—and show our guarantee of satisfaction, you take orders right and left. You collect a big cash profit in advance on every order, and build up fine permanent income for yourself in spare or full time.

YOUR OWN SUITS WITHOUT 1¢ COST!

Our plan makes it easy for you to get your own personal suits, topcoats, and overcoats without paying 1¢—in addition to your big cash earnings. Think of it! Not only do we start you on the road to making big money, but we also make it easy for you to get your own clothes without paying one penny. No wonder thousands of men write enthusiastic letters of thanks.

Just Mail Coupon

You don't invest a penny of your money now or any time. You don't pay money for samples, for outfits, or for your own suit under our remarkable plan. So do as other men have done—mail the coupon now. Don't send a penny. Just send us the coupon.

NO EXPERIENCE NEEDED

It's amazingly easy to take measures, and you don't need any experience to take orders. Everything is simply explained for you to cash in on this wonderful opportunity. Just mail this coupon now and we'll send you this big, valuable outfit filled with more than 150 fine fabrics and everything else you need to start. You'll say this is the greatest way to make money you ever saw. Rush the coupon today!

PROGRESS TAILORING CO., Dept. E-276
500 S. Throop Street, Chicago 7, Illinois

Progress Tailoring Co., Dept. E-276
500 S. Throop St., Chicago 7, Illinois

Dear Sir: I WANT MONEY AND I WANT A SUIT TO WEAR AND SHOW, without paying 1¢ for it. Rush Valuable Suit Coupon and Sample Kit with actual fabrics ABSOLUTELY FREE.

Name_____ Age_____

Address_____

City_____ State_____

91

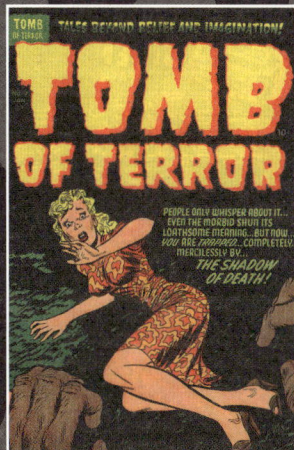

Witches Tales
April 1954 - Issue #24

Cover Art - Lee Elias

Undertaker
Script - Howard Nostrand
Pencils -Howard Nostrand
Inks - Howard Nostrand

Mutiny On The Boundary
Script - Bob Powell
Pencils - Bob Powell
Inks - Bob Powell

Eye Eye, Sir
Script - Unknown
Pencils - Sid Check
Inks - Sid Check

Monumental Feat
Script - Unknown
Pencils - Manny Stallman
Inks - Joe Certa

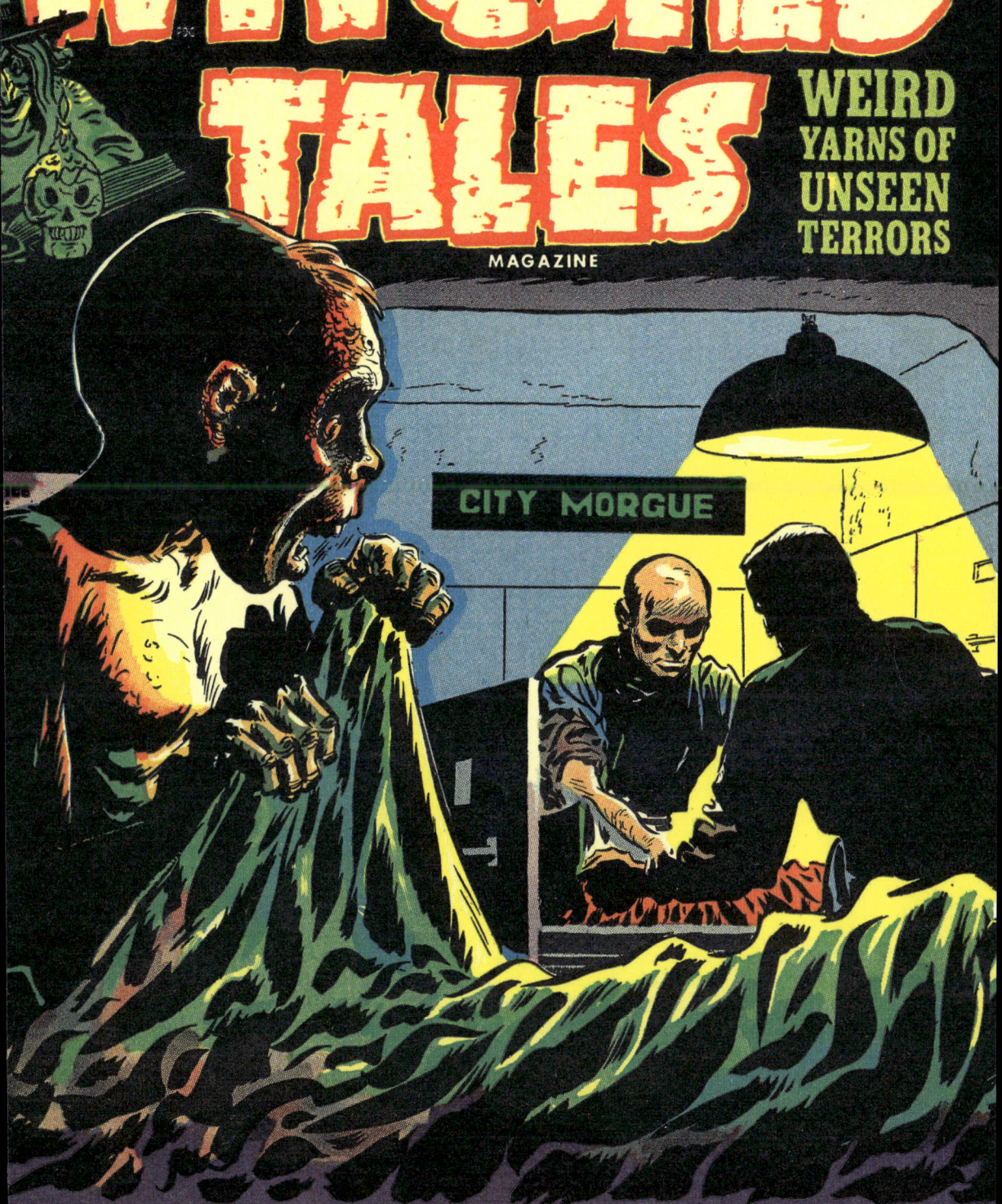

START A FINE BUSINESS IN SPARE TIME!

RUN THE BEST
"SHOE STORE BUSINESS"
IN YOUR TOWN!

FREE! SELLING OUTFIT

QUICK-START SELLING OUTFIT FREE!
YOU DON'T INVEST A CENT!

Now you can have a profitable "Shoe Store Business" right in your hands! None of the expenses of rent, light, fixtures, etc. of the ordinary shoe store. You just make money—up to $84 a week *extra* on just 3 easy sales a day! You're independent, with an opportunity to make a handsome income as long as you care to take orders in a business with a never-ending demand, because EVERYBODY WEARS SHOES.

Just rush the coupon—I'll send you my Quick-Start shoe outfit right away, ABSOLUTELY FREE. Start by selling to friends, relatives, neighbors, to people where you work. Valuable actual samples, and demonstrators of calf skin leather are furnished free of cost to qualified men.

My Professional Selling Outfit contains cut-away demonstrator so your customers can actually *feel* the restful Velvet-eez Air Cushion innersole. Special measuring device—National Advertising reprints—door opener kits—polishing cloths—actual shoes—everything you need to build a profitable repeat business. Here's your chance to join me and get into the BIG MONEY shoe business now!

OVER 160 FAST-SELLING STYLES
FOR MEN & WOMEN!

Satisfy the needs and tastes of almost every person in your community. Sell air-cooled Nylon Mesh shoes with Velvet-eezair cushion innersoles—horsehide, kid, kangaroo leather shoes, slip-resistant Gro-Cork soles, oil-resistant Neoprene soles—every good type of dress, sport and work footwear—over 160 styles for men and women! Your customers will be amazed at the comfort they get from walking on 10,000 tiny air bubbles in Velvet-eez shoes. Also special steel shanks. You're way ahead of competition—you draw on our huge stock of over 200,000 pairs—thus your customers get the EXACT style, size and width they order! Your service ends tiresome shopping from store to store trying to find a shoe that fits in a style the customer wants. Special features make it *extra* easy to sell gas station men, factory workers, waiters, etc. Because Mason Shoes are *not* sold in stores, people must buy from YOU and KEEP buying from you!

Start Right NOW!

Just mail the coupon . . . I'll rush your FREE Starting Outfit that includes EVERYTHING you need to start making exciting cash profits *right away!*

TOP MEN MAKE $5 TO $10 IN AN HOUR!... YOU DON'T INVEST A CENT ... MAKE BIG PROFITS...NO STORE OVERHEAD ... EXCLUSIVE SALES FEATURES BUILD YOUR REPEAT BUSINESS!

Get Exciting EXTRA Awards This Year!

This year we are celebrating our "Golden Anniversary" . . . 50 years of bringing top quality shoes to the men and women of America. Mason Shoe Counselors will share in thousands of dollars of EXTRA prizes . . . including valuable *free* merchandise awards and bonus checks! Right NOW is the perfect time to start in this profitable business!

NATIONAL ADVERTISING CREATES HUGE DEMAND FOR VELVET-EEZ SHOES!

Due to our National Advertising, millions have seen Mason Velvet-eez Shoes in magazines and on Television. Now we need more good men to satisfy that demand and make plenty of extra cash for themselves. Just show the wonderful exclusive Velvet-eez Air Cushion that brings such comfort to men and women who stand on their feet all day. The Velvet-eez-demonstrator you'll get free will make easy sales for you, as it has for others. The famed Good Housekeeping Guarantee Seal is another Mason "extra" that keeps steady profits rolling in!

Guaranteed by Good Housekeeping

DON'T DELAY

SEND FOR FREE OUTFIT!

MR. NED MASON, DEPT. MA-306
MASON SHOE MFG. CO.
CHIPPEWA FALLS, WISCONSIN

Please rush me your FREE Quick Start Shoe Selling Outfit featuring Air Cushion shoes, other fast sellers, *everything* I need to go into this profitable business, and start making immediate cash profits!

Name_____ Age_____

Address_____

Town_____ State_____

MASON SHOE MFG. CO.
DEPT. MA-306 CHIPPEWA FALLS, WISC.

WITCHES TALES, APRIL, 1954, VOL. 1, NO. 24, IS PUBLISHED BI-MONTHLY
by WITCHES TALES, INC., 1860 Broadway, New York 23, N. Y. Entered as second class matter at the Post Office at New York, N. Y., under the Act of March, 3, 1879. Single copies, 10c. Subscription rates, 10 issues for $1.00 in the U. S. and possessions, elsewhere $1.50. All names in this periodical are entirely fictitious and no identification with actual persons is intended. Contents copyrighted, 1954, by Witches Tales, Inc., New York, City. Printed in the U.S.A. Title registered in U. S. Patent Office.

WELCOME

The four greatest weird books, in announcing a new policy, have pulled one of the most terrifying coup d'etats in the sanctified realm of horror.

For, CHAMBER OF CHILLS, WITCHES TALES, TOMB OF TERROR, and BLACK CAT MYSTERY have joined together in a four-power horror pact.

And this package of unbeatable shock will come to you in a cyclical pattern of doom, with four distinctive terror books getting to you during a two-month period. Thus, a mag belonging to this group will appear on your newsstands every two weeks -- each one a king of shock.

Just look at this shock king's domain...

BLACK CAT MYSTERY will offer you a package of real-life horror, where man meets man in a mad clash of reality...

WITCHES TALES is designed to tickle your funny bone and chill your spine, the strangest and most different terror mag ever created.

TOMB OF TERROR will consist of stories told out of this world, an unmistakeable unit of horror ripped from the many unexplored voids...

CHAMBER OF CHILLS will carry you to the incredible sphere of the supernatural whose teller is as weird as his stories!

Look for them!

UNDERTAKER

PA HAS TOLD ME A LOT! HE'S TOLD ME THAT THE WORLD OUTSIDE IS HARD...CRUEL... ROTTEN TO THE CORE! HE'S ALSO TOLD ME TO STAY AS FAR AWAY FROM IT AS I CAN. THEREBY HANGS A TALE! YOU SEE...

I...LIKE... IT... OUTSIDE...!

DOXY!

THIS IS PA...

GET AWAY FROM THAT WINDOW!

TCH! TCH! WHY DO YOU DO FOOLISH THINGS? HAVEN'T I ALWAYS TOLD YOU WHAT'S OUTSIDE, CHILD? BITTERNESS...RANCOR! EVIL PERSONIFIED! COME AWAY, CHILD!

YES, PA!

FIRES AND BRIMSTONE AWAIT YOU...OUTSIDE!

Y-YES...!

HERE...IS...FINALITY!

DEATH!

I--I SEE, PA!

YES...! IS THIS IS PA!

SO...FOR ALL MY LIFE...MY WHOLE WORLD WAS CONFINED TO AN UNDER-TAKING PARLOR! CAN YOU IMAGINE SUCH A WORLD? AGE-WORN CARPETS...CONTINUAL SILENCE...DEAD BODIES...SWATHED WITH RIGOR-MORTIS...BEING ROLLED TO A WAITING COFFIN...

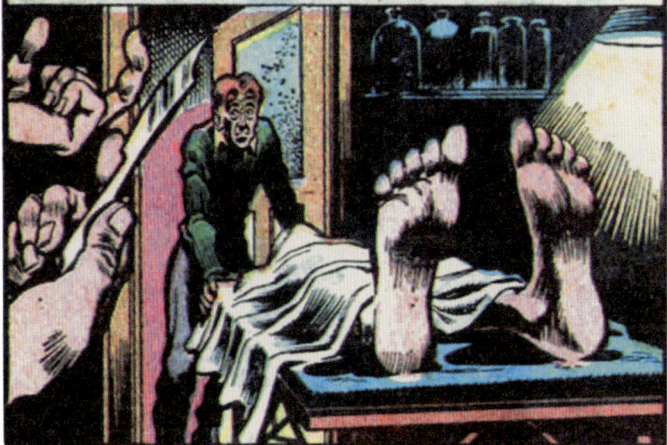

...DRESSED IN SUNDAY'S FINEST...HANDS CLASPED ANGELICALLY...REPOSING ON A BED OF WOOD...SOFT SATIN RUFFLED TO CARESS ITS FACE...

...THEN THE LID SLAMMING SHUT... TIGHTLY SHUT...

SLAM!

RRRRRMMMM

WHAT A LIFE! WHAT A DECREPID... NO-GOOD...GERM-EATEN...STAGNANT ...MUTE LIFE! I CAN'T...

...TAKE IT...

...ANY MORE...!

WHAM

I LAY IN THE COFFIN...QUIET...HUSHED...STILL! NO MUSCLE WITHIN ME STIRRED! PA CALLED TO ME...

DOXYYYY! YOO HOO! THIS...COFFIN'S GOT...TO GO! DOXYYYY!

PA COULDN'T FIND ME! HE DID ALL THE WORK BY HIM-SELF...NOT KNOWING HOW CLOSE I WAS TO HIM...

WHERE...IS...THAT...CHILD?

WE'RE OFF! SOON AS WE...HAHAHA...GET TO THE CEMETERY...AND PA DELIVERS THIS COFFIN...

...I'LL BREAK OUT OF THIS COFFIN...AND...RUN...LIKE A BEAVER...FREE...HEEHEEHEE...I'LL BE FREE...

ONLY...

I FORGOT...

THE FIRES...

CREMATORIUM

THE END

PICTURES

Driblets of clouds floated by the moon, casting the street in moving, dark shadows. Harry Peck waited, fingering the camera ever so slightly. *They're still talking...*

He inched forward, out of the building's protective corner, coming nearer the opened window. *Get it right,* Peck thought, *snap it when they plunge the knife into him!*

Peck was out in the open now, standing immediately in front of the window; he held the camera to his eye. He saw the three figures: the sleeping man, the blonde woman with her fiendish gleam, and the other man, his face broken out in beads of glistening sweat, gripping the knife.

Suddenly, the knife fell. Peck snapped the shutter. There was the grating sound of steel into flesh, followed by a throaty death grunt. Then, Peck ran, away from the house, away from the murder; he ran, his breath coming hard. He held the camera tightly in his hand, not wanting to lose it now ... not after he got his picture.

Then, he stopped, resting his frame against a tree. It was quiet, the air about him hushed and still. *No good,* he thought. Peck wasn't satisfied. *The boss wouldn't like it.* He had to have the right one ... with the right tone ... with the right spirit! "Real gore!" that's what the boss said.

He took out a cigarette, lit a match and, out of the corner of his eye, caught a glimpse of a woman in the middle of a street. She was alone. *Too alone!* Instinc-tively, Peck shot the camera to his eye level and caught the woman in its square sights.

I knew it! Another murder! The woman was trapped in the glare of a car's headlights, webbed inescapably in the twin orbs of the machine-monster that bore down on her with the speed of a death projectile.

Peck caught the action. The car hit the woman head-on, sending her tumbling to the the floor and then, in a clash of gears, zooming on. The woman lay on the ground, her head smashed in a pool of blood. She was dead.

Peck was dejected, though. *It's not what I want. Not what the boss wants! Gore ... real, ugly, horrible gore ...!* He felt despondent, walking along the residential street.

Abruptly, he shivered. His spine tingled. The cold, clammy, invisible hand of fear tore across his face, leaving him frozen to the spot he was standing at. He stared wide-eyed at the scene before him.

....T-there it is! He slowly lifted the camera, his fingers twisted with fright. *God, how horrible!* His tongue felt as though it was swollen as he licked his lips. *Get it over with ... and run!* Peck snapped the shutter.

Later, Peck flung the finished, glossy photographs on his boss's desk.

The boss looked at them, wincing. "Yeow!" The boss shuddered. "That's what I want!"

Peck smiled. "Yeah," he said, "I knew you'd like it. Nothing so horrible to us ... like CHILDREN PLAYING!"

The boss looked at Peck. They both smiled. Peck and his boss were ghouls, ugly, torn ghouls — and pictures of children playing, for ghouls, are real gore.

STATEMENT OF THE OWNERSHIP, MANAGEMENT AND CIRCULATION REQUIRED BY THE ACT OF CONGRESS OF AUGUST 24, 1912, AS AMENDED BY THE ACTS OF MARCH 3, 1933, AND JULY 2, 1946, OF WITCHES' TALES published Monthly at New York, N. Y. for October 1, 1953.

1. The names and addresses of the publisher, editor, managing editor, and business managers are: Editor: Leon Harvey, 1860 Broadway, N. Y. C.; Managing Editor: Alfred Harvey, 1860 Broadway, N. Y. C.; Business Manager: Robert B. Harvey, 1860 Broadway, N. Y. C. Publisher: Witches Tales, Inc. 1860 Broadway, N. Y. C.

2. The owners are Witches Tales, Inc., 1860 Broadway, N. Y. C.; Leon Harvey, 1860 Broadway, N. Y. C.; Alfred Harvey, 1860 Broadway, N. Y. C.; Robert B. Harvey, 1860 Broadway, N. Y. C.

3. The known bondholders, mortgagees, and other security holders owning or holding 1 percent or more of total amount of bonds, mortgages, or other securities are: None.

4. Paragraphs 2 and 3 include, in cases where the stockholder or security holder appears upon the books of the company as trustee or in any other fiduciary relation, the name of the person or corporation for whom such trustee is acting; also the statements in the two paragraphs show the affiant's full knowledge and belief as to the circumstances and conditions under which stockholders and security holders who do not appear upon the books of the company as trustees, hold stock and securities in a capacity other than that of a bona fide owner.

(signed) ROBERT B. HARVEY, Business Manager

Sworn and subscribed to before me this 30th day of September, 1953.

Moe J. Mescheroni (My commission expires March 30th, 1954)

Mother Mongoose's NURSERY CRIMES

"PUSSY CAT, PUSSY CAT WHERE HAVE YOU BEEN?"

SAID THE CAT—"I'VE GONE TO SEE ONE OF MY KIN!"

"PUSSY CAT, PUSSY CAT, HAS YOUR KIN A NAME?"

"NO," SAID THE CAT, "BUT I LIKE HIM ALL THE SAME!"

Mother Mongoose's NURSERY CRIMES

DOCTOR FOSTER WENT TO GLOUCESTER

IN A TORRENT OF RAIN! THE BRIDGE—IT HAD TUMBLED,

THE HORSE—IT HAD FUMBLED, SO DOCTOR FOSTER

NEVER WENT TO GLOUCESTER AGAIN!

NOW WE GO TO THE BOOK-SHELF AND PULL OUT ONE OF THE WORLD'S MOST FAMOUS STORIES, AND SHOW YOU HOW *WITCHES TALES* WOULD DO IT!

MUTINY ON THE BOUNDARY

A BOO OF THE MONTH

THE HMS *BOUNDARY*, BOUND FOR TAHITI AND THE SOUTH SEAS, WAS A TOMB OF TORTURE FOR ITS MEN -- FOR RULING WITH AN IRON FIST AND A BLACK SOUL WAS ITS POWER-CRAZED CAPTAIN, THE TYRANT, WILLIAM BLAH!

MITH-TER GOBBLE! THAT IS *HOW* WE *MUST DEAL* WITH THESE *CURTH.* AS MY *FIRST MATE* -- YOU *SHOULD* HAVE DEALT OUT *PROPER PUNISHMENT!*

BUT, SIR! THE MAN HAS NOT BEEN WELL FOR TWO DAYS NOW. HE COULDN'T HAVE TURNED THE WHEEL MUCH MORE QUICKLY--

DLEATH DO NOT TAKE *ITH-THUE* WITH MY *ORDER-TH,* MITH-TER GOBBLE! I AM *STILL CAPTAIN* OF THITH *SHIP!* I SHALL NOT BE THITH LENIENT WITH *ANY* OF *THESE MEN* AGAIN. *I* AM THE *LAW* HERE. I MUST BE *OBEYED* -- TO THE *LETTER!*

YES, CAPTAIN!

DAY AFTER DAY.. HOUR AFTER HOUR.. A RAVING, RANTING MADMAN STRODE UP AND DOWN THE DECKS, HOLDING THE POWER OF LIFE OVER A HUNDRED TERROR-STRICKEN, SULLEN MEN...

THITH BRATH-RAILING IS *FILTHY*, THCUM! YOU *HAVE NOT CARRIED OUT MY ORDERTH!* DO YOU *KNOW* THE *PENALTY* FOR SUCH *CARE-LETHNETH! DEATH! YETH!* I CAN *PRONOUNCE* DEATH ON YOU! MITHTER GOBBLE! MITHTER GOB-BLE!

HERE, CAPTAIN. BEGGING THE CAPTAIN'S PARDON-- BUT WON'T YOU HAVE *PITY* AND *COMMUTE* HIS SENTENCE, SIR?

PERHAPTH YOU ARE RIGHT! WE HAVE NEED OF ALL HANDTH! UP, TWINE -- YOU'LL HANG BY THE YARD-ARM INSTEAD!

NO! N-NO! PLEASE, CAP'N.. PLEASE--! NOT THAT! I-- I'LL BE DEAD BY MORNIN'!

NO! NO...UGH! NO-O-O-O..!

LIFT HIM *HIGHER*... THERE! LET HIM *FEEL* THE *WIND* ON HITH *TREMBLING* FACE!

YOU *DIRTY*... FAT *DOG!* MAY YOU *ROT* IN *HADES* FOR YOUR *BLACK HEART!*

YOU DARE THPEAK BACK TO ME? MITHTER GOBBLE! CLAP THIS ROGUE IN IRONS! WE SHALL TAKE HIM BACK TO ENGLAND FOR HANGING!

RISE UP! CRUSH THIS *CRAZED* HOUND, LADS! UP... AT... HIM..!

BLAH LISTENED TO THE SCREAMING SAILOR- CALMLY LISTENED AS HE WIPED HIS BROW-CALMLY LISTENED, AS A TIC IN THE CORNER OF HIS EYE BOTHERED HIM- CALMLY LISTENED, AS HE WITHDREW A FLINTLOCK FROM HIS BELT-AND FIRED...

THE BALL ENTERED THE SAILOR WITH A SUDDEN THUD,...TOPPLING HIM OVER...DEAD! BLAH BREATHED HEAVILY A FEW TIMES - AND THEN TURNED TOWARDS HIS FIRST MATE...

CLEAR THE *DECK* OF THITH... *CARRION*, MITHTER GOBBLE! WE *SHALL NOT* THTAND FOR *INTHUBORDINATION* ON THITH *SHIP!* FOLLOW ME OUT, THIR!

NIGHT CAME AND WITH IT, SURCEASE! CAPTAIN BLAH RETIRED TO HIS CABIN AFTER A HEARTY MEAL...AND SLEPT SOUNDLY! MEANWHILE...A FEW MEN SPOKE IN HUSHED WHISPERS...THEIR FACES LIT BY PALE LANTERN LIGHT...

HEAR ME OUT, HUGH. WE MUST KILL HIM! WE CANNOT CONTINUE UNDER HIS WILL MUCH LONGER!

LOWER...YOUR...VOICE, LAD! HMM! AYE... 'TIS THE BEST WAY!

NO, JAMIE. 'TIS THE WRONG WAY-- BECAUSE IT IS *MUTINY!* HAVE PATIENCE! WE SHALL FIND HARBOR AT TAHITI SOON.

TAHITI--SONG--WOMEN FOR ALL OF US! HAPPINESS-- LAUGHTER..AY--IT IS LIKE A DREAM OF HEAVEN. ALL RIGHT, HUGH.. WE'LL WAIT!

YES.. WE MUST WAIT...WAIT!

THE MEN BIDED THEIR TIME... SAVORING THE SWEET DREAM OF REACHING A MISTY ISLAND... CRANING THEIR NECKS TOWARDS THE CROW'S NEST WHERE THE FIRST WORD WOULD COME FROM! THEN IT CAME... AND WHEN THE "BOUNDARY" DROPPED ANCHOR...!

ALL *LEAVES* ARE *CANTHELLED,* MITHTER GOBBLE! THESE MEN ARE *CONFINED* TO THEIR *QUARTERTH..* FOR THEIR THURLY THLIPSHOD *DITHOBEDIENCE!* I AM GOING *ASHORE*...TO *PRETHENT* MY *CREDENTIALS!*

A-AYE, SIR...!

BUT NEWS OF THE *BOUNDARY'S* APPEARANCE HAD REACHED THE NATIVES, AND SOON...

PLENTY OF WINE, FOOD, AND SPICES, LADS. STOCK UP BEFORE HIS ROYAL LOWNESS RETURNS! *YAHHAOOO!*

BUT AS FATE WOULD HAVE IT, CAPTAIN BLAH RETURNED PRE-MATURELY, AND...

THIS IS *RANK* INTHUBORDINANCE, MITHTER GOBBLE! I HOLD YOU *RETHPONTHIBLE* FOR THIS *SHOCKING OCCURENTH!* YOU SHALL BE *DOCKED THIX* MONTHS *PAY.* ATH FOR THE *RETHT*--THE LEMONS...FRUIT... AND FOODSTUFFS....*ALL* ARE TO BE CATHT *OVERBOARD!*

BUT, CAPTAIN BLAH.. SIR.. WE NEED LEMONS BADLY. SCURVY MAY BREAK OUT.. AND --

THILENTH! I AM *WELL AWARE* OF THAT! HOWEVER, ORDERTH ARE TO TRANTHPORT *POTTED PALMS* BACK TO ENGLAND. WE HAVE NO ROOM FOR...LEMONS!

BUT...FOR *DARING* TO *QUESTION* MY AUTHORITY...YOU WILL BE *PLACED* IN THE BRIG ON... *BREAD* AND *WATER*...FOR THE *DURATION* OF OUR *VOYAGE!* OUT OF MY THIGHT! I AM SHACKLED WITH STUPID FOOLS!

THE DAY OF RECKONING WILL COME, BLAH! I *SWEAR* IT!

NOW BEGAN THE LONG VOYAGE HOME..AND BLAH GREW INCREASINGLY WORSE...

LAY ON, YOU DECK LICE! MARK WELL YOUR ENERGIES! I'LL *NOT* HAVE A *LAZY MAN* ON BOARD THITH SHIP! *LAY..ON*..

HEAVE... *HEAVE*...

WE CAN *THROW* HIM *OVERBOARD* AND SET *COURSE* FOR THE ISLANDS, HUGH. HE'LL *KILL* US ALL *BEFORE* THIS TRIP'S *FINISHED*!

NO, JAMIE! I HAVE A *BETTER* IDEA. HAVE PATIENCE, MAN-- AND...*WAIT*... *WAIT*...!

ONE WEEK LATER, AS THE BOUNDARY NEARED THE STORM-TOSSED ARCHIPELAGOS...

YOU *DATHTARDLY* FOOL! I'LL *TEACH* YOU TO POLISH MY BOOTS WITH VIGOR FROM NOW ON. MITHTER GOBBLE... *MITHTER GOBBLE* I *WANT* THIS MAN *LASHED* TO THE *WHEEL*!

SPARE ME, SIR! THE WIND *WILL CUT* ME TO RIBBONS!

THEN THAT *WILL* BE TO YOUR *DITHADVANTAGE*, MY JACKANAPETH! WELL! WHAT ARE YOU *THWABIES TNTARING* AT ME FOR? *GET ABOUT YOUR WORK!* HALF FOOD RATIONS FOR *ALL*, MITHTER GOBBLE!

DID YOU *HEAR*? MITHTER GOBBLE! ANSWER ME, SIR... AT ONCE! GIVE THE ORDER FOR THESE DECK THCUM TO DITHPERTH! *AT...ONCE...THIR--* OR BY HEAVEN, I'LL ...

MITHTER GOBBLE... DO YOUR *DUTY*! I'M... *CAPTAIN*...HERE! YOU MEN...GO *BACK*.. I'LL HAVE...YOU ALL *HANGED*...FOR... *M-MUTINY*...

AND NOW.. AS IF SHOT OUT OF A CANNON, THE HMS *BOUNDARY* SURGED FORWARD LIKE A SOARING BIRD, SWIFTLY AND BUOYANTLY TOWARD HOME...

LAY TO, MATIES! CAPTAIN BLAH HAS GIVEN US A *FULL ROUND* OF *GROG* TONIGHT!

YOUR ORDERS ARE TO RAISE SAIL? AYE...AYE...SIR!

TWO DEGREES NOR' BY NOR'WES; CAPTAIN! WE'RE... *STRAIGHT*...ON COURSE!

AND FOUR MONTHS LATER-- ENGLAND!

I AM LORD TREWAINE, GENTLEMEN... COMMISSIONER OF HIS HIGHNESS' HARBOR! WE HAVE *RECEIVED* A *LETTER* BY *CLIPPER SHIP* FROM YOUR CAPTAIN BLAH...WHILE IN *TAHITI*...THAT HE FEARS *MUTINY* ON BOARD SHIP! *PREPARE* TO STAND *INSPECTION*!

MUTINY IS A *SERIOUS* OFFENSE, GENTLEMEN. IF CAPTAIN BLAH'S *CHARGES SHOULD PROVE* TO BE *MERITED*...YOU MUST *STAND TRIAL* FOR *TREASON!* I DO NOT SEE HIM. WHERE IS HE?

THERE IS *SOME MISTAKE!* THE CAPTAIN HAS HAD A *SUCCESSFUL VOYAGE*. HE HAS BEEN WITH US *CONSTANTLY!*

AYE, THAT HE HAS, SIR! BY YON MIZZEN-MAST HE *WAITS* TO *RECEIVE* YOU!

WE HAVE ALWAYS OBEYED HIS ORDERS--AND NOT ONCE HAVE WE GONE AGAINST HIM.

NOR *HAS* HE HAD ONE *PERVERSE* WORD TO SAY *ABOUT* US, SIR. AND WE *HAVE CARRIED* OUT EVERY *COMMAND* TO THE *LETTER!* HE HAS *REMAINED* ON THE *QUARTER DECK*--IN *FULL CHARGE*. THERE HAS BEEN....NO MUTINY... WAS THERE, CAPTAIN?

FOR THERE STOOD THE TERRIBLE, THE MIGHTY, THE TYRANT, *CAPTAIN BLAH*, NAILED TO THE MAST IN ALL HIS HORRIBLE GLORY-- WATCHING OVER ALL AS WAS HIS RIGHT--AND AGREEING WITH ALL IN *DEATH* AS HE HAD FOR *FIVE MONTHS!*

THE END

110

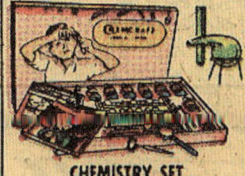

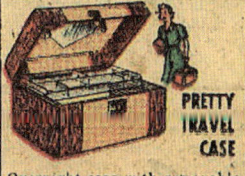

TERROR IS SIGHT-UNSEEN IN...

EYE EYE, SIR

ME? I'M RUDY CRANE, PRIVATE DETECTIVE! THE STORY OF MY LIFE IS A SNAPPY TALE. YOU SEE, THEY KICKED ME OUT OF COLLEGE WHEN I WAS ABOUT TWENTY-SEVEN —FOR TRYING TO HAND MISS DUNCAN, MY BIOLOGY PROF, A COUPLE OF LAUGHS— AFTER SCHOOL...

THE DEAN SAID HE COULDN'T PUT ME BACK IN COLLEGE, BUT I COULD HANG AROUND THE OFFICE AND SWEEP OUT AND WASH WINDOWS. BUT IT WAS NO GO! I WANTED TO BE ON MY OWN— SO I HIT DAD FOR A COUPLE OF MILLION AND OPENED UP THIS SMALL BUT MODEST PRIVATE DICK FIRM! SETTLE BACK AND LISTEN TO MY FIRST CASE! IT'S A REAL PIP...

OUCH!

Panel 1: SHE WAS MY FIRST CUSTOMER, TALL AND THIN, SOMETHING TO LOOK AT AND THINK ABOUT! AS FAR AS I WAS CONCERNED, THERE WAS NO ONE ELSE IN THE ROOM. I PLAYED IT COOL, THOUGH! CASUAL-LIKE I GREETED HER...

WOW! WEE-HOO! ZOWIE! GO...GO..!

HELLO! MY NAME'S LUCY LATOUR!

Panel 2: STILL KEEPING EVERYTHING INSIDE ME LIKE A JACK-IN-THE-BOX, I SEATED HER AND GOT DOWN TO THE BUSINESS OF THE DAY...

YEAH? WHAT CAN I DO FOR YOU? NAME IT AND IT'S YOURS!

LAY OFF, BUSTER! I WANT YOU TO FIND MY HUSBAND! I HAVEN'T SEEN HIM SINCE HE WENT FOR A LOAF OF BREAD THREE YEARS AGO! FIND HIM. YOU SEE, I DON'T LIKE STALE BREAD!

Panel 3: HOW COULD YOUR HUSBAND LEAVE SOMETHING LIKE — YOU? HE MUST HAVE BEEN OFF HIS ROCKER! IF IT WASN'T FOR YOUR GLASSES, YOU'D BE A REAL KNOCKOUT! AS IT IS, YOU AREN'T TOO BAD!

NEVER MIND WHY! JUST FIND HIM! MAYBE AFTERWARDS WE CAN PLAY A GAME WE BOTH LIKE!

Panel 4: THAT WAS ENOUGH FOR ME! I CAN TAKE A HINT! THE LAST PLACE LUCY'S HUSBAND WAS SEEN WAS A BAR UP THE BLOCK AND AROUND THE CORNER — A SMALL DIVE THAT EVEN THE COCKROACHES DIDN'T HAVE GUTS TO GO INTO! ANYWAY, WE WENT THERE...

WOW! ZOWIE! ZSA ZSA GABOR! LOVE IT! GO... GO..!

SIMMER DOWN, BUSTER!

Panel 5: THE BARTENDER WAS TOUGH, BUT NOT TOUGH ENOUGH. I HIT HIM. HE WENT DOWN LIKE A STACK OF DISHES. WHEN HE GOT UP, I GRABBED HIM BY THE COLLAR. I WISHED IT WAS HIS THROAT.

WE'RE LOOKING FOR MRS. LATOUR'S HUSBAND! HAVE YOU SEEN HIM?

NO, I AIN'T SEEN HIM! EVEN IF I DID, I WOULDN'T SAY SO!

Panel 6: HOW COULD A GUY LEAVE SOMETHING LIKE THAT? HE MUST HAVE BEEN OFF HIS ROCKER! IF IT WASN'T FOR HER GLASSES SHE'D BE A REAL KNOCKOUT! AS IT IS, SHE ISN'T TOO BAD!

LET'S GO, LUCY! HE DON'T KNOW ANYTHING!

TOO BAD...

2

THE GROWL IN MY STOMACH TOLD ME I WAS HUNGRY. WHEN LUCY BIT ME IN THE EAR, I KNEW SHE WAS TOO! WE FINISHED UP A FILET IN LIKITY-SPLIT TIME. AND RETURNED TO THE BUSINESS OF THE DAY...

FIGHT IT, RUDY, FIGHT IT WITH ALL YOU GOT! FIND MY HUSBAND FIRST! MAYBE THEN..?

YOU'VE GOT GUTS, LUCY, REAL GUTS! HOW COULD A GUY LEAVE YOU!!! IF IT WEREN'T FOR YOUR GLASSES...

IT WAS NO USE! I HAD TO FIND LUCY'S HUSBAND! HE HAD BELONGED TO A MEN'S CLUB, A SLICK PLACE WITH MILE-HIGH CARPETS THAT SUBBED FOR A MAUSOLEUM AT NIGHT. WE WENT THERE. ALL I COULD FIND WAS A DIGNIFIED JOE...

WOW! ZOWIE! WEE WEE WEE! LUCIUS BEEBE! GO...GO...!

GUY'S ON HIS LAST LEGS! HASN'T AN OUNCE OF LIFE LEFT IN HIM!

YOU'RE RIGHT! BUT HE MIGHT BE A LEAD. ASK HIM, RUDY BABY, ASK HIM — FAST!

THE WAY LUCY SPOKE, I KNEW SOMETHING WAS UP! I GAVE THE JOE A SHORT RIGHT UNDER THE HEART. I LIKED IT! IT WAS A GOOD ONE! HE BLUBBERED FOR A WHILE AND QUIETED DOWN. BUT, LIKE I SAID, IT WAS NO USE.

LATOUR? DEVILISH GOOD SORT! REAL BATTLESHIP! MISSING, YOU SAY? RAN OUT ON YOU, EH? BLOODY, INFAMOUS DEED! NO, I HAVEN'T SEEN HIM FOR THREE MONTHS!

IT'S NO GO, LUCY! BLOCKED AGAIN!

YES...

WE LEFT! THE CORRIDOR WAS DARK AS WE ENTERED IT! THE OLD GUY WAS TALKING TO HIMSELF. I WANTED TO GIVE HIM A QUICK JAB IN THE TEETH, BUT I CHANGED MY MIND. I HAD OTHER THINGS ON IT!

DEVILISHLY GOOD-LOOKING WOMAN! LATOUR'S WIFE, EH? LEFT HER, TOO! BEYOND ME HOW HE COULD HAVE DONE A THING LIKE THAT! CONFOUNDED BLACKGUARD! TOO BAD ABOUT THOSE GLASSES THOUGH...

LIKE I SAID, THE CORRIDOR WAS DARK. THINGS KEPT RUNNING THROUGH MY BRAIN, THINGS I WANTED TO THINK ABOUT!

SUDDENLY, I GRABBED HER. SHE FELL INTO MY ARMS LIKE AN AIR-FOAM CUSHION. THE SWEET SCENT OF HER PERFUME REMINDED ME OF SPINACH. I HAD TO HAVE HER, SO I KICKED HER IN THE SHINS. I LOVED IT. SHE FOUGHT BACK LIKE A TIGER...

NO, NO... MY HUSBAND'S NOT FOUND. HONEY, NOT YET! NOT YET!

WHACKY, YOU'RE DRIVING ME WHACKY! HOW LONG CAN I WAIT?

3

SURGERY

The smooth marble floor of the sanitarium echoed with the steps of a tall man. The corridor funneled down into twin doors, over which was the sign: SURGERY. The man walked towards them, a slight twang of nervousness humming through his body. He knew, though, that it would disappear with thought . . . thought . . . and memory . . .

He remembered the cell, its walls padded with heavy material, its small, barred window allowing a spike of light to enter, its heavy iron door, which was just slammed shut: all this he remembered. Then, with a shiver, the man recalled his twin brother, Bob Laycoe, seated on the floor and mumbling to himself. Laycoe looked up.

"Well, Paul, did you expect," his voice cracked, "to find your brother in this sordid condition?"

"I'd like to talk to you, Bob," Paul Laycoe whispered, his voice as tender as possible. He tried to subdue the horrible fact that this wreck of a man, this beaten, broken remnant was once Robert Laycoe, the famous surgeon.

"Don't be so superior!" Bob screamed. "Say what you mean. You want to operate on my brain. That's it, isn't it?"

"Well, I . . . yes!" Paul said, a little ashamed.

"I won't allow it," Bob bellowed. "Do you hear? I won't allow you, a pipsqueak surgeon, to touch my brain with a knife!"

"The disease has to be cut out," Paul said quietly.

Bob had run into the shadows that were bunched in the corner of the room like a heavy cloak; but, even through them, his eyes gleamed. When he spoke, his voice seemed to come from blackness. "No, you're wrong. As soon as I get back into the swing of things, I'll be okay again. Let me perform one more operation . . . just one! That'll set me right!"

Paul winced with the suggestion. "You know that's impossible," he stated, peering into the glob of darkness that enveloped Bob.

Paul caught his breath, He was now on the fringe of the heavy blackness. He made out Bob's outline: the hunched shoulders, his head tucked in between them. Through the dense darkness that Paul now penetrated fully, he felt Bob's groping hands, clawing at him like talons.

He was horribly aware that Bob looked like something, something other than a man or a human being, looked like a mammoth bird, a gargantuan bird of prey. Paul screamed. Bob looked like a vulture and he was about to spring.

Even Bob's voice now assumed a squawk. "One more operation," it said. "One more!" That was all. Through the silent, black shadows, there came a guttural sound of held, choked breath.

The figure entered the swinging doors and saw the clean, white surgical room. Someone was on the operating table, etherized into unconsciousness. The figure donned a surgical mask and walked to the table. He leaned over it.

It spoke, its voice muffled through the mask. "Well, Paul," it said, "I told you all I needed was one more operation. Too bad no one could ever tell us apart. Heh?"

MONUMENTAL FEAT

THE FALL WINDS HIT HARD INTO CHAPPIE HALSTEAD'S CHEEKS, MAKING THEM TINGLE. HE FELT INVIGORATED AND ALIVE — AND HE LOOKED FORWARD WITH AN ALMOST TANGIBLE SENSE OF ANTICIPATION TO THE FOOTBALL GAME HIS FRIENDS INVITED HIM TO! THIS WAS THE FIRST ONE IN HIS LIFE HE WAS GOING TO SEE...

HEY, CHAPPIE— HOW'S IT *FEEL?* BET YOU CAN HARDLY WAIT TO GET TO THE FIELD?

GOT THAT OLD *ACHE* IN YOUR GUTS, EH? ME, TOO..!

YES... YES...!

DON, WHAT ARE THOSE... *MONUMENTS...* FOR?

MAN, DON'T YOU KNOW? YOU *REALLY* HAVEN'T BEEN *AROUND!* WHY, THE GREATS...THE *REAL GREATS...* ARE *BURIED* OUT THERE! THEY WERE SOMETHING!

CHAPPIE'S HEART SKIPPED A BEAT! HE COULDN'T TAKE HIS EYES OFF THE MONUMENTS, FEELING DRAWN TO THEM, FEELING A KINSHIP WITH THEM! EVEN AFTER THE GAME STARTED, HE STARED...

IN MEMORY OF CHOO CHOO CONROY

HE WAS OBLIVIOUS TO THE CHEERS... THE GROANS...THE HUSHED SILENCES THAT ACCOMPANIED TRICKY MANEUVERS! ALL HE SAW THAT DAY WERE THE MONUMENTS...

THE IMMORTALITY OF THE THREE GREATS BURIED THERE DUG INTO HIM LIKE THE PLAYERS' CLEATS INTO THE TURF...CHEWING HIM UP...TEARING HIS SOUL INTO LITTLE CHUNKS...

IN MEMORY OF BULL DOE AFVEY

AND...WHEN THE GAME WAS OVER...

HEY, CHAPPIE, WHAT'RE YOU SO QUIET ABOUT? DIDN'T YOU LIKE THE GAME?

HE DIDN'T EVEN SEE IT! HE KEPT ON STARING AT THE MONUMENTS...STARING AT 'EM...AND STARIN' AT 'EM!

BOY! I'D LOVE TO HAVE A MONUMENT... DEDICATED...TO ME!

EXIT

THAT NIGHT...

I'VE GOT TO HAVE A MONUMENT—GOT TO HAVE MY NAME ON ONE... GOT TO BECOME A FOOTBALL GREAT...!

CHAPPIE THOUGHT...AND THOUGHT

WHEN THE NEXT DAY CAME, CHAPPIE BOUGHT A FOOTBALL, HIS FIRST ONE, CARESSING ITS PIGSKIN WITH TENDER FINGERS...

SP

IT WAS A WEEK DAY AND THERE WAS NO FOOTBALL AT THE BEAVER FIELD. A SILENCE...ALMOST LIKE A PALL...PERVADED THE STADIUM AS CHAPPIE ENTERED IT AND WALKED TO THE MONUMENTS, HIS NEW FOOTBALL FIRMLY GRIPPED IN HIS HANDS...AND THEY LOOKED LIKE TOMBSTONES IN THE BRISK, AUTUMN LONELINESS...

SOME DAY... MY NAME WILL BE ON A MONUMENT... RIGHT ALONG SIDE HERE...!

IN MEMORY OF

IN MEMORY OF

IN MEMORY

AND... HE MADE A VOW...

2

THEN, AS THE DAYS PASSED, CHAPPIE LOOKED FORWARD TO PLAYING FOOTBALL WITH A FANATIC GLEE...THAT TOOK UP ALL HIS TIME...THAT PUSHED OTHER THINGS TO THE DISTANT BACKGROUND! THE NEWNESS OF THE FOOTBALL RUBBED OFF WITH CONSTANT USE...AND IT ACQUIRED A DIGNIFIED GLOSS THAT CHAPPIE LOVED TO LOOK AT.

I'M *LEARNING!* I'M LEARNING...*REAL WELL...!*

HE PRACTICED IN EVERY SPARE MOMENT...LEARNING PASSING...RUNNING...KICKING. HE SHARPENED HIS REFLEXES...STRENGTHENED HIS ANKLES...MADE HIS LEGS INTO LOCOMOTIVE GRANITE! HE PLAYED IN PICK-UP GAMES, WHERE HE EXCELLED, THEN, ONE DAY...

THAT'S IT, CHAPPIE!

THROUGHOUT THE WHOLE GAME, A SOLEMN-FACED MAN WATCHED CHAPPIE. THEN, AFTER IT WAS OVER, THE MAN AMBLED TO HIM AND SPOKE QUIETLY...WITHOUT EMOTION...STATING PLAIN FACTS...FACTS THAT MADE CHAPPIE'S DREAM MORE REAL...NEARER...EVER NEARER....

I *LIKE* THE WAY YOU PLAY, CHAPPIE... LIKE IT *VERY MUCH!* HOW'D YOU LIKE TO *PLAY* FOR...THE *BEAVERS?* I'M ONE OF THEIR *SCOUTS!* NAME'S HYATT...LEM HYATT!

PLAY...FOR...THE ...BEAVERS?!! ARE YOU *KIDDING?* I'D *LOVE* IT! THIS... IS...THE...*DAY!*

SO, LATER, IN THE PRESENCE OF WITNESSES, CHAPPIE SIGNED A CONTRACT TO PLAY FOR THE BEAVERS...

GOOD BOY...!

...TO START ON ONE OF THE BEAVERS' FARM TEAMS...

LATER, CHAPPIE'S VOW WAS REPEATED...STRESSED... REITERATED...FOR THE SAKE OF THE DEAD!

I'M...COMING...(CHOKE)...!

IN MEMORY OF TIGER WALSH

IN MEMORY OF

DOG YEY

3

So, LATER, CHAPPIE HAD HIS FIRST TASTE OF PROFESSIONAL FOOTBALL – AND THE TASTE WAS BITTER. HE SWALLOWED IT, THOUGH! HE HAD TO...

C'MON, GO ... GO...!

HE DROVE FORWARD – DRIVING, EVER-DRIVING – WANTING TO GET TO THE TOP...IMPATIENT TO GET THERE...

..UGH...'

GET OFF YOUR FEET! C'MON, MOVE...!

UNTIL, HE WAS READY! HE KNEW IT... FELT IT...

GOOD ...GOOD...'

YEA!

HURRAH!

CHAPPIE...

CHAPPIE...

HAWKS

CHAPPIE HALSTEAD'S NAME GOT TO BE KNOWN – AND ITS RING BEGAN TO SOUND LIKE GREATNESS! HE WAS CLIMBING THE LADDER AND THE TOP WAS IN SIGHT! SO, ONE DAY...

CHAPPIE, WE'RE BRINGING YOU UP!

YEAH! YOU'RE TOO GOOD TO STAY WITH THESE BUSH-LEAGUERS!

THE BEAVERS WANT YOU!

LATER...

THE GOAL WAS NEARER. HE COULD ALMOST TOUCH IT!

SO, CHAPPIE HALSTEAD WENT INTO HIS FIRST GAME, PLAYING WITH THE BEAVERS! EXPECTATION POUNDED WITHIN HIM... THE CROWD ROARED... THE HUDDLE WAS FORMED! THE FIRST PLAY... THE BEAVERS HAD THE BALL... AND CHAPPIE WAS TO CARRY IT...

38-2! YOU'VE *GOT* IT, CHAP!

THE LINE FORMED... THE BALL WAS SNAPPED BACK TO THE QUARTERBACK... AND ON A QUICK-HAND-OFF... CHAPPIE FOUND A HOLE IN THE LINE... AND RAMMED THROUGH IT...

HE DODGED ONE TACKLER... STIFF-ARMED ANOTHER... REVERSED HIS FIELD... CHANGED AGAIN... SIDE-STEPPED A LUNGING MAN... AND HEADED FOR THE GOAL LINE! HE COVERED FIVE YARDS... TEN... THIRTY... FIFTY... SIXTY... HEARD THE CLOMPING CLEATS OF THE OPPOSITION'S SECONDARY BEHIND HIM... AND, SUDDENLY, AT THE GOAL LINE... WAS TACKLED...

HE FELL FORWARD, THE WORLD SPINNING AROUND HIM! THERE WAS THE CLEAR SIGHT OF THE HEAVY GOAL-POSTS BEFORE HIM... HE HEARD THE THUNK OF HIS HEAD BANGING UP AGAINST THEM... SAW THE HAZE... THE BLACKNESS... THE SPINNING, NEVER-ENDING BLACKNESS...

THIS WAS THE WORLD OF BLANKNESS... AND BLACKNESS ... FOR CHAPPIE HALSTEAD... THE WORLD WITHOUT WORDS... WITHOUT FEELING... WITHOUT LIFE!

LORD! HE'S... DEAD!

BOY! WHAT A *RUN* HE *MADE!* IT WAS... *GREAT!*

EVERYONE SAW THAT CHAPPIE HAD THE TOUCH OF GREATNESS ... AND THAT IT HAD TO BE REMEMBERED! SO, A VOW MADE MANY LONG YEARS AGO...

IN MEMORY OF CHAPPIE HALSTEAD

IN MEMORY OF TIGER WALSH

...WAS *FINALLY* REALIZED!

THE END

127

129

TALES OF TERROR AND SUSPENSE

CHAMBER OF
CHILLS

Collect all 4 Volumes of Chamber of Chills from PS Artbooks

Chamber of Chills
Volume One

Chamber of Chills
Volume Two

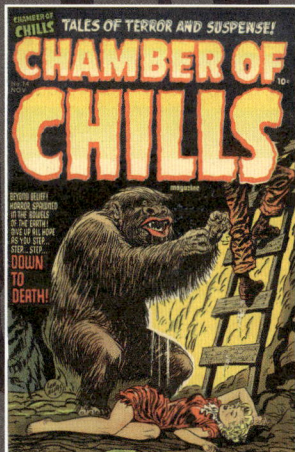

Chamber of Chills
Volume Three

Chamber of Chills
Volume Four

Witches Tales
June 1954 - Issue #25

Cover Art - Howard Nostrand

The Ticket
Script - Unknown
Pencils - Manny Stallman
Inks - Manny Stallman

Ali Barber and the Forty Thieves
Script - Bob Powell
Pencils - Bob Powell
Inks - Bob Powell

What's Happening at 8.30pm
Script - Howard Nostrand
Pencils - Howard Nostrand
Inks - Howard Nostrand

Monopoly
Script - Unknown
Pencils - Manny Stallman
Inks - Manny Stallman

TCHES
ALES
WE DARE YOU
TO READ THESE EERIE TALES
OF SUPERNATURAL HORROR!
WITCHES
TALES
WEIRD
YARNS OF
UNSEEN
TERRORS
HAT HAPPENS AT 8:30 P.M.?

hands tied?

... because you lack a High School diploma?

YOU CAN GET A High School education AT HOME FOR ONLY $6⁰⁰ A MONTH!

WITCHES TALES, JUNE, 1954, VOL. 1, NO. 25, IS PUBLISHED BI-MONTHLY by WITCHES TALES, INC., 1860 Broadway, New York 23, N.Y. Entered as second class matter at the Post Office at New York, N. Y., under the Act of March, 3, 1879. Single copies, 10c. Subscription rates, 10 issues for $1.00 in the U. S. and possessions, elsewhere $1.50. All names in this periodical are entirely fictitious and no identification with actual persons is intended. Contents copyrighted, 1954, by Witches Tales, Inc., New York, City. Printed in the U.S.A. Title registered in U. S. Patent Office.

WELCOME

WE WANT YOUR LET-TERS! All kinds... big ones, fat ones, skinny ones, all sizes and shapes! And... what do we want you to write about?

We want your opinion on that new, terrific, four-power horror pact that CHAMBER OF CHILLS, TOMB OF TERROR, BLACK CAT MYSTERY and WITCHES TALES have entered into... sort of a blood pool! How do you rate this shock king's domain?

Tell us what you like a-bout these four distinctive books that now come to you during a two-month period, a mag appearing on your newsstands every two weeks.

What is the impact of BLACK CAT MYSTERY, where man meets man in a mad clash of reality? How different is the design of WITCHES TALES, the mag that chills your spine and tickles your funny bone? How far are you sent by TOMB OF TERROR, whose stories are ripped from the many unexplored voids? How deep are you in the in-credible sphere of the super-natural, which CHAMBER OF CHILLS takes you to?

We want the answers to these questions in your let-ters. Don't choke up... let us have it, both barrels. All you do is, write to:

WITCHES TALES, INC.
1860 Broadway
New York 23, N. Y.

WITCHES TALES

CONTENTS NO. 25

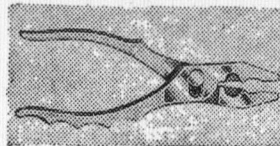

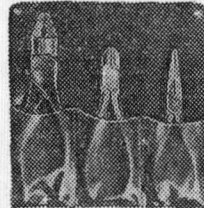

THE TICKET

YOU'RE A *GUNMAN*, LOLLO GIBRIDA. YOU'RE FAST WITH THE TRIGGER ... AND YOU'RE *WANTED* BY THE *LONDON POLICE*. YES, LOLLO, *YOU'RE BEING CHASED* ...

TWEEEET

YOU'VE JUMPED THE FENCE, LOLLO ... BUT WHERE TO NOW? IT'S NIGHT AND A ROTTEN CHILL BITES INTO YOU LIKE A SNAKE. FOG'S ALL AROUND, YOU FEEL *TRAPPED* AND YOU *CAN'T SEE* ...

WH ... WHERE AM I? CAN'T ... (GASP) ... RUN ANY MORE!

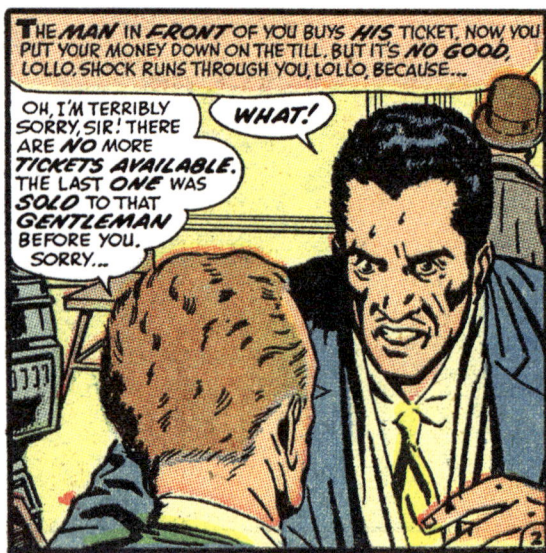

WHAT'S IN A NAME?

The editor was balling out Tom Powers once again.

"Listen, Tom," he shouted. "If you're going to write stories about ghouls and vampires and such, at least give them proper names. Sam, the vampire; Sadie, the witch; Gregory, the ghoul; Morris, the mummy! What kind of stuff are you giving me?"

Tom Powers smiled. "Listen, Gordon," he said, "Don't those names give a touch of realism to the stories? Doesn't Morris, the mummy, sound better than Garffo, the mummy? Don't you think it's more probable to meet a vampire named Samuel than one called Krako?"

"Don't you hand me any of that tommyrot!" said Gordon. "If you want to deal with the stupid supernatural, go ahead and do it. If it's a good story, I'll buy it. But you give your creatures names that would fit. Yes, Krako, Garffo, Ygor, Barto may sound silly to your half-baked brain, but those are the names I want!"

"Listen, pal," said Tom Powers, trying to calm the editor. "There's no reason to get excited."

"But I've gone over this with you a hundred times!"

"I know. Easy, take it easy. Let me explain a misconception to you. Don't you understand why people expect supernatural creatures to have those crazy names of yours?"

"I'm not asking for a lecture," protested the editor.

"Just let me finish, Gordon. Those names were used because most of those supernatural stories grew up in foreign countries. So foreign or pseudo-foreign names seem natural for the characters."

"So I have no objections," said Gordon.

"But you should have!" said Tom Powers. "Don't you see what I'm trying to do? I'm trying to give supernatural stories an American flavor. I want people to think it could happen here. So you've got to give the people in your supernatural stories popular names!"

Gordon couldn't take any more. "Get out of here," he told Tom Powers. "And don't come back till every one of your monsters have the right names. Leave American names to the historians! We deal in fiction, and the fictional supernatural creature is a foreigner!"

Tom Powers didn't wait for another word. Bread and butter was more important to him than any whim. He tipped his hat, said good-bye, and told Gordon he'd be back with the most foreign names ever made.

The editor smiled when Tom Powers had exited. "Got to give the guy credit," he said. "He's sure got spunk."

"Who's got spunk?" said a voice.

"Huh?" Gordon swung round in his chair to face two ghoulish figures in vampire-like capes.

"Who are you?" the editor said in a startled voice.

"Just a couple of vampires," answered one of them. "My name's Thomas. My partner's name is Eddie. And you've got a case, boy."

The last words Gordon heard as teeth dug into his neck were: "You traitor, you!"

SO ALI WAS UP AGAINST THE WALL. AND WHAT MADE IT EVEN MORE GALLING WAS THAT OF ALL THE NEIGHBORS ON HIS BLOCK, ALI BARBER WAS THE POOREST, MOST MISERABLE FAILURE OF THEM ALL!

ALL OF THEM ARE MAKING OUT! ALL OF THEM BUT *ME!* SOMETHING HAS TO BE DONE! THEY CAN'T KEEP ME DOWN! I *KNOW* I'LL BE FAMOUS. I JUST *KNOW* IT! I'LL PROVE IT!

BUT ALI WAS AT THE END OF HIS ROPE. HE TOSSED AND TURNED IN HIS SLEEP! HE MOANED AND GROANED AND WAILED WHEN OTHERS COULDN'T HEAR HIM. HE TRIED TO THINK OF A WAY OUT--*ANY* WAY OUT. AND THAT NEXT MORNING, AS HE CAME TO OPEN HIS SHOP...

NO MORE CUSTOMERS! HOW AM I GOING TO BUILD UP MY TRADE? HOW AM I GOING TO PAY MY BILLS, AND BUY MY WIFE A NEW HAT, AND BE FAMOUS? HOW AM I-- WAIT! I'VE GOT IT!

WHY NOT GO TO THESE FELLOWS DIRECTLY? SURE-- IT'S A FORMAL DINNER. THEY *HAVE* TO BE SHAVED, DON'T THEY? AND IF I WORK FAST, I'LL MAKE A MINT. WHY NOT?

BAR SHOP

BUSINESSMAN'S DINNER
BLUE ROOM ... 4 P.M.
FORMAL

SO ALI LOOKED AT THE REGISTER, FOUND FORTY NAMES SIGNED THERE AS BUSINESSMEN, GATHERED ALL HIS SHAVING KITS TOGETHER, AND MINUTES LATER, FACED THE DOOR OF HIS FIRST PROSPECT...

FORTY BUSINESSMEN AT A DOLLAR A HEAD WILL GIVE ME FORTY DOLLARS-- I'LL HAVE ENOUGH FOR---

REMEMBER--- WE'RE ALL BUSINESSMEN, SEE? WE'RE MEETIN' TO DISCUSS BUSINESS!

HA, HA... SOME BUSINESS! HOW WE'RE GONNA BUMP OFF RIVAL MOBS!

SHADDUP, LOU! NOW EVERYONE GO TO YOUR ROOMS! IF THE BULLS EVER GET WISE THAT THE FORTY MOST WANTED CRIMINALS ARE HERE UNDER ONE ROOF, THEY'LL HAVE A FIELD DAY. WE GOTTA BE CAREFUL! *VERY CAREFUL!* THE MINUTE SOMEONE GETS SUSPICIOUS, WE *BLOW!* UNDERSTAND?

GOOD LORD--!

I WON'T TELL ANYONE! I'LL JUST COLLECT MY REWARD WITHOUT A FUSS. DEAD OR ALIVE... THERE'S A PRICE ON EACH OF THEIR HEADS! *DEAD OR ALIVE!*

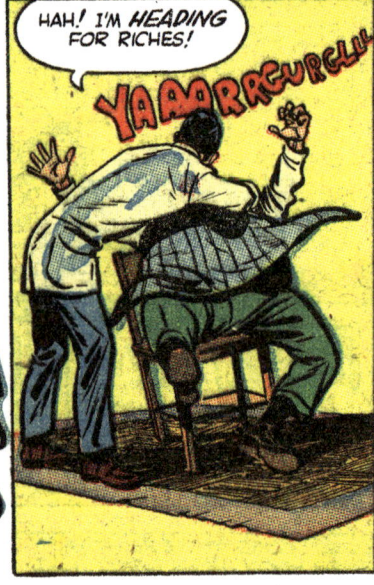

149

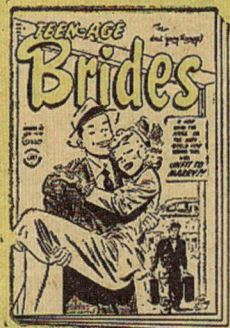

Panel 1: EVEN AS HE ROUNDED A CORNER, FACING A DILAPIDATED STREET, THERE WAS A STILLNESS AND AN EMPTINESS THAT DISTURBED HIM. SUDDENLY, A SHAFT OF LIGHT PEEKED DOWN. A YOUNG BOY WAS LOOKING OUT, TOWARDS HIM...

HEY!

Panel 2: QUICKLY, AS IF TERROR WERE GOADING HER, THE BOY'S MOTHER PULLED HIM AWAY...

TOMMY! WHAT'S THE MATTER WITH YOU? DON'T STAY THERE!

Panel 3: TWO SHUTTERS SLAMMED, KNIFING THE SHAFT OF LIGHT INTO DARKNESS...

WHAT GIVES HERE?

SLAM!

Panel 4: PERPLEXED, AGITATED BY THE EMPTINESS THAT HUNG LIKE A SHROUD OVER EVERY STREET HE WALKED UPON, THE MAN SEEMED TO WANDER AIMLESSLY, A BELFRY CLOCK SOMEWHERE TOLLED EIGHT TIMES...

BONG BONG BONG BONG BONG BONG BONG BONG

SHLEP SHLEP SHLEP SHLEP SHLEP SHLEP

Panel 5: THEN HE STOPPED, A CREASE OF A SMILE EASING INTO HIS FACE. A SHORT DISTANCE AWAY WAS A MAN, WARMING HIMSELF BY A BRIGHT, ORANGE FIRE...

WELL, HALLELUJAH! A PERSON!

Panel 6: HE DIDN'T KNOW WHY HE SHUFFLED SILENTLY TO THE FIRE. IT JUST SEEMED TO FIT THE VILLAGE'S FOREBODING TONE. SLOWLY, HE TAPPED THE MAN ON THE SHOULDER. THE MAN TURNED AROUND, THE LOOK OF FEAR ON HIS FACE...

UM, EXCUSE ME.

TAP TAP

YEOWWW!!!

Panel 7: HE EXPLAINED, WANTING TO KNOW WHERE EVERYBODY WAS. THE STRANGER EASED UP A LITTLE, STILL SLIGHTLY CAUTIOUS. HE WAS INVITED TO SIT DOWN. THE FIRE'S GLOW WAS WARM...

SURE, IT'S LONELY, BUSTER! YOU BETTER SIT DOWN. DON'T YOU KNOW WHAT'S HAPPENING AT 8:30 PM?!

THANKS.. WHAT DO YOU MEAN... 8:30?!! WHAT'S GOING ON? WHAT'S HAPPENING?!!

THE GUY WAS RUNNING. HE WAS SURE OF IT. SUDDENLY, HE FELT A SCURRYING BEHIND HIM AND THE TRAMPLE OF FEET MOVING RAPIDLY...HE WHIRLED...

SHLOP SHLEP SHLEP SHLUP SHLOP

SOMETHING WAS HAPPENING. IT WAS LIKE A SNOW-BALL ON A HILL, ROLLING DOWNWARD AND GETTING BIGGER. SOMEBODY ELSE BRUSHED BY HIM...AND RAN OFF...

HE PUT HIS GRIMY FINGERNAILS TO HIS MOUTH. SWEAT BEADS FORMED ON HIS INKY BROW. FEAR...COLD AND ABSOLUTE ...CHOKED HIM, KNOTTING HIS THROAT IN AN UNCONSUMING BALL...

LORD...LORD....!

AND...HE BEGAN TO RUN...

SHLEP SHLUP SHLEP SHLUP SHLEP SHLUP SHLEP SHLUP SHLEP SHLUP SHLOP

BUT...HE DIDN'T KNOW WHERE TO GO. EVERY AVENUE SEEMED BLOCKED, EVERY DIRECTION SEEMED TO END IN A MAZE. HE HEADED FOR AN ALLEY, TRIPPING OVER AN ASH-CAN. THE METALLIC DIN RESOUNDED IN CLAMOR...

CRASSHH!

SHLEP SHLUP SHLEP SHLUP SHLUP SHLUP SHLUP

HE VEERED, SLUSHING AWAY FROM A RED GLASS EYE, AND RAN WITH INCREASED FERVOR. HE CHURNED THE GROUND BENEATH HIM IN HUGE GLOBS OF WETNESS, HEADING INTO DARKNESS AND BLIND DIRECTION...

DEAD END

UNTIL HE FACED AN EMPTY FETID STREET. HE STOOD ALONE...HORRIBLY ALONE...IN THE MUCK THAT HAD THE SWEET SCENT OF HOME...

WH-WHERE CAN I GO? WHY AM I RUNNING? WHAT THE BLAZES IS GOING ON, ANY HOW?

4

HIS MIND DANCED WITH CRAZINESS. HE WAS CAUGHT, HYSTERICALLY CAUGHT BY A DEATH HE KNEW WAS COMING, DAZED, UNBELIEVING, HE BACKED UP AGAINST A STORE WINDOW, TRYING TO GET HIS BEARINGS, TO SET THINGS RIGHT...

GOT TO THINK...! IT'S GOING T HAPPEN...AT...8:30! WH-WH TIME IS IT...NOW?

THE STORE'S INTERIOR WAS LIT BY A SINGLE BULB. HE LOOKED INSIDE, NOTICING THE CLOCK HANGING ON THE WALL. HE GULPED, THEN SCREAMED...

YEOW!

THE UGLY MYSTERY, BLACK AND IMPENDING, BEGAN TO CLOSE IN. HIS BLOOD POUNDED FURIOUSLY. IT WAS ALL SO HORRIFYING THAT A WHITE DROP THAT SPLATTERED ON HIS SHOULDER SEEMED UNCOMMON...SEEMED OUT-OF-PLACE...

EH? WHA--? RAIN?!!

IT WASN'T RAIN THOUGH! THE DROPS WEREN'T COOLING! THEY WERE HOT, COMING DOWN IN A STEADY STREAM... SEARING EVERYTHING AROUND HIM IN WHITE-HEAT...

NO, NO! NOT RAIN...

THE STREAM POURED DOWN IN ENDLESS, SEARING PATTERNS...SEARING EVERYTHING...SCORCHING THE STREET. HE SMELLED HIS OWN FLESH...IN ITS SCORCHING, ROTTED MIASMA...AND HE REALIZED WHAT WAS HAPPENING...AND WHAT HE WAS...

I KNOW...I KNOW! IT'S...8:30...

HE WAS A GERM!

THE STREAM...NOW STREAKS...BEGAN TO BURN HIM... BURN HIM ALIVE...

EIGHT...THIRTY... EIGHT...THIR... YEOOWWWW!

AND THE STREAKS WERE...ALL-CONSUMING...ALL POWERFUL...X-RAYS!
THE END.

157

Mother Mongoose's NURSERY CRIMES

HICKORY DICKORY DOCK TRIED TO STEAL THE CLOCK...

TICK TICK TICK TICK TICK TICK

AT A QUARTER TO FOUR, HE GOT TO THE DOOR

TICK-SQUEERP TICK-SQUEERP

BUT THE DOOR HAD BEEN JUICED, AND THE SPRINGS BROKE LOOSE!

TICK... WHOOOMP!

NOT THE CLOCK'S... BUT HICKORY DICKORY DOCK'S!

Mother Mongoose's NURSERY CRIMES

LITTLE JACK HORNER SAT IN A CORNER

EATING A STRANGE LOOKING PIE.

BUT HE WASN'T WELL-FED TILL HE PULLED OUT THAT HEAD...

AND SAID:

WHAT A *GHOUL* BOY AM I!

LOVE PROBLEM

The man and woman could only live and love by moonlight. Night was their day, and day their night. Yet they never minded it. This was natural to vampires.

But Cecelia and Gregory had another problem, a problem that could destroy their love.

That problem was expressed clearly one clear and beautiful night as they walked together near the marshes.

"Gregory," Cecelia said. "You must get money somewhere. We can't go on this way any longer."

Gregory looked at her, and said, "Darling, I know you're right. And believe me, I do want to marry you. But I just can't seem to make ends meet. And I surely don't want you to live in any old tomb. You've got to have the best."

He kissed her then, a cold and wonderful kiss that chilled her with a vampire passion.

"Be patient," he said. "It won't be too much longer."

But the weeks flew by, and there was no change. Gregory couldn't hold a job. They all ended up in the same way as that night watchman stint. He couldn't control his great lust for blood, and instead of staying on the job, he travelled the city seeking a snack here, a snack there. It was obvious they had to fire him.

So this time Cecelia had to give an ultimatum. She realized she wasn't getting any younger.

"Gregory," she told him one black night. "It hurts to say this; but I must. I can't wait any longer for you. You must get enough money to marry me or we will have to part."

The words hurt Gregory even more. But he knew she was right. "I will make one last effort," he promised. "You will see that our love will not fail."

The next night, Gregory put his efforts to work. He got a job in a bakery rolling rolls and baking cake. The salary wasn't bad, and it looked as if it could build into something big.

He promised Cecelia he would control his desire for blood, curbing it to weekends. And Cecelia was thrilled. She was sure that he had at last found his niche in society.

She was right, but not as right as she expected to be. He had found his niche in society, all right, Lenore Society, the baker's daughter! And Lenore didn't care if he worked or not. Her father's bakery was doing a rolling business.

So that was the way the love problem was resolved. Cecelia was a vampire who couldn't keep her man. And Lenore Society was a vamp who knew her way.

FOR DARBY DAY, BUSINESSMAN, THERE ARE THE USUAL FOUR SEASONS PLUS A FIFTH... VAMPIRE SEASON, AND... DURING THAT ONE... HE HAS A...

MONOPOLY

DARBY DAY COULD NOT HELP THE FAILURE OF HIS PICKLE WORKS. HE HAD TRIED HIS BEST, BUT WHEN HE HAD TO LOOK AT THE RAMSHACKLE BUILDING, WITH ITS DELECTABLE SCENT OF SPICE STILL WAFTING OUTWARDS, HE COULD NOT HELP BUT THINK HE WAS SAYING GOOD-BYE TO A LONG, FAITHFUL FRIEND...

SO LONG... CHUM...

DARBY DAY
107 VARIET

HEAD BOWED, DARBY DAY SHUFFLED THROUGH THE STREETS, NOT EVEN THE EVEN THE EXCITED SHOUTS OF FLEEING PASSER-BYS MENDED HIS BROKEN HEART.

VAMPIRES...

VAMPIRES!

VAMPIRES, SHAMPIRES! WHO CARES?

WHEN HE REACHED HIS APARTMENT HOUSE...AND HE WAS CLIMBING THE STAIRS TO HIS SINGLE ROOM...HE WAS STILL OBLIVIOUS TO ANYONE...OR ANYTHING...

GOT TO LOOK FOR A NEW BUSINESS...

NO VAMPIRE... IS...GET-TING ME!

HE SWITCHED ON THE LIGHT ONCE HE REACHED HIS ROOM. OUTSIDE, IT SEEMED LIKE A SMALL, YELLOW SQUARE OF PAINT...PALING WITH INATTENTION...

V-V-VAMPIRES!

BUT... WHAT--?

V-V-VAMPIRES! THAT'S IT!

AN IDEA HAD TAKEN HOLD IN DARBY DAY'S BRAIN. IMPATIENTLY, HE RAN TO THE BOOKSHELVES BEHIND HIM... HIS HAND REACHING OUT FOR A SINGLE BOOK...

WHY...WHY DIDN'T I THINK OF THIS SOONER? DARBY DAY...YOU'RE A FOOL!

VAMPIRES

REVISED EDITION

HE GRABBED THE WITHERED, DUSTY TOME, PLACING IT ON A TABLE BEFORE HIM. WILDLY, DARBY DAY FLIPPED ITS PAGES...MURMURING TO HIMSELF...

VAMPIRES? HMMM! VAMPIRES! LET'S SEE...VAMPIRES... AND THEIR... DEATH!

REACHING THE PLACE HE WANTED IN THE BOOK, HE SLAPPED IT DOWN ON THE TABLE. THEN, THROUGH THE NIGHT, HE STUDIOUSLY READ...

SILVER BULLETS! STAKES... THROUGH THE HEART! SEEMS TO BE THE ONLY WAY TO KILL THEM!

HA! WHY NOT? CAPITALIZE ON THIS VAMPIRE EPIDEMIC... BY MANUFACTURING...SILVER BULLETS...AND STAKES! HEH-HEH! A...SURE-FIRE SCHEME...TO KILL VAMPIRES...AND MAKE MONEY! I'LL HAVE A...MONOPOLY...ON IT!

IT WAS ALMOST TWO MONTHS LATER... TWO MONTHS OF HARD LABOR, WORKING ON HIS SILVER BULLETS AND TAPERED STAKES... THAT DARBY DAY DECIDED TO TRY OUT HIS PRODUCT IN THE LOCAL VAMPIRE CASTLE...

GULP... THE PRICE OF FORTUNE...!

HE PENETRATED THE CASTLE'S SUFFOCATING DARKNESS, GOING DEEPER AND DEEPER INTO IT. SUDDENLY, DARBY DAY HEARD A SHUFFLE AND A THROATY, RAVENOUS GROWL. HE WHIRLED... READYING HIS GUN AND CROSS-BOW... TO FACE TWO VAMPIRES...

HEE-HEE-HEE HEE-HEE-HEE

YEOW! LET'S HOPE... THESE THINGS ...WORK...!

FOR A MOMENT THERE WAS SILENCE. THEN HE SWUNG INTO CONCENTRATED ACTION, HIS GUN, HOLDING THE SILVER BULLET, SWEPT UP... AND FIRED...

BLAM!

THERE WAS A SCREAM. THEN EFFORTLESSLY, DARBY PLUCKED A FEATHERED, TAPERED STAKE FROM HIS SHEATH, APPLIED IT TO HIS CROSS-BOW... AIMED...

...AND LET LOOSE. THERE WAS A SPLIT-SECOND OF SINGING DEATH BEFORE THE STAKE STRUCK INTO THE CHEST OF THE SECOND VAMPIRE. IT WAS OVER.

BLOOOOOM

MOMENTS LATER, DARBY DAY LOOKED DOWN UPON TWO FIGMENTS OF DEATH... WHO LAY BEFORE HIM... ONE WITH A BORE IN HIS CHEST CREATED BY A SILVER BULLET... AND THE OTHER WITH A CHEST FEATURING AN ALIEN FEATHERED STAKE...

IT... WORKS! IT WORKS!

VICTORIOUSLY, DARBY DAY HOISTED THE IMPLEMENTS OF VAMPIRE-DEATH ABOVE HIS HEAD. THERE, IN THE SHADOWS, HE LOOKED LIKE A KING WHO HAD COME HOME...

HA HA HA! IT WORKS! NOW... TO GO INTO... PRODUCTION!

IN A SMALL, MODEST WAY, DARBY DAY STARTED HIS VAMPIRE EXTERMINATING BUSINESS...

...AND THE FRIGHTENED PEOPLE RESPONDED...

...BUILDING HIS FIRM INTO BIGGER AND BETTER THINGS ...MUCH BIGGER...

...AND, AGAIN, THE SCARED PEOPLE RESPONDED!

DARBY DAY ADVERTISED HIS EERIE PRODUCT...

...ON THE ROAD...

USE DARBY DAY BECAUSE...

...IN THE AIR...

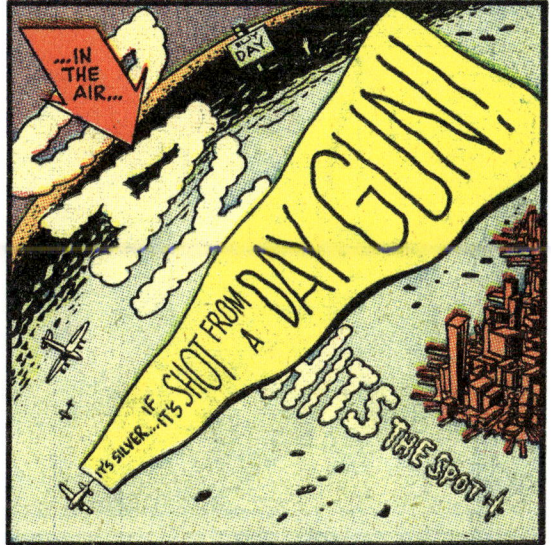

IT'S SILVER...IF IT'S SHOT FROM A **DAY GUN!** ...HITS THE SPOT 4

SLOWLY, THE VAMPIRES WERE BEING EXTERMINATED. EACH NIGHT, ONE WOULD GET KILLED BY A DARBY DAY PRODUCT...

EEIIAA

UNTIL DARBY DAY WAS A MADE MAN. THE PEOPLE HAD BOUGHT UP HIS SILVER BULLETS AND FEATHERED STAKES WITH AN INSANE FRENZY. DARBY, SEATED IN HIS PLUSH OFFICE, RELISHED HIS IMPORTANCE...

YOU CAN SEND IN THAT DELEGATION NOW, MISS HARRIS!

YES, SIR!

IN THESE PLUSH DAYS, DARBY HAD SEEN MANY DELEGATIONS. HE LOOKED AT THE THREE MEN ENTERING HIS OFFICE, NOTICING NOTHING UNUSUAL ABOUT THEM...

GOOD DAY GENTLE-MEN!

GLAD WE...

...CAN GET...

...TOGETHER, MR. DAY!

HUMPH! YES, OF COURSE! WHAT CAN I DO FOR YOU?

THEN, SUDDENLY, AN UGLY TRANSFORMATION TOOK PLACE IN THE THREE MEN. THEIR HAIR BECAME LONGER...THEIR EARS POINTIER...THEIR TEETH SHARPER. THEY BECAME RAVENOUS VAMPIRES...

YOU CAN...

...STOP...

...KILLING US!

THE THREE VAMPIRES LUNGED AT DARBY DAY. THEIR FANGS WERE BARED FOR THE THROATY KILL. DARBY QUICKLY GRABBED A GUN AT HIS SIDE...AND FIRED...

TH- THE GUN... IT DOESN'T WORK!

BANG!

BAM!

BAM!

CRASH

KRUMP!

HURRIEDLY, HE REACHED FOR THE LOADED CROSS-BOW. HE LET FLY A FEATHERED STAKE...BUT...

THE CROSS-BOW HAS FAILED! NO! NO!

A DARBY DAY PRODUCT

THE VAMPIRES BACKED A QUIVERING, SLOBBERING DARBY DAY INTO A CORNER. HE COWERED, THE TASTE OF DEATH RANK IN HIS MOUTH. THE BLOOD-THIRSTY BEINGS LOOKED HUNGRILY AT HIS THROAT...TAKING TIME OUT TO ANSWER HIS QUESTIONS...

WHY DIDN'T YOU DIE? WHAT HAPPENED? WHY??!!

YOU SEE...

...MR. DAY...

....WE'VE GOT...

BULLET-PROOF VESTS ON!

THE END

5

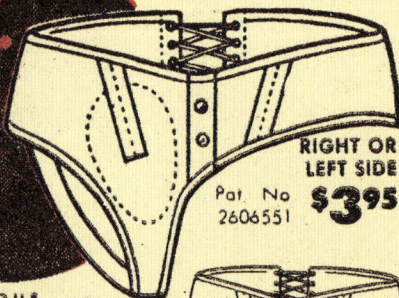

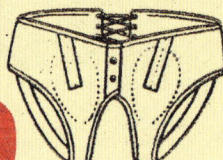

166

THEN, WAH-WAH
BUDD JUMPED...

Witches Tales
August 1954 - Issue #26

Cover Art - Lee Elias

Long Shot
Script - Unknown
Pencils - Manny Stallman
Inks - Ross Andru

Withering Heights
Script - Bob Powell/Howard Nostrand
Pencils - Bob Powell
Inks - Howard Nostrand

Go Vampire
Script - Unknown
Pencils - Unknown
Inks - Unknown

Up There
Script - Unknown
Pencils - Joe Certa
Inks - Joe Certa

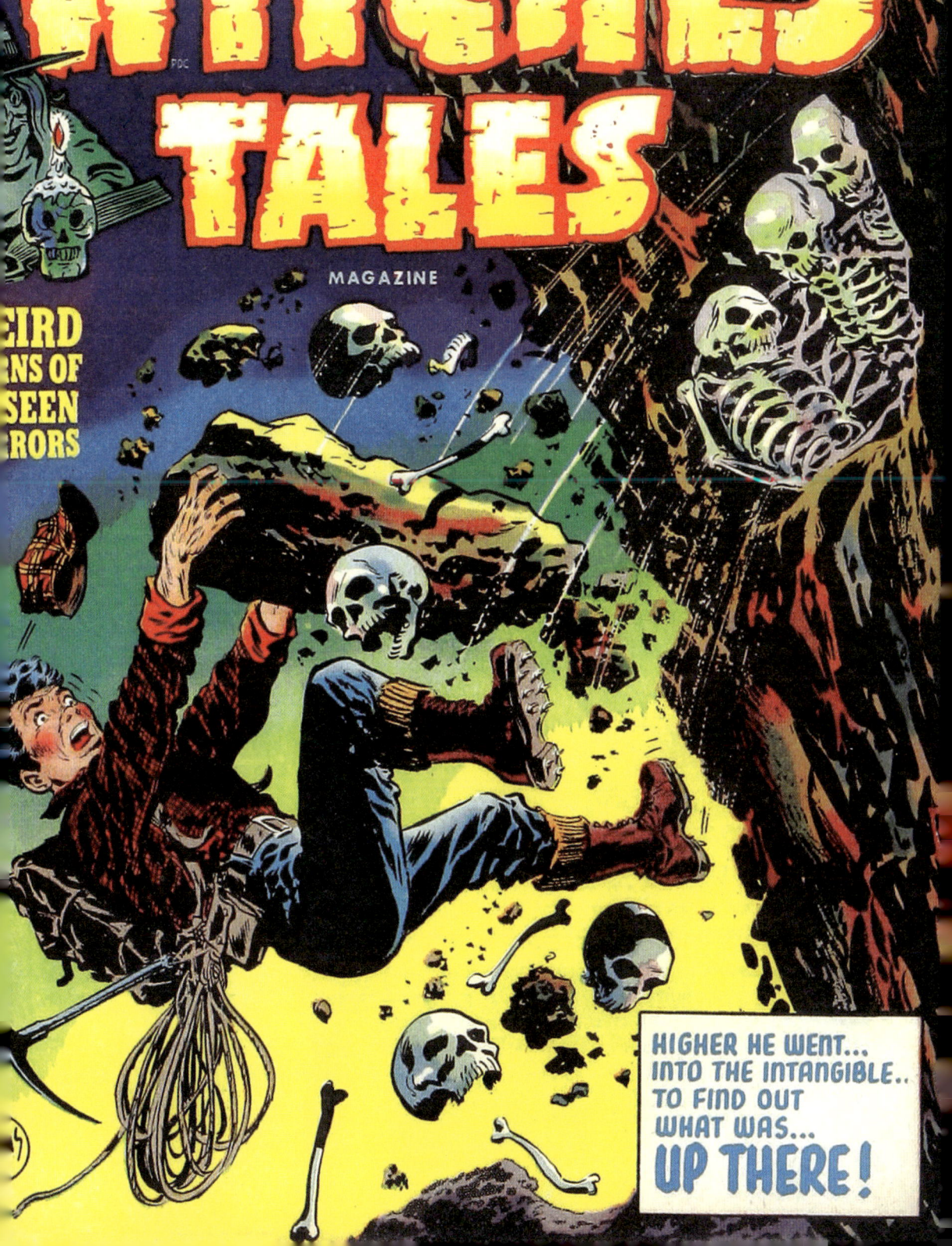

WITCHES TALES, AUGUST, 1954, VOL. 1, NO. 26, IS PUBLISHED BI-MONTHLY by WITCHES TALES, INC., 1860 Broadway, New York 23, N. Y. Entered as second class matter at the Post Office at New York, N. Y., under the Act of March, 3, 1879. Single copies, 10c. Subscription rates, 10 issues for $1.00 in the U. S. and possessions, elsewhere $1.50. All names in this periodical are entirely fictitious and no identification with actual persons is intended. Contents copyrighted, 1954, by Witches Tales, Inc., New York, City. Printed in the U.S.A Title registered in U. S. Patent Office.

Dig in a messy grave and you'd find terror, wouldn't you? Well, that's what we offer! Crawl through a dark dungeon with time-gnawed walls and you're bound to come out shocked. Right? Well, we give you that feeling . . . plus! Look through these stories and you'll find the real thing . . . the intangible that makes your blood bubble and your eyes white. This is . . . TERROR!!

Every ounce of artificiality has been extracted . . . every particle of the synthetic has been subtracted . . . and every semblance of the unreal has been protracted. For in these stories, you'll find that distilled element . . . the kind that only makes for pure horror.

This is the "distilled element" that makes your reading matter different . . . that makes it unique . . . that makes it tense . . . that makes you come back for more. It's what you want.

And these yelling yarns are the kind that makes the small hours smaller . . . and has the chill of doom that only one cold, gray hand could create. These needling narratives have come to you from the nether region, where every step forward takes the reader to an acre that he should stay away from . . . but yet is compelled to go. These stories are different. They have the distilled element of fear!

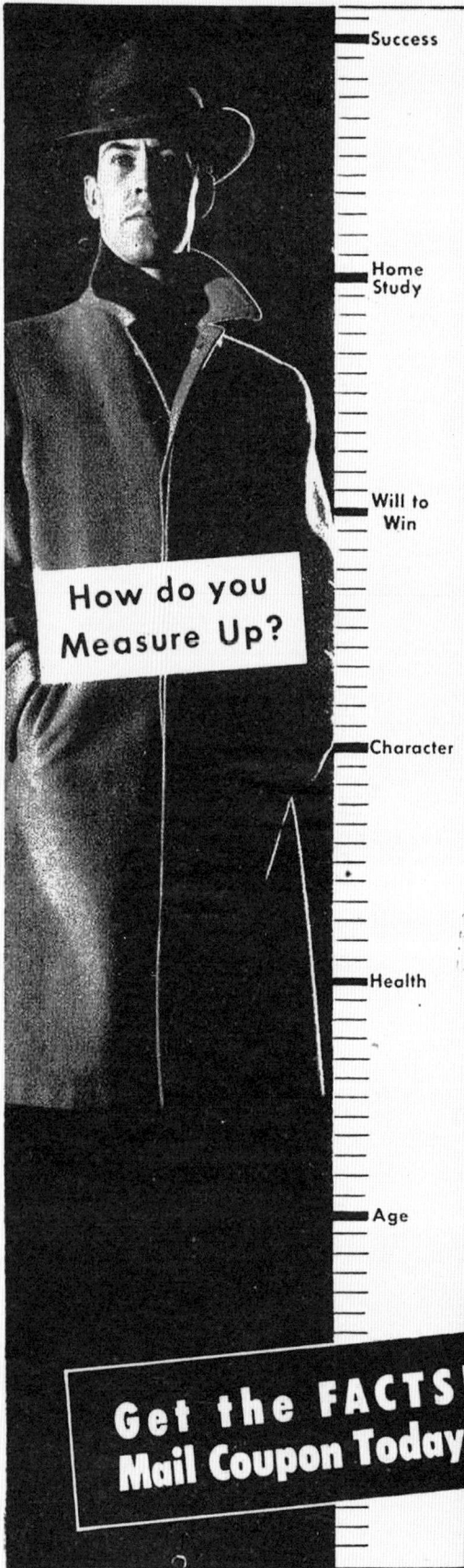
174

EVER FAINTLY, WARREN BUDD SMILED. THEN ROUTINELY...

TRUE, THERE IS NO EARTHLY REASON FOR THE FEELING. IT SEEMS TO BE ALMOST SUPER-NATURAL. HOWEVER, I AM WILLING TO PUT MY... UHMM!...PROWESS TO THE TEST. SHALL WE SAY, I SHALL DIE... TO PROVE THAT I CAN'T?!!

1, 2, 3, 4, 5, 6, 7

CAN WE UNDERSTAND MR. QUIMBY'S ABASHED REACTION TO WARREN BUDD? CAN WE SEE WHY HE FELL INTO HIS CHAIR, SIGHING HEAVILY? I AM SURE WE CAN.

YOU SIGH, MR. QUIMBY, GOOD...VERY GOOD. IT SHOWS YOU ARE OVER YOUR INITIAL RELUCTANCE. MR. QUIMBY, THERE ARE FANTASTIC PROFITS TO BE MADE FROM MY... UHMM,...GIFT, THEY CAN BE...ENORMOUS.

YOU'RE A LUNATIC!

BUDD WENT TO THE COAT RACK, HOLDING QUIMBY'S COAT OUT FOR HIM...

CALL ME WAH-WAH! ALL MY FRIENDS DO...! I THINK A BRISK WALK OUTSIDE WILL DO US BOTH GOOD. I'VE ALWAYS FOUND FRESH AIR QUITE CONDUCIVE TO BUSINESS. MUCH BETTER THAN A STUFFY OFFICE. SHALL WE GO?

Y...YES, OF COURSE. AIR... MUCH BETTER!

TO DESCRIBE MR. QUIMBY AS "TROUBLED" WOULD BE AN UNDERSTATE-MENT. HE WAS, RATHER, FRENZIED. OUTSIDE, WALKING BESIDE HIS TALKATIVE BOOK-KEEPER, MR. QUIMBY FOUND THE SUNNY DAY AND COOL BREEZE SECONDARY TO THE CONVERSATION...

WAH-WAH, I HATE TO SEEM INQUISITIVE...BUT...COULD YOU TELL ME HOW YOU ACQUIRED THIS...UHMMM... POWER OF NOT DYING? I DO HOPE I'M NOT PRYING.

NOT AT ALL, MR. QUIMBY. A RATHER CORRECT QUESTION AT THIS POINT, I SHOULD SAY.

REALLY, IT'S NOTHING ASTOUNDING. YESTERDAY MORNING I AWOKE....AND THERE I HAD IT. FELT RATHER STODGY...A STOMACH TIC... BUT I QUICKLY ADJUSTED. THAT'S ABOUT IT, MR. QUIMBY.

BUDD!

MAD-MAN-MAX YOUR FRIENDLY INSURANCE AGENCY

GUNS FOR HIRE

CRASH!

COULD IT HAVE BEEN A TRICK? A MIRAGE? COULD THE SAFE HAVE MISSED? MR. QUIMBY HAD TO ANSWER IN THE NEGATIVE, FOR THERE, IN FRONT OF HIM AND AS BIG AS LIFE, WAS WAH-WAH BUDD, ANALYTICALLY SHOOING AWAY A FLECK OF DUST FROM HIS SLEEVE...

2

Panel 1: WITH A BURST OF EMOTION, MR. QUIMBY GRABBED WARREN BUDD TOWARDS HIM, JIGGLING THE BOOK-KEEPER'S PINCE-NEZ...

SENSATIONAL, BUDD... ABSOLUTELY SENSATIONAL!

PLEASE, MR. QUIMBY... CONTROL YOURSELF! THIS IS SO UNLIKE YOU.

Panel 2: MR. QUIMBY RELEASED BUDD, STRAIGHTENED HIS TIE, AND SUCCESSFULLY REGAINED HIS BUSINESS-LIKE COMPOSURE. BUDD SMILED...

UH...EXCUSE ME, WAH-WAH. IT... IT'S JUST THAT I GET SO EXCITABLE WHEN I SEE A CHANCE TO MAKE SOME... WHAT'S THE EXPRESSION... MOOLAH! B...BUT...CAN WE MAKE SURE? WILL YOU LIVE IN THE FACE OF... ANYTHING?

MOOLAH IT IS, MR. QUIMBY. AND... AS FOR SURETY... WELL, I THINK THAT CAN BE ARRANGED. IT REALLY IS AN EASY MATTER.

Panel 3: CORROBORATION, MR. QUIMBY... CORROBORA-TION! THEN, OFF WE GO... TO A HUGE FORTUNE. HOW-EVER, LET US HAVE SOME DINNER FIRST... AND TONIGHT YOU SHALL HAVE YOUR EVIDENCE, MR. QUIMBY. ...TONIGHT..!

Panel 4: MR. QUIMBY GULPED DOWN HIS MEAL. HE WAS NOT RAVENOUS; MERELY IMPATIENT. THAT NIGHT, IN A QUIET, DESERTED CARNIVAL, HE WATCHED AS WAH-WAH BUDD LED TO TO A HIGH-DIVE...

WAH-WAH, WHY DID YOU LEAD ME...HERE?

YOU WANTED PROOF, MR. QUIMBY. I AM GIVING IT TO YOU.

Panel 5: HE WATCHED AS WAH-WAH BUDD STARTED TO CLIMB THE LADDER. HE COULD HARDLY BELIEVE WHAT HE HEARD.

I WILL CLIMB THIS LADDER, MR. QUIMBY. I WILL CLIMB TO THE TOP... AND STAND THERE, MR. QUIMBY. THEN, I WILL JUMP INTO A...DAMP RAG! A DAMP RAG, MR. QUIMBY.

BUDD! DON'T BE AN IDIOT!

Panel 6: HE STOOD FROZEN AS HE SAW BUDD ATOP THE HIGH-DIVE, HIGH IN SPACE...

DO NOT WISH ME LUCK, I'M SURE I DON'T NEED IT!

BUDD.... WAIT! IT'S... FOOLISH... INSANE..!

Panel 7: THEN, WAH-WAH BUDD JUMPED...

3

THE PURSUIT

Hector McCloy still remembered the woman. He couldn't get her out of his head. Despite her good looks, the clear blue eyes as deep as quicksilver, the smart, pert dress, the velvety voice — despite these things, there was still something odd about her.

There, that day in his private detective's office, when she had given him all that money to track the man down, he recalled the strangeness about her. What was it?

He found the man. Some routine checking, putting together some odd facts, adding two-and-two, making the pieces fit, and he finally found him. That part wasn't too hard. The stiff part was knowing what the man looked like. How can a private detective really track a guy without knowing what he looks like? It was all so weird.

And there he was, no more than twenty-five feet ahead of him. McCloy had the man boxed into an alley. He didn't want it that way. You can't face a quarry when you're both boxed in: only one guy can leave. But he had no choice. The man had led him to this corner where there was no light. The moon wasn't even on his side. The heavy clouds, dragging across the sky like clods of damp rags, shrouded it. McCloy breathed silently. There was nothing. No, correct that! There were shadows, shuffling shadows — his and the man he hunted down.

McCloy slid the gun out from his shoulder holster. It felt firm, nice, in his hands. He always felt a hundred-percent better with a gun in his hand. Gives a guy a warm feeling of satisfaction. McCloy quivered, though. He had the gun; he hunted down the guy. Still, he was scared.

He edged forward, slicing the distance between him and the guy. Why doesn't he turn around? He gripped the gun with all his might, feeling the hard steel cut into the palm of his hand. He gritted his teeth. The time had come.

"NICHOLAS!" he called.

The man turned around swiftly. McCloy jumped. He had a light, an unearthly light, a crazy mixture of red and blue — and it was smack-dab in the middle of his forehead. It wasn't real.

The man shuffled forward, nearer to McCloy. The detective began to make out other assortments. The guy's face was metallic, like aluminum, and he had no mouth — just a microphone, a round one, that looked like an orange pushed into the face. He spoke:

"Leave, earthling!" It was no voice; just sound. McCloy went for the trigger, but he felt himself flying through the air, felt himself flat on his back, and the guy's cloyish, sickly fingers holding his wrists with the grip of a wrench. And McCloy was staring into that metallic face. It was horrible.

"You fool!" the guy said. "You fall for Marta's feminine wiles — and you find yourself confronted with a Martian!"

Marta! That was the girl's name, the weird girl. What did she have to do with a — Martian? The question was answered for him.

"You're going to die, earthling," the guy said, "for finding me out!" McCloy felt the blackness closing in, and before it was really black, he heard: "Didn't you know Marta was a Venusian? That Venus and Mars both have spies on Earth?"

ONCE AGAIN WE RE-TELL A FAMOUS STORY AS WITCHES TALES SEES IT...
WITHERING HEIGHTS
BLAST THESE MOORS!!! CAN GET LOST TOO EASILY!!
A BOO OF THE MONTH
THE FIGURE WAS LOST ON THE MOORS. THE DRIVING WIND AND BLINDING SNOWSTORM LASHED ABOUT HIM IN UNABATED FURY. A WARM LIGHT, BREAKING THROUGH THE STORM IN A YELLOW GLOW, DREW HIM ON, A BEACON OF SAFETY IN THIS HORRIBLE ENGLISH WEATHER...
1

THE FIGURE OPENED THE MASSIVE DOOR- CREST. HE FACED A WARM BUT CHEERLESS INTERIOR...AND A HANDSOME MAN...

GOOD EVENING TO YOU, SIR! THE MOORS ARE LONELY THIS TIME OF YEAR...LONELY AND MYSTERIOUS!

HOW SAY YOU, SIR? WHAT'S WRONG? YOU'RE AS PALE AS A SHEET!

I COULD HAVE SWORN...I HEARD A VOICE...OUT THERE ON THE HEATH! A...WOMAN'S VOICE...! THE WIND PLAYS TRICKS, THOUGH...!

~A WOMAN'S VOICE! TELL ME MORE!.. YOU MUST..!

TH...THERE IS NOTHING... MORE! NOTHING, I TELL YOU! M...MY COACH BROKE DOWN... AND I'VE WANDERED HERE! MY NAME IS GREGORY PARSON! WHAT MORE CAN A STRANGER...SAY?!!

DID YOU SEE HER? SHE CALLED OUT MY NAME! TELL ME, MAN... DID YOU SEE HER?

SUDDENLY, AS IF HIT BY A STROKE, THE LANDLORD PUT HIS FACE TO HIS HANDS... AND SOBBED HEAVILY...

FORGIVE ME! I...I'M NOT MYSELF! I'VE BEEN ALONE SINCE SHE...CATHERINE ...DIED! MY...CATHY..!

I...SEE! I'M VERY SORRY! BUT...IF YOU'LL SHOW ME MY ROOM, I'LL BE OBLIGED!

THE LANDLORD OF WITHERING HEIGHTS LED HIS LODGER TO HIS ROOMS. HIS FLICKERING CANDLE DARTED SHADOW PATTERNS ON THE COLD, GREY WALLS...

THIS WAY, SIR!

Y...YES! ..(GULP!)..~

THEN, AS THE STRANGER ENTERED HIS ROOM AND SHUT THE DOOR BEHIND HIM, HEAT- CLIFF SOBBED INAUDIBLY. HIS WHOLE FIGURE WAS ONE OF DEJECTION AND DESPONDENCY...

CATHERINE... MY DARLING! COME BACK TO ME! CATHERINE, DARLING! CATHY...!

THE WIND RATTLED THE SHUTTERS OF THE HOUSE. IT MOANED HUNGRILY OUTSIDE. THEN IT CAME...SOUNDING LIKE A SIGH AT FIRST...THEN A MURMUR...FINALLY A NAME...

...HEATCLIFF... HEATCLIFF...!!

I HEARD IT! *HER* VOICE!

IT GOT LOUDER...

HEATCLIFF! HEATCLIFF!!

I'M COMING! I'M COMING, DARLING! CATHERINE!

HEATCLIFF!

I'M HERE, CATHERINE! *I'M HERE!*

HE RAN OUT SHOUTING! HE RAN OUT FLAILING THE WIND AND CRUSHING THE SCRAGGLY CARPET OF BLUE-GREEN GRASS UNDERFOOT. HE RAN, HAIR TOUSLED, CHEST HEAVING, ARMS SWINGING, CALLING...CALLING TO HIS LOVED ONE!

CATHERINE! CATHERINE!

CATHY! ANSWER ME, DARLING! WHERE ARE YOU? CATHY! CATHY!

WHAT'S THE TROUBLE? CAN I HELP?

NO! I...IT'S JUST MY IMAGINATION PLAYING TRICKS ON ME, SIR! THE WIND HAS DECEIVED ME!

WELL THEN... GOODNIGHT!

AY! GOODNIGHT!

THE WAILING WIND PUSHED THE DARK STORM CLOUDS OUT OF THE SKY AND THE PALE, SILVERY MOON CAME OUT! MIDNIGHT CAME TO WITHERING HEIGHTS,... AND HEATCLIFF SIPPING TEA! SUDDENLY...

HEATCLIFF.... HEATCLIFF!

I HEARD IT THIS TIME! I CANNOT DENY IT NOW EVEN TO MYSELF! *SHE'S* OUT THERE ON THE MOORS!

CATHY! CATHY! I'M COMING TO YOU, DARLING! WHERE ARE YOU?

HEATCLIFF...

HE RAN OUT...STUMBLED...BUT SAW HER...

HEATCLIFF! HURRY, HEATCLIFF!

YES! I'M COMING, DARLING! WAIT! ..OOF..!

HEATCLIFF! HURRY! HURRY, DARLING!

YES! ALL RIGHT... I'M COMING...! ..GRUNT..!

DARLING! COME ..TO...ME..! ..HEAT...CLIFF..F..F..!

ALL RIGHT... ALL RIGHT... HOLD ON,..! I'M RUNNING..TO... YOU..! ..CHOKE..!

HE FLUNG HIS ARMS AROUND THAT WONDROUS SHAPE!

CATHY! YOU DON'T KNOW HOW MUCH I'VE MISSED YOU! CATHY..!

THEY WALKED SLOWLY BACK TO WITHERING HEIGHTS, ARMS AROUND EACH OTHER, LOST IN THE ECSTASY OF LOVE-- TREADING THEIR WAY ACROSS THE MOORS!

NOW THAT I'VE FOUND YOU AGAIN, SWEETHEART-- I'LL NEVER LET YOU GO!

ALWAYS AND FOREVER, HEATCLIFF MY LOVE!

4

I COULDN'T SLEEP AT NIGHTS, CATHY. EVER SINCE YOU WERE TAKEN AWAY FROM ME, I KNEW YOU'D COME BACK! I KNEW IT SOMEHOW!

YES, DEAREST. I CAME BACK!

AND THEN--IMPELLED BY AN EAGER CURIOSITY GREATER THAN HIS OWN PATIENCE, HEATCLIFF STOPPED AND PULLED THAT SWIRLING SHAPE CLOSER...

I MUST LOOK AT YOU, DARLING. I'VE THOUGHT OF YOU SO MUCH-- SO MUCH!

NO, HEATCLIFF! NOT YET! I MUST TELL YOU SOMETHING FIRST--SOMETHING *IMPORTANT!*

IT CAN WAIT! LET ME LOOK AT YOU, CATHY. MY WONDERFULLY SWEET CATHY!

YOU WON'T LIKE WHAT YOU SEE, DARLING. I'VE... CHANGED. WE HAVE BEEN PARTED A LONG TIME!

BUT THE BURNING HUNGER OF REMEMBRANCE WAS TOO STRONG FOR THE GASPING MAN. HIS FINGERS DUG DEEP INTO YIELDING FLESH, SWINGING AROUND THE SHAPE OF HIS BELOVED...

I DON'T CARE! I *MUST,* DARLING! YOU'RE MY LIFE!

THEN LOOK--!

OH--H!

I TRIED TO TELL YOU, HEATCLIFF! I'VE BEEN *DEAD,* MY DARLING! DEAD--FOR YEARS! BUT I CAME BACK TO WARN YOU! NO--DON'T RUN AWAY FROM ME!

BUT HEATCLIFF BROKE AND RAN--HIS NERVE SHATTERED BACK TO REALITY. STILL THE THING PURSUED HIM TOWARDS THE VERY DOOR OF WITHERING HEIGHTS...

GET BACK! DON'T TOUCH ME!

DARLING! DARLING! I LOVE YOU! THAT'S WHY I CAME BACK TO SAVE YOU--TO TELL YOU ONLY WHAT THE *DEAD* KNOW. YOU'VE BEEN HOST TO... A...

--VAMPIRE!

AIIIIEEEEE!

THE END

STOP SMOKING

TOBACCO COUGH—TOBACCO HEART—TOBACCO BREATH—TOBACCO NERVES...
NEW, SAFE FORMULA HELPS YOU BREAK HABIT IN JUST 7 DAYS

No matter how long you have been a victim of the expensive, unhealthful nicotine and smoke habit, this amazing scientific (easy to use) 7-day formula will help you to stop smoking—IN JUST SEVEN Days! Countless thousands who have broken the vicious Tobacco Habit now feel better, look better—actually feel healthier because they breath clean, cool fresh air into their lungs instead of the stultifying Tobacco tar, Nicotine, and Benzo Pyrene—all these irritants that come from cigarettes and cigars. You can't lose anything but the Tobacco Habit by trying this amazing, easy method—You Can Stop Smoking!

HOW HARMFUL ARE CIGARETTES AND CIGARS?

Numerous Medical Papers have been written about the evil, harmful effects of Tobacco Breath, Tobacco Heart, Tobacco Lungs, Tobacco Mouth, Tobacco Nervousness . . . Now, here at last is the amazing easy-to-take scientific discovery that helps destroy your desire to smoke in just 7 Days—or it won't cost you one cent. Mail the coupon today—the only thing you can loose is the offensive, expensive, unhealthful smoking habit!

• YOU CAN STOP

- Tobacco Nerves
  STOP
- Tobacco Breath
  STOP
- Tobacco Cough
  STOP
- Burning Mouth
  Due To Smoking
  STOP
- Hot Burning Tongue
  Due To Smoking
  STOP
- Poisonous Nicotine
  Due To Smoking
  STOP
- Tobacco expense

SEND NO MONEY

Aver, 1½-Pack per Day Smoker
Spends $125.90 per Year

Let us prove to you that smoking is nothing more than a repulsive habit that sends unhealthful impurities into your mouth, throat and lungs . . . a habit that does you no good and may result in harmful physical reactions. Spend those tobacco $$$ on useful, healthgiving benefits for yourself and your loved ones. Send NO Money! Just mail the Coupon on our absolute Money-Back Guarantee that this 7-Day test will help banish your desire for tobacco—not for days or weeks, but FOREVER! Mail the coupon today.

ATTENTION DOCTORS:

Doctor, we can help you, too! Many Doctors are unwilling victims to the repulsive Tobacco Habit. We make the guarantee to you, too, Doctor. (A guarantee that most Doctors dare not make to their own patients) . . . If this sensational discovery does not banish your craving for tobacco forever . . . your money cheerfully refunded.

YOU WILL LOSE THE DESIRE TO SMOKE IN 7 DAYS...OR NO COST TO YOU

Don't be a slave to tobacco. . . . Enjoy your right to clean, healthful, natural living. Try this amazing discovery for just 7-Days. . . . Easy to take, pleasant, no after-taste. If you haven't broken the smoking habit forever . . . return empty carton in 10 Days for prompt refund. Mail the coupon now.

Here's What Happens When You Smoke . . .

The nicotine laden smoke you inhale becomes deposited on your throat and lungs . . . (The average Smoker does this 300 times a day!) Nicotine irritates the Mucous Membranes of the respiratory tract and Tobacco Tar injures those membranes. Stop Tobacco Cough, Tobacco Heart, Tobacco Breath . . . Banish smoking forever, or no cost to you. Mail the coupon now.

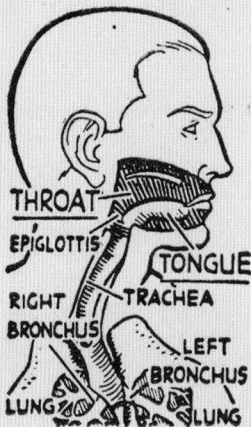

THROAT
EPIGLOTTIS
TONGUE
RIGHT
BRONCHUS
TRACHEA
LEFT
BRONCHUS
LUNG
LUNG

STOP SMOKING--MAIL COUPON NOW!

NO SMOK COMPANY, Dept HNS
400 Madison Ave., N.Y. 17, N.Y.

SENT TO YOU IN
PLAIN WRAPPER

On your 10 day Money-back Guarantee, send me No Smok Tobacco Curb. If not entirely satisfied I can return for prompt refund.

Send 7-Day Supply. I will pay Postman $1.00 plus Postage and C.O.D.

Enclosed is $1.00 for 7-Day Supply. You pay postage costs.

Enclosed is $2.00 for 25-Day Supply for myself and a loved one. You pay postage costs.

NAME _____
             (Please Print)
ADDRESS _____

TOWN _____ ZONE ____ STATE ____

187

LIVE TOY CIRCUS

With Performing CHAMELEON -- FREE!

Now, — for the first time ever — you can have a real live circus of your own. Just dozens of fine toys, each wonderful in itself, make up this circus set for the "Greatest Show on Earth." You and your friends can have hours of fun setting up the props for the circus, placing the Ringmaster, clowns, performing animals, and wild animal cages for the many exciting acts. You can even put on a real live trained animal act with the live, performing chameleon who will walk a tight rope, swing on a trapeze and change color right before your eyes from bright green to brown and back again.

Just look at all the things you get for only $1.00. Big Circus Ring, Wild Animal Cages, colorful plastic animals, Kangaroo with baby in pouch, clowns, Ringmaster, Chameleon Leash and Halter, Performing Platform, Tight Rope and Poles, Trapeze, 27 Wonderful pieces in all PLUS — FREE — THE LIVE PERFORMING CHAMELEON, who will not only act in your circus but will make a fine pet too.

Order today at our risk. If you are not satisfied that here is the best toy — the most fun ever — then just return it after 10 days free trial for a full refund of the purchase price — and keep the Chameleon as our gift to you.

only
$1.00

ALL THIS INCLUDED FOR ONLY $1.00

15 animals from our wide assortment including Clowns, Bears drinking a bottle of milk, Bunnies, Elephants, Horses, Lions, Tigers, Kangaroos, Monkeys, Deer, Flying Fish, Giraffes, Pelicans and other birds. 10 are made of bright, colorful break-resistant plastic.

3	Cages on Wheels
1	Tightrope
1	Ring Master with Whip
15	Circus Animals
1	Trapeze
1	Circus Ring
2	Clowns
1	Chameleon Leash and Halter
1	Performing Platform
1	Set Poles for Tightrope

You get 27 pieces in all, including simple instructions . . . . AND the LIVE CHAMELEON FREE!

Chameleons are real fun. They love to perform. You'll laugh with delight as they run with delicate balance along the tight rope or swing on the trapeze. They are harmless, clean and no trouble at all to keep as pets. Your friends will really gape with surprise when they see him riding on your shoulder. Your parents will be charmed with this small, clean pet. You'll love him. Sold normally for about 75c, you get this live chameleon FREE with the purchase of your Toy Circus.

LIVE Performing Chameleon included FREE

Here is our offer. Send us your order for the Live Toy Circus Today. We will send you one of these cute, harmless, performing pet chameleons free with each order. You pay only $1.00 and you must be 100% delighted or your money back.

190

GET UP...AND GIVE IT THAT OLD COLLEGE TRY IN...

GO VAMPIRE

His arguments were futile, his protestations impossible. The father could not see his son's view. So, that night, the son went out into the dark night, feeling unimportant in his quest. He heard the click-clack of the woman but he felt no zest in what he was about to do....

She's frightened. Well that's good!

The woman was upon him. He jumped from the shadows....

YEOWW!

Go ahead, run! Nobody's going to hurt you!

He howled but to no avail. The woman ran...and the son simply watched her go....

Then he went home. His father faced him, pride on his face.

How's the boy? Gave 'em the old one-two, huh? That's the spirit. I like the old college try! Gave 'em a nip for vampire U!

Dad, I...I...!

You don' know what you've got, boy! Fire...vim and vitality! That's youth! Dickerdoo... dickerdoo?...hollyhollyhoo! Bleed 'em! Bleed 'em...booboo-boo! Ahh those were the days, boy!

Can I say something, dad...please?

He watched the exuberance ebb from his father's face...

I had a victim, dad,...a girl! B-but...I...I didn't do anything! She ran...and I saw her run! I didn't follow her! I just saw her go! Dad, I--I couldn't..! I don't want to be a vampire!

Oh!

The vampire grabbed his son, clutched him to his bosom. Then he held him out at arm's length, looking at him. There was encouragement in the father's eyes...

Never mind, boy! We'll go out there...and show those people what a vampire from vampire U is capable of. Up we go, lad...outside...and for a nip.

B-but, dad, I...I..!'Oh, all right..!

3

193

THE VAMPIRE AND HIS SON WALKED TO AN ALLEY. IT WAS QUIET, ALMOST SOMBER. AT THE ALLEY'S END THERE CAME A MAN. THE VAMPIRE TURNED TOWARDS HIS SON AND SPOKE TO HIM IN WHISPERS...

NOW, WATCH, BOY! HERE'S THE WAY WE DID IT BACK IN THE OLD DAYS!

YES, DAD...!

THE ELDER VAMPIRE SPRUNG...

THE VAMPIRE ACHED FOR THE MAN'S THROAT. BUT HIS INTENDED VICTIM FOUGHT BACK, BOTH LOOKING LIKE TWIN OGRES IN THE SHADOWS.

THE VICTIM FREED HIMSELF AND GALLOPED AWAY. THE VAMPIRE WATCHED, TRYING TO CATCH HIS BREATH...

UNN-H...HUFF! PUFF!

THE VAMPIRE TURNED TOWARDS HIS SON, WHEEZING, TRYING TO CONTROL HIS RAMPANT BREATH. THE SON MERELY SMILED...

COULDN'T...HUFF...QUITE GET THE RASCAL...(GROAN!) NOT WHAT...PUFF...I USED TO BE, SON! BUT...YOU GET THE IDEA, BOY! THAT'S THE WAY ROCKO USED TO GO... HUFF...AT IT!

I SEE, DAD! IT WAS A GREAT EXHIBITION!

SUDDENLY THE VAMPIRE LOOKED AT HIS SON, HE HAD NEVER SEEN HIM LIKE THAT...SO SERIOUS...SO UNATTENTIVE...

WH - WHAT'S THE MATTER, BOY?

I THINK IT'S ABOUT TIME I TOLD YOU, DAD!

TOLD ME... WHAT?!!

I TRIED TO SAY IT BEFORE...BUT YOU WOULDN'T LISTEN! YOU'VE GOT A PICTURE OF VAMPIRE U...AND I CAN'T CHANGE IT...NO MATTER WHAT I DO... OR SAY! WELL, DAD...VAMPIRE U'S CHANGED!

4

Panel 1: THE SON GREW SOMBER. HE HUNCHED HIS SHOULDERS. A VICIOUS SMILE CROSSED HIS FACE...

VAMPIRE U HAS KEPT ABREAST WITH THE TIMES. THINGS HAVE COME AND GONE! NEW THINGS HAVE TAKEN ITS PLACE. THE YOUNGER GENERATION IS TAKING OVER!

Panel 2: HOW DO YOU MEAN, BOY? VAMPIRE U WILL ALWAYS REMAIN THE SAME..!

YOU'RE WRONG, DAD! WE'VE LEARNED DIFFERENT THINGS! VAMPIRE'S ARE PAST! SOMETHING...SOMEBODY NEW....IS COMING!

Panel 3: THE BOY THEN TORE OFF HIS VAMPIRE WINGS...

FORGET YOUR CHEERS, DAD! NO MORE BITE 'EM! NO MORE BLEED 'EM...!

Panel 4: HE BLUNTED HIS POINTED EARS...

IT'S A NEW DAY... A GOLDEN DAY..!

Panel 5: HE RUBBED HIS HANDS OVER HIS FACE...

I OWE A LOT TO VAMPIRE U, DAD! A GREAT DEAL..!

KEEP OUT

Panel 6: THE VAMPIRE BACKED AWAY AS HIS SON CAME OUT OF THE SHADOWS. HE KNEW SOMETHING WAS CHANGED... SOMETHING HE NEVER SUSPECTED...

BOY... BOY... WHAT HAVE YOU DONE?

NO, DAD... NOT WHAT I'VE DONE! YOU SHOULD ASK...WHAT HAS VAMPIRE U TAUGHT ME...HOW THEY MADE ME PART OF A NEW AGE!

Panel 7: VAMPIRE U TOLD ME HOW TO BECOME... A ...GHOUL!

MY BOY, WHAT HAVE THEY DONE TO YOU!

THERE IS A MORAL TO THIS STORY. IT'S...VAMPIRES COME AND GO...BUT GHOULS ARE HERE TO STAY. SO... RAISE A CHEER! GHOULA ...GHOULA... *The End*

195

HUMPTY DUMPTY SAT ON A WALL,

HUMPTY DUMPTY HAD A GREAT FALL;

ALL THE KING'S HORSES AND ALL THE KING'S MEN

COULDN'T PUT HUMPTY DUMPTY TOGETHER AGAIN!

BIRDS OF A FEATHER FLOCK TOGETHER,

AND SO DO PIGS AND SWINE;

RATS AND MICE WILL HAVE THEIR CHOICE,

BUT I DON'T HAVE MINE!

FORTUNE HUNTER

Steve Thompson had figured it out perfectly. He wasn't going to let anyone stop him now. It was like a well-executed end-around-end football play, and he was carrying the pigskin for the touchdown.

Only the pigskin was a petite red-haired beauty, and the goal-line was the million dollars she was heir to.

He smiled as he thought of this imagery in football terms. It made his doings sound like true sportsmanship.

He was walking with his red-haired heiress now, passing a pleasant Sunday afternoon through the city's carnival. He put his arm around her, and she looked up at him.

"Oh, Steve," she said. "Just think of it. Only one more week, only seven more days."

"I wish it was today, Marsha," he said. "I hate every one of my days without you . . ." And your money, he finished silently.

She smiled her agreement. Then suddenly she became excited. "Oh look, darling! Look! A Gypsy fortune teller! Let's have our fortune told?"

"But, Marsha. You know that stuff is silly. It's nothing but a waste of time." A touch of fear had gripped him. Sure the stuff was a pack of lies, but what if that Gypsy really tipped her off? It was better if he played it safe.

"But, darling," she pleaded. "Just this once. I really want to."

Maybe it was better giving in this time, he decided. Show her what a compromising guy I am.

"I guess you can't say no to the woman you love," he lied so beautifully.

The Gypsy greeted them at the front of the tent. She showed them in and sat Marsha behind the crystal ball.

"I almost think she's going to tell me the truth," Marsha whispered to Steve.

"I'd kill her if she did," Steve told himself.

The Gypsy went to work. Her phoney mystic ways brought a smile to Steve's face. And her words made him feel even better.

"I see a great occasion coming into your life, young lady," she began. "I see a very lucky day coming your way. Why, it is just a week away. The two of you are there. There are many, many other people. Lots of friends and relatives. It is taking place in the city's biggest church."

Wow, is this a set-up, Steve thought. He could have kissed the Gypsy. Marsha reached for his hand. He smiled and kissed her on her forehead.

Yes, Steve Thompson was happy. Even the Gypsy was with him. At least, he thought she was.

For, you see, Steve Thompson had an accident that next week. And the following Sunday, a really lucky day in Marsha's life, there were many, many people at the city's biggest church. There were loads of friends and relatives of both Steve and Marsha. It was quite an occasion. It was . . . Steve Thompson's funeral.

UP THERE

YOU'D BLOW YOUR STACK IF YOU FOUND OUT WHAT WAS...

GENTLEMEN, ON THIS FILM IS MAURICE SHMEERZ'S SECRET. I PLAN TO SHOW IT TO YOU. UNFORTUNATELY, SHMEERZ IS NOT HERE TO SEE IT! HE IS ... UMM... DETAINED!

DETAINED! A PSYCHIATRIST'S POLITE WORD FOR BEING COMMITTED. OH, EXCUSE ME! I'M MAURICE SHMEERZ. I CLIMBED LANAPURNA MOUNTAIN!

FOR THOSE WHO DON'T KNOW, LANAPURNA IS 29,602 FEET HIGH...AND IS THE MOST DANGEROUS OF THE HIMOLYA CHAIN! I ... MAURICE SHMEERZ...AM THE ONLY MAN WHO REACHED ITS PEAK...WHO KNOWS WHAT'S ...UP THERE!

1

"IT WAS ALMOST FIFTEEN MONTHS AGO THAT I SET OUT FROM MY NATIVE FRANCE...TO CLIMB LANAPURNA. THE FRENCH PRESIDENT WISHED ME GOOD LUCK..."

GOOD CLIMBING, MAURICE!

"MY WIFE WISHED ME GOOD LUCK..."

COME BACK SOON, MAURICE!

"MY FRIENDS WISHED ME GOOD LUCK..."

AU REVOIR, CHERI!

..MMMMM!..

"I WENT WINGING OFF TO THE HIMOLYA COUNTRY. THIRTY-SIX HOURS LATER I FOUND MYSELF IN A SMALL RUSTIC TOWN...WHERE I SHOOK HANDS WITH THE REST OF MY ASSOCIATES..."

WE'RE WAITING, MAURICE.

YES, MAURICE...AND SO IS...LANAPURNA!

"I TURNED AROUND...TO GAZE AT THE MIGHTY MOUNTAIN. SHE STOOD IN SPLENDOR...AN ALMOST INSURMOUNTABLE BARRIER. MY HEART POUNDED AS I SAW HER. YES, THERE SHE WAS... LANAPURNA!"

"IT TOOK US ALMOST TWO MONTHS OF SOLID PREPARATIONS BEFORE WE BEGAN THE CLIMB, BUT WHEN WE FINALLY DID START OUT, I KNEW WE LOOKED LIKE FOUR ANTS TRYING TO CONQUER A GIANT..."

"BUT, I, MAURICE SHMEERZ, KNEW THAT I WOULD DEFEAT HER. IT WAS MY DESTINY. WHAT I DIDN'T KNOW WAS...WHAT WAS UP THERE..."

"SOON, MY COMPANIONS AND MYSELF FOUND OUT THAT LANAPURNA WAS LIKE A FICKLE WOMAN. ONE MOMENT SHE WAS SWELTERING..."

"AND ...8,000 FEET HIGHER,...SHE WAS LIKE AN ICE-BOX..."

"FULL OF TREACHEROUS STREAMS AND DANGEROUS GULLEYS..."

"BUT I, MAURICE SHMEERZ, WAS ALWAYS ON HAND TO TAKE PICTURES OF THE DESTINY THAT WAS MINE."

"AT 10,000 FEET, THE GLARE OF THE SUN BOUNCING OFF THE SNOW WAS TREMENDOUS. WE HAD TO DON SUN GOGGLES TO PROTECT OUR EYES..."

"IT WAS SLIGHTLY HIGHER THAT WE EXPERIENCED AN AVALANCHE."

"BUT OFF WE SET AGAIN, UNDAUNTED...UNAFRAID..."

3

"IT WAS AT 16,002 FEET THAT I SAW THAT MY COMPANIONS DID NOT SHARE THE SAME DESIRES AS I. THEY WERE FRIGHTENED IN OUR PALTRY PITCHED-TENT THAT WAS SUPPOSED TO BE CAMP..."

I'M SORRY, MAURICE... FRANCOIS AND I CANNOT GO ANY FURTHER. WE'RE FRIGHTENED.

I SEE. AND YOU... MARIUS...ARE YOU FRIGHTENED, TOO?

NO, MAURICE, I WILL GO WITH YOU... TO THE TOP!

"SO, THE NEXT MORNING, MARIUS AND I STARTED OUT...CLIMBING HIGHER... EVER HIGHER..."

"SUDDENLY THE ROPE THAT HELD MARIUS TO ME BROKE...AND THAT WAS THE LAST I SAW OF HIM..."

YAAAAAA!

"I WAS ALONE...ALONE ON THE TERRIBLE DRIFTS OF LANAPURNA...BUT STILL I WENT ON..."

"I WAS EXHAUSTED. I COULD NOT BREATHE. I STRUGGLED TO REACH LANAPURNA'S TOP, THEN, AS IF BY MAGIC, I SAW IT..."

"LANAPURNA'S PEAK..."

"THE FIRST MAN TO REACH IT...THE THOUGHT RAN THROUGH MY HEAD. HIGHER I WENT... HIGHER... UNTIL I STOOD ON ITS SUMMIT..."

4

201

"ONCE ON TOP, I HEARD SOMETHING SNAP. I GUESS IT WAS MY MIND. FOR...ON LANAPURNA'S WINDBLOWN PEAK, 25,000 FEET HIGH...I FOUND OUT...FOUND OUT WHAT WAS ...UP THERE..."

HA..HA! HA..HA HA HA..HA! HA.. HA

"I COULDN'T RESIST THE TEMPTATION. I HAD TO TAKE MY MOVIES OF THE SCENE...TO SHOW IT TO THE PEOPLE. IT WOULD BE SOMETHING TO CONVINCE THEM...WHY I WENT CRAZY ON LANAPURNA..."

WELL, THERE YOU HAVE IT. THAT'S MY STORY...MAURICE SHMEERZ'S STORY. NOW... TAKE A LOOK AT WHAT THE PSYCHIATRISTS ARE GOING TO SEE~!

GENTLEMEN, WE ARE ON LANAPURNA MOUNTAIN NOW. MR. SHMEERZ TOOK THESE MOVIES. LET US SEE WHAT MADE HIS MIND GO!

WE ARE HIGHER NOW... NEARING THE PEAK!

NOW... WE ARE ON THE PEAK. LET US SEE ...

"I TOLD YOU. CAN YOU SEE WHY I WENT CRAZY CLIMBING LANAPURNA MOUNTAIN, AN OLD FRANKFURTER STAND WAS ...UP THERE!"

The End.

8

203

204

205

I really couldn't blame
The Other Girl

> It was my own ugly skin that chased him away — but it was a Doctors Formula that won him back

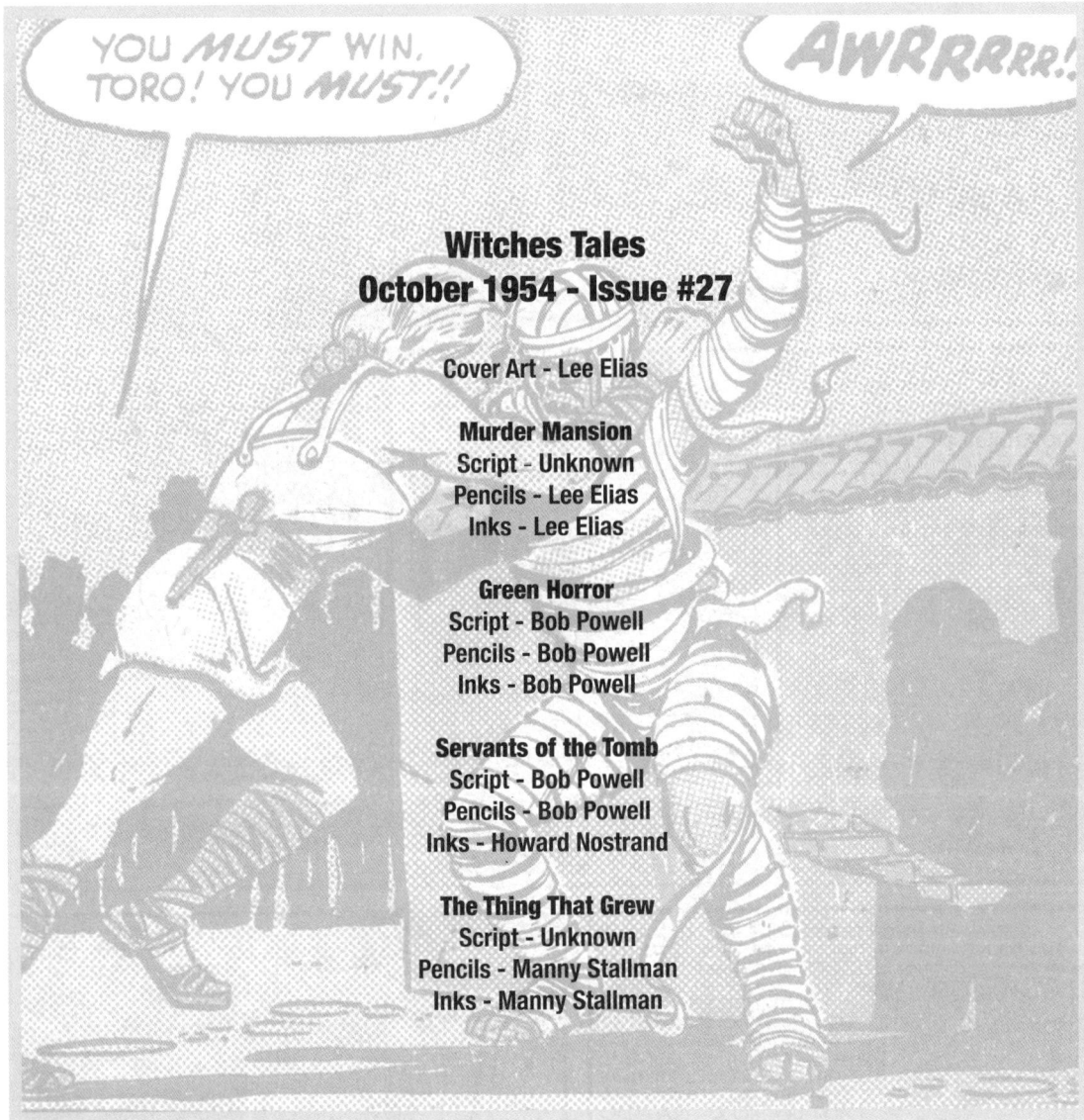

YOU *MUST* WIN, TORO! YOU *MUST*!!

AWRRRRR!

Witches Tales
October 1954 - Issue #27

Cover Art - Lee Elias

Murder Mansion
Script - Unknown
Pencils - Lee Elias
Inks - Lee Elias

Green Horror
Script - Bob Powell
Pencils - Bob Powell
Inks - Bob Powell

Servants of the Tomb
Script - Bob Powell
Pencils - Bob Powell
Inks - Howard Nostrand

The Thing That Grew
Script - Unknown
Pencils - Manny Stallman
Inks - Manny Stallman

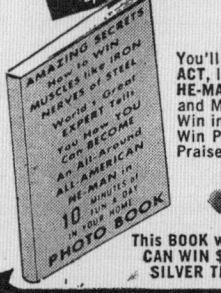

WITCHES TALES, OCTOBER, 1954, VOL. 1, NO. 27, IS PUBLISHED BI-MONTHLY
by WITCHES TALES, INC., 1860 Broadway, New York 23, N. Y. Entered as second class matter at the Post Office at New York, N. Y., under the Act of March, 3, 1879. Single copies, 10c. Subscription rates, 10 issues for $1.00 in the U. S. and possessions, elsewhere $1.50. All names in this periodical are entirely fictitious and no identification with actual persons is intended. Contents copyrighted, 1954, by Witches Tales, Inc., New York, City. Printed in the U.S.A. Title registered in U. S. Patent Office.

THE WITCH'S MESSAGE

Heh! Heh! How many times the pot of evil has boiled! But, this time, the brew I have bubbling in it is special . . . it has ALL the ingredients of shrieking horror, savage suspense and blood-curdling action!

Never before have I gathered such a collection of tales. Never before has your sanity been called upon to withstand such terror as appears in this issue!

What is the secret of MURDER MANSION? Why do its walls tremble? Who does the dance of death?

Then, in THE THING THAT GREW, you will see right before your bulging eyes a monster that defies nature. You will find yourself twisting from under its deadly foot as it tries to crush thousands. A tidal wave could have no greater fury.

But, can there be a greater mad-masterpiece of horror than the SERVANTS OF THE TOMB? See dead men walk, giants battle, and thousands riot in panic! Cringe when the Tomb of Zombies is opened!

Heh! Heh! Wait! There is more! Read about the two who thought they could know the mysteries of the unknown. Read what happens when they meet the Frogmen!

Heh! Heh! Heh! You can't wait, can you? Very well, turn the page and take the journey through fear!

MURDER MANSION

MURDER MANSION

The CREATURES WHO RULE THE *DEAD* DID NOT SLEEP QUIETLY BENEATH THE *ROTTING* HOUSE! THEY REACHED FROM ANOTHER WORLD, CALLING THROUGH THE SHADOWS, WAITING... WAITING TO CLAIM TENANTS FOR THE...

LUCY AND JERRY WILLIAMS SPED THROUGH THE NEW ENGLAND NIGHT TO SPEND THEIR HONEY-MOON IN LUCY'S FAMILY MANSION— A HOUSE SHE HAD INHERITED...A HOUSE SHE HAD NEVER SEEN!

OH, DARLING, I HOPE WE LIKE MOON MANSION.

IT'S PROBABLY A SWEET LITTLE PLACE... AND IT'S ALL OURS!

BUT AS THE YOUNG COUPLE WENT OUT INTO THE NIGHT AIR, LUCY WAS UNEASY! A SOLITARY CAB DRIVER WAS THE ONLY FIGURE IN THE DESERTED DEPOT...

WHAT A *DREADFUL PLACE!* WHAT A *QUEER* OLD MAN!

HERE WE ARE, DARLING...OH, DRIVER! CAN YOU TAKE US TO MOON MANSION?

MOONVIL

NO-DON'T- *ARRRGHH!*

THE *SCREAMING DARKNESS* OF THE PIT CLOSED OVER LUCY, AND WHEN SHE EMERGED, SHE WAS A *WALKING CORPSE...A WITCH* OF EVIL!

NOW I KNOW WHAT CALLED ME... *HEE HEE!* I MUST-- KILL! I--MUST KILL--JERRY-- *HEE! HEE! HEE!*

JERRYYY... JERRYYYYY... I AM COMING UP TO YOU NOWWW...

WHA-! WHO IS THAT? LUCY---WHERE ARE YOU, LUCY?!!

LUCY! WHAT'S THE MATTER?? YOU LOOK SO *STRANGE!* YOU LOOK SO *DIFFERENT!* WHAT'S HAPPENED... LUCY!!

IT'S ALL RIGHT NOW, MY DARLING...JUST LET ME PRESS THIS LITTLE BUTTON! *HEE, HEE!*

STOP! THE BED...IT'S GOING TO *CRUSH ME...* YOU'RE NOT LUCY! WHAT ARE YOU? *STOP!!*

THIS IS WHAT CALLED ME, MY DARLING... *DEATH! HA HA HA HARRGH! DEATH! DEATH!*

LIKE A HORRIBLE VISE, THE BED CANOPY LOWERED, BRINGING THE *CRUSHING SOUNDS* OF *BLOODY DEATH!*

NO! NOOORRRGRGG...

HA HA! MOON MANSION IS *NOT* FOR THE *LIVING!* IT SHALL BE THE *HOME OF DARKNESS* UNTIL THE *DAY OF DOOM!*

WHERE BE YER HUSBAND, MRS. WILLIAMS?

HE HAD TO GO AWAY-BUSINESS! HEE HEE! GIVE ME MY THINGS AND LET ME GO!

WHY WOULD THEY WANT TO LIVE IN THE BLACK PLACE? MY, BUT SHE ACTED STRANGE-LIKE!

ENCLOSED IN THE BLACKNESS OF MOON MANSION, LUCY CALLED TO THE SPECTERS THAT HAUNTED THE MUSTY ROOMS OF DEATH... BUT...

COME TO ME, SPIRITS OF EVIL! COME FOR HOURS OF...WHA-? WHO COULD BE CALLING HERE...!

KNOCK! KNOCK!

WHO ARE YOU? WHAT DO YOU WANT HERE AT THIS TIME OF NIGHT?

THE PEOPLE IN THE VILLAGE TOLD US THIS PLACE IS FOR SALE...MAY WE COME IN? IT'S A BAD NIGHT!

I DON'T LIKE THIS PLACE, JOHN...IT SCARES ME!

HUSH, DEAR, SHE'LL HEAR YOU!

THEY LIED TO YOU! THERE IS SOME MISTAKE! THIS PLACE IS NOT FOR...YOU! PLEASE GO!

BUT THE "THINGS" HAD COME AT LUCY'S CALL! EVEN THOUGH SHE COULD NOT SEE THROUGH THE SHADOWS THAT CLUSTERED ABOUT LUCY, THE WOMAN COULD SENSE THE PRESENCE OF EVIL...

EEEEEE-JOHN! I THOUGHT I SAW SOMETHING BEHIND HER... SOMETHING HORRIBLE...TAKE ME AWAY!

WHA-! PLEASE, DEAR, IT'S JUST THE LIGHTNING!

Panel 1:
THEY HAVE SEEN THE POWERS OF THE MANSION... THEY MUST NOT LEAVE HERE ALIVE!

PLEASE CALM YOUR-SELVES...THERE IS NOTHING HERE! IF YOU WILL EXCUSE ME FOR A MOMENT...!

Panel 2:
WHILE THE VISITORS WAITED, LUCY PRACTISED THE *BLACK ARTS!* HER PURPOSE WAS THE PURPOSE OF... *MURDER!..*

SLAVE-SPIRIT OF MY MURDERED HUSBAND! OUTSIDE IS THE CAR IN WHICH THE VISITORS HAVE COME... *DESTROY* IT! LET THEM NOT ESCAPE THE TOMBS OF MOON MANSION...

IT...SHALL BE... DOOOOONE...

Panel 3:
CRASH!
CR-RACK

Panel 4:
WHAT HAPPENED!

OUR CAR...OUR CAR HAS BEEN DESTROYED BY LIGHTNING!

OH, JOHN... I'M FRIGHTENED!

Panel 5:
YOU HAD BEST STAY HERE...IT'S A *WILD NIGHT!* I ONLY HAVE TWO BEDROOMS THAT CAN BE... USED! BUT, ONE OF THE GIRLS WILL HAVE TO STAY IN MY ROOM!

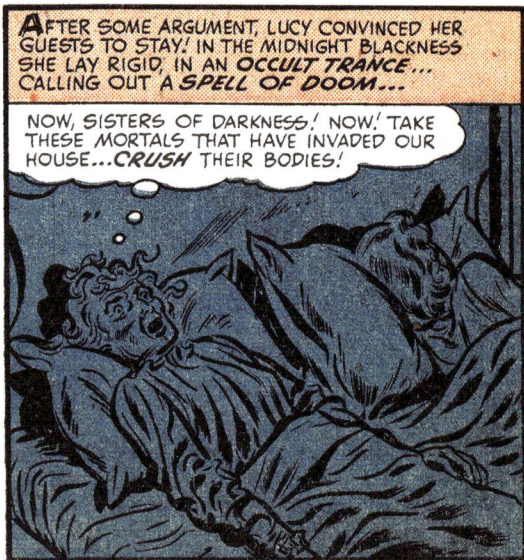

Panel 6:
AFTER SOME ARGUMENT, LUCY CONVINCED HER GUESTS TO STAY! IN THE MIDNIGHT BLACKNESS SHE LAY RIGID, IN AN *OCCULT TRANCE...* CALLING OUT A *SPELL OF DOOM...*

NOW, SISTERS OF DARKNESS! NOW! TAKE THESE MORTALS THAT HAVE INVADED OUR HOUSE...*CRUSH* THEIR BODIES!

AND IN LUCY'S BEDROOM, THE OTHER GIRL SAT UP, WIDE AWAKE WITH SUDDEN TERROR!
EEEEEEE-UGH!
WHAT WAS THAT SCREAM!? THOSE FLAMES... WHERE ARE THEY COMING FROM?!
AS SHE SPRANG FROM THE BED OF DEATH, THE GIRL ACCIDENTALLY TOUCHED THE SECRET BUTTON!
WHAT IS THAT IN THE BED?!! I MUST BE LOSING MY MIND!! NO! NO! THOSE FLAMES...
LUCY WAS KILLED! KNOCKING OVER THE CANDLE, THE GIRL RAN FROM THE ROOM LIKE A SHRIEKING TORCH!
THE BED... IT KILLED HER! OH! OH! THE CANDLE! I'M BURNING... NOOO! NO! EEEEYAAAHHH!
EEEYAARGHH!
THE MANSION OF THE DEAD BECAME A MASS OF DEVOURING FLAME... THE VILLAGERS CAME TOO LATE TO STOP THE FIRE, AND AS THEY WATCHED THE DESTRUCTION OF THE BLACK PLACE...
YAAAAAAAAOOOOOOOO!
THE SCREAM OF DEATH!
WHAT WAS THAT?
I TOLD THEM NOT TO GO THERE... I FEEL SORRY FOR THE YOUNG COUPLE! WHAT A WAY TO DIE!
THE HUSBAND WAS AWAY... T'IS THE LASS I FEEL SORRY FOR! SHE WAS SO YOUNG AND SWEET! BUT AT LEAST THE BLACK PLACE IS NO MORE! IT WAS A MURDER MANSION!
THE END

WHAT ARE THE *APPALLING* CREATURES THAT EMERGE FROM THE WILD, BEATING HEART OF THE SWEATING JUNGLE?... WHY DO EVEN THE BEASTS SHRIEK IN TERROR AT THE SIGHT OF THE...

GREEN HORROR

DEEP IN THE JUNGLES OF BRAZIL, WHERE HUMANS SHOULD NOT *DARE* TO VENTURE, WHERE *FEAR* AND *DANGER* WAIT BROODING IN EVERY CORNER, TWO PEOPLE MOVE SLOWLY TOWARDS A PERILOUS ADVENTURE...

HURRY, RUTH!! THAT RIVER SHOULDN'T BE VERY *FAR* NOW!!

I'M TIRED, FRANK! I STILL DON'T BELIEVE THOSE *FROG MEN* REALLY EXIST!!

THIS MUST BE IT!! WE CAN CAMP BY THE BANK!

I DON'T LIKE IT, FRANK!! THE WATER LOOKS SO... *STRANGE!!*

WHEN DAY COMES, THE EXPLORERS LOOK AGAIN AT THE MYSTERIOUS RIVER...
I MUST ADMIT THE RIVER LOOKS BETTER THIS MORNING! AND I DON'T SEE ANY OF YOUR FOOLISH FROG MEN ABOUT!!!
I GUESS I DRAGGED YOU ON THIS EXPEDITION FOR NOTHING, RUTH! BUT THOSE SECRET RECORDS SAID THEY EXISTED---
THINK I'LL GO IN FOR A SHORT SWIM! WANT TO COME, "PROFESSOR"?
NO, I WANT TO LOOK OVER THESE MAPS. WE MIGHT HAVE THE WRONG RIVER!!
OH, WHAT I HAVE TO GO THROUGH BEING THE WIFE OF AN EXPLORER... IS THAT YOU, FRANK??
SUDDENLY, A REPULSIVE CREATURE, HALF-MAN, HALF-FROG, APPEARS IN THE WATER, ITS WEIRD VOICE RAISED IN A CHILLING CHANT OF DEATH!...
FRANK!!! HELP!!! HELP!!
KRAAGHHH-HHH!! KRAAAGGHH-HH!!
A HUMAN FROG! I'M COMING, RUTH!!
AHH-H-H..
KROWWGG-HH-H-H-H!
KILL HIM, FRANK!!!
AWRRRGHH-H-H-H-H!!

FIERCELY, DESPERATELY, THE EXPLORER AND THE UNEARTHLY BEING GRAPPLE IN THE WATER, DEATH A GRIM SPECTATOR!

AAARRR-GHHHH-H-H!!

HURRY UP, RUTH! WE'LL HAVE TO GET OUT OF HERE!!

ERGH-H-H!! I SWALLOWED SOME OF HIS--HORRIBLE BLOOD!!

WE'LL HAVE TO GO ACROSS THE RIVER! BUT HOW...WAIT! LOOK--A STRAY WAR CANOE!

FRANK, LOOK AT THEM! WILL WE EVER ESCAPE??

FRANTICALLY LAUNCHING THE CANOE, THE TWO EXPLORERS RUSH INTO THE WATER, FLEEING THE SLIMY WET CLAWS OF THE DIABOLICAL FROG MEN!...

THEY'RE GAINING ON US!!

KEEP ROWING!!! WE MUSTN'T STOP!!!

THEY'VE CAUGHT US!!!

FIGHT THEM OFF, FRANK!! MAYBE WE CAN MAKE IT TO SHORE!!

KROWGG-GH-H-H.

ON AND ON, THE STRANGE BATTLE *RAGES*, HUMAN BEINGS AGAINST *GHASTLY* HALF-HUMAN BEINGS BENT ON *TEARING THE FLESH* OF THOSE WHO *DESTROYED* ONE OF THEIR NUMBER...

RAAGH-H-H-H!!!

KRAGH-H-H!!

ROWGGHH-H-H!!

WE MADE IT.!! ARE YOU ALL RIGHT, RUTH?

YES, YES!! BUT LET'S GET OUT OF HERE!!

WHERE WILL WE *RUN*?? I'VE LOST OUR *MAPS* AND--- WH--??

FRANK.!!! KRAWKK-K-K! KRAWK-K-K!!!

BEFORE HIS *TERRIFIED* EYES, THE EXPLORER WATCHES HIS WIFE BECOME A *LOATHSOME* BEING, A *WALKING GREEN HORROR!!*

SHE SWALLOWED THE *BLOOD* OF THE FROG I KILLED!!! UGH-H-H!!

WHAT'S HAPPENING TO ME? KRAGGH-H-H!! KROWGH-H!!!

YOU MURDERED ONE OF MY *BROTHERS*.!! YOU MUST *DIE!!!*

N-N-O-O-O.!! ARRRGH-H-H.!!

...AND NOW, IN THE *WILD, BEATING HEART* OF THE SWEATING JUNGLE, A *MONSTER* GOES TO JOIN HER *FELLOW CREATURES*, LEAVING BEHIND HER THE REMAINS OF AN ILL-FATED ADVENTURE!

KROWGGHHH-H-H-H.!! KROWGGG-HH-H-H.!! KRAWGGH-H-H!!!

THE END.

225

ONE MILLION *VOLTS!*

"Do you have anything to say?"

"Get it over with, you stinking cops!"

"Put the head-piece on."

"Ready, Warden."

"When the red light goes on above the chair, you know what to do."

The red light blinked on.

ZZZZZZZZIIIIII!!!!

"Warden, look. He's glowing!"

"More electricity."

"We've got it up to a million volts now, sir."

"Something has gone wrong. Oh no! He's getting up . . . he's ripping the straps."

The police in the electrocution room huddled against the walls. Standing before them, his body bristling with electricity, was Pretty Boy Wills.

Finally, the warden found his voice.

"Everyone out of here. We'll lock him in."

Everyone tried to escape the monster at once. They jammed at the door but before they could all get out, Wills had staggered over and grabbed one of the policemen.

"Quick! Slam that door shut!"

The warden and the others clustered around the window, looking in on the room. Their minds were confused . . . almost frozen with horror.

"Look! He's got Lewis. He's holding him in his arms. The electricity from his body is burning Lewis to a crisp!"

"Doctor," gasped Warden Trent, "what happened?"

"I don't really know, but I think his body somehow has absorbed the electricity and is using it as we would blood. It's a medical miracle . . . Watch out! Get away from these metal walls!"

The doctor's warning came just in time. Wills was nearing the door. The minute he touched it, the walls became charged with deadly electricity.

"What do we do now?" shouted one of the attendants, "he's battering down the door!"

No one could move! If Wills got out, he would never be stopped. Suddenly, the sound of sizzling electricity behind the door stopped. The walls were no longer charged.

"Open the door," ordered the doctor. The huge door swung open. The men fell back in terror.

"Just as I thought," exclaimed the doctor. "our bodies are only so strong. After several minutes the electricity finally killed him."

The doctor pushed his foot through the pile of dust that had once been a man!

DUEL AT DAWN !

"The sun's hot."

"Yeah. These bags are getting heavy."

"Quite a place, this canyon."

"It's gonna take some traveling to get out of it."

"Just think, Spider, we've got enough gold in these bags to make us millionaires."

"I been thinking about that, Joe. Look, why don't you throw that gun away. It makes me nervous."

"This gun makes me feel safe, Spider. You were okay — helping me kill that prospector who struck it rich and getting his gold — but that's done. Now, you'd slit me in two to get all the gold!"

And so the two men rode on. As the days passed the friction between them increased. Joe knew he needed Spider to lead him out of the Gold Mountains. Spider knew he could have everything if he could get the gun.

When they bedded down for the nights, they tried to fight off sleep in order to watch each other. One night. . . .

"Just a little more . . . little more . . . oops. . . ."

Spider had kicked loose some stones as he crawled towards Joe. The other murderer fell back with a start.

"So, you tried to finish me! Looks like I don't get to sleep anymore."

"Aw, look, Joe, I'll tell you what. Give me three quarters of the gold an' I won't touch you."

"No!"

More hot, dust-filled days passed. Now both men did not dare to sleep. One wanted to kill. The other wanted to live.

Spider was the bigger and stronger of the two. He knew that sooner or later Joe would have to give in. His chance came.

Night wore on to dawn. Joe, his face drawn, his brow fever-charged, could barely keep awake. Suddenly, he pitched forward, unconscious.

With a mad lunge, Spider was upon him, his hands ripping the gun from Joe's.

"Now, I got him."

Spider rose and backed away a few feet. He leveled the gun at Joe's head.

BLAM!

Spider began to laugh insanely. Then, his laughter changed to shrieks of terror. The vibrations set up by the gun's explosion had started a landslide!

Tons of rock began to cascade down the canyon walls. In minutes, Spider was crushed under the avalanche. Just then, the sun rose and its rays caught a small piece of ore. It sparkled—the last remains of a buried treasure!

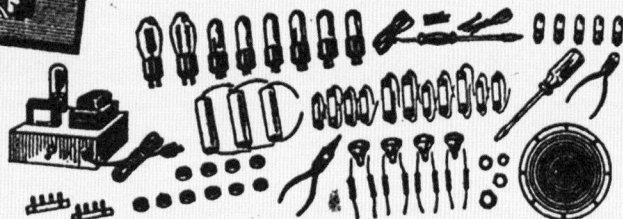

228

LET THE GODS BE ANGRY NOW!! ALL THOSE WHO ARE AFRAID OF THEIR WRATH HAVE BEEN KILLED!!!

WE MUST HURRY! THE MOON WILL BE OUT SOON!!

DO NOT STOP UNTIL THE WALL HAS BEEN BROKEN!!

TORO WILL WALK THE STREETS OF THE CITY-- TONIGHT!!!

WE'VE DONE IT!!! NOW WE MUST LET THE MOON SHINE DOWN UPON OUR DEAD FRIEND!!!

THE MOON IS BRIGHT THIS EVENING! IT SHOULD HELP US IN OUR---WORK...

IT WON'T BE LONG NOW!!! LOOK-- IT STIRS!!

STEADILY, THE MOON SHINES UPON THE LOATHESOME FIGURE ON THE SLAB... UNTIL THE CHILL OF DEATH BEGINS TO FADE... AND LIFE BEGINS TO STIR IN THE TREMENDOUS BODY!...

A-A-W-W-R-R-R-R!!

HE'S ALIVE AGAIN!!

--AND HE BELONGS TO US!!

THE VAMPIRE'S RETURN

"George, move the lantern closer to the coffin!"

The yellow, misty light fell fully upon a rusting red coffin. A huge triangular shield could be seen on one side of the decaying box. On the shield was inscribed . . .

"HERE LIE THE REMAINS OF THE HUMAN VAMPIRE. THE WOODEN STAKE THAT PIERCES ITS HEART WILL FOREVER QUIET ITS THIRST FOR BLOOD."

"Ha-a-a-a, George, look, look at that stupid inscription. I, Doctor Chandu, have found the lost notebook of that great master of life and death, that supreme juggler of natural existence, Professor Bartok. He is dead but his notes will tell me how to bring life to the . . . HUMAN VAMPIRE!"

"What I like, Doctor, is how I choked the keeper of the vault where this coffin was. His eyes bulged so when I dug my fingers into his th. . . ."

"Shut up, you idiot! We can't stand here! The moon will rise soon and the stake must be removed!"

"Yes, master!"

"But, first, is IT ready?"

"If the emergency arises, it will be ready!"

Then, the horrible work began. Slowly, the top of the coffin was lifted. And, as the fresh air seeped into the box, a strange, heavy air was pushed out. Finally, the coffin was open!

"Oh, master!"

"Yes, George, he doesn't look very pretty, does he? How long it has been since his lips have tasted the sweetness of human blood!"

The two men continued to look down on the monster. What did it look like? Imagine a man whose body is thin and long. Imagine a man whose arms, covered by a black cloak, look like the wings of a bat. Imagine a man whose lips are thin and blue . . . lips which hide teeth as sharp as razors.

"All right, George, help me take out the body and place it on this slab. The moonlight must fall directly on the body!"

After the vampire was placed on the specially constructed slab, the doctor retreated to a corner and began to chant strangely. Again and again he would look at the notebook. Then, he removed a hypodermic needle from his bag. In it was a serum prepared in his laboratory from notes in Bartok's book. All was ready now.

"Master, the moon."

The full, silvery moon was rising. The vault began to grow light . . . to shimmer in the strange glow. Doctor Chandu approached the human vampire. He uttered some words. Then, he plunged the needle into the arm of the vampire.

George watched in dumb horror as Chandu began to pull the stake out of the vampire's heart. Slowly . . . slowly, the wooden stake was eased out.

"HA-HAH-HA . . . So. I have life again. But I need blood . . . blood . . . blood!"

The vampire was alive. Quickly, it jumped from the coffin, grabbed George, who was standing nearby, and began to tear at his throat.

"Master . . . help . . . arrrgh. . . ."

"Drink deeply, my pretty. As my slave, you will have much work to do!"

"I, your slave? Ha-ha-ahaaaa. Do you think I would let a human tell me what to do, now that I have been released from death?"

"Stay back! I am your master! I gave you life! STAY BACK!"

The vampire began to come forward. In mad desperation, Doctor Chandu ran to an object he had prepared before.

"It is good I took this precaution. I thought you might be hard to handle. I. . . ."

The vampire was hypnotizing Chandu. In seconds, Chandu was like stone. However, in that state, the doctor could not stand. He pitched forward, slamming heavily into his machine.

"AAAARRRGH!!!"

Back staggered the human vampire, a huge stake driven completely through its chest! The machine was a large sling, capable of shooting wooden stakes!

The monster slumped to the ground, dead! Then, Doctor Chandu dizzily rose to his feet, still in the hypnotic trance. By chance, he rubbed against the coffin and wiped the rust off the *rest* of the inscription.

". . . AND HE WHO IS HYPNOTIZED BY THE VAMPIRE AND IS NOT BROUGHT BACK TO NORMAL BEFORE THE NEXT FULL MOON BY THE VAMPIRE WILL CHANGE INTO A VAMPIRE HIMSELF."

THE THING THAT GREW!

FROM THE SPINE-CHILLING SLEEP OF A LIVING DEATH... FROM THE UNBELIEVABLE HORROR OF A MILLION YEARS AGO... FROM A FORGOTTEN ICE-CAVE DEEP IN THE TOMB OF THE EARTH COMES THE MONSTROUS TERROR OF...

GREAT SCOTT! A PERFECTLY PRESERVED *BABY DINOSAUR*... FROZEN INTO THE ICE A MILLION YEARS AGO! I MUST TAKE IT BACK TO MY LABORATORY... MAYBE I CAN *BRING IT TO LIFE*...!!

DR. MARVELLE, THE WORLD'S MOST BRILLIANT EXPLORER AND SCIENTIST, TOOK THE DINOSAUR BACK TO HIS *SECLUDED LABORATORY* IN VERMONT. IN SECRECY, HE TINKERED WITH THE STAGGERING SECRETS OF LIFE...

IF ONLY I AM DOING THE *RIGHT THING*... IN THE INTEREST OF SCIENCE! I THINK...THIS EXPERIMENT WILL BRING THE *BEAST* BACK TO LIFE...!

I'VE FOUND IT! THIS IS IT...*THE SECRET OF LIFE*!!

237

NOW TO LET IT *SLEEP* IN THE LIQUID I HAVE JUST DISCOVERED!

BUT WHEN DR. MARVELLE CAME INTO THE LAB THE NEXT MORNING, HE FELT THE *HAND OF HORROR* TOUCH HIS TINGLING SPINE...

IT'S- IT'S GONE! THAT WINDOW...*SOMETHING* HAS GONE THROUGH THAT *WINDOW!*

GASP!...THE MONSTER HAS *GROWN!* WHAT IF IT DOESN'T STOP GROWING..! WHA--! WHAT WAS THAT NOISE FROM THE MOORS--?!

AAOOWWWWWW

GRAAAOOWWWWWRR!!

GOOD LORD! THERE-THERE IT IS! I MUST FIND SOME WAY TO KILL IT BEFORE IT *GROWS* ANY MORE!!

Spurred BY *TERROR,* DR. MARVELLE WORKED ALL DAY TO FIND A FORMULA THAT WOULD *KILL* THE DINOSAUR BUT, THAT NIGHT...

GRAAAOOW

IT'S...NO USE... I CAN'T KILL THE MONSTER I'VE CREATED! WHAT'S *THAT* AGAINST THE SKY...NO! OH, *NO! IT CAN'T BE!..!*

IT'S- COMING BACK HERE...HELLO! HELLO! OPERATOR! GIVE ME THE POLICE... *EMERGENCY*... I'VE GOT TO RUN! IT'S COMING *NEARER!*

YAAARRRR

RORR

238

241

242

You, Too, Can Be Tough!
GREATEST SELF-DEFENSE OFFER EVER MADE!

LIGHTNING JU-JITSU

Master Ju-Jitsu and you'll be able to overcome any attack—win any fight! This is what this book promises you! *Lightning Ju-Jitsu* will equip you with a powerful defense and counter-attack against any bully, attacker or enemy. It is equally effective and easy to use by any woman or man, boy or girl—and you don't need big muscles or weight to apply. Technique and the know-how does the trick. This book gives you all the secrets, grips, blows, pressures, jabs, tactics, etc. which are so deadly effective in quickly "putting an attacker out of business." Such as: Hitting Where It Hurts—Edge of the Hand Blow—Knuckle Jab—Shoulder Pinch—Teeth Rattler—Boxing the Ears—Elbow Jab—Knee Jab—Coat Grip—Bouncer Grip—Thumbscrew—Strangle Hold—Hip Throw—Shoulder Throw—Chin Throw—Knee Throw—*Breaking* a Wristlock, or Body Grip, or Strangle Hold—*Overcoming* a Hold-up, or Gun Attack, or Knife Attack, or Club Assault, etc. etc.—Just follow the illustrations and easy directions, practice the grips, holds and movements—and you'll fear no man.

If This Should Happen to You

Would You Know This Quick Defense?

only **$1.00**

HOW TO PERFORM STRONG MAN STUNTS

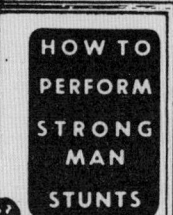

included **FREE!**

FREE 5 DAY TRIAL

BEE JAY, Dept. HM-78
400 Madison Ave. N.Y. 17, N.Y.

FREE
How to Perform STRONG MAN STUNTS

With every order we will send you ABSOLUTELY FREE this exciting book! It shows you the *secret way* in which YOU will be able to: tear a telephone book in half—hammer a nail into a board with your bare fist—rip a full deck of cards into two parts—crush and shatter a rock with a blow of your hand—and many other stupendous strong man stunts! All this will be easy for you using the confidential, hidden way shown in this amazing book! Don't miss this amazing combined offer—on our FIVE DAY TRIAL! If not delighted with your results, your money back at once.

243

244

PS
Artbooks

Collect all 4 Volumes of Chamber of Chills from PS Artbooks

HARVEY HORRORS
COLLECTED WORKS
CHAMBER OF CHILLS
VOLUME TWO

CHAMBER OF CHILLS
TALES OF TERROR AND SUSPENSE!
CHAMBER OF CHILLS
No. 8 MAY
NOW PUBLISHED MONTHLY
MAGAZINE 10¢
THE HORROR OF AGES
...THE SLIME OF HELL...
THE MADNESS OF GENIUS!
MIX WELL FOR THE...
FORMULA FOR DEATH!

May - October 1952
Issues 8 - 13

Foreword by
Michael T. Gilbert

Chamber of Chills
Volume Two

Witches Tales
December 1954 - Issue #28

Cover Art - Unknown

Toys of Terror
Script - Unknown
Pencils - Lee Elias
Inks - Lee Elias

The Witch Who Wore White
Script - Unknown
Pencils - Unknown
Inks - Unknown

The Man Who Had No Body
Script - Unknown
Pencils - Rudy Palais
Inks - Rudy Palais

Demon Flies
Script - Unknown
Pencils - Joe Certa
Inks - Unknown

Information Source: Grand Comics Database!
A nonprofit, Internet-based organization of international volunteers dedicated to building a database covering all printed comics throughout the world.
If you believe any of this data to be incorrect or can add valuable additional information, please let us know www.comics.org
All rights to images reserved by the respective copyright holders. All original advertisement features remain the copyright of the respective trading company.

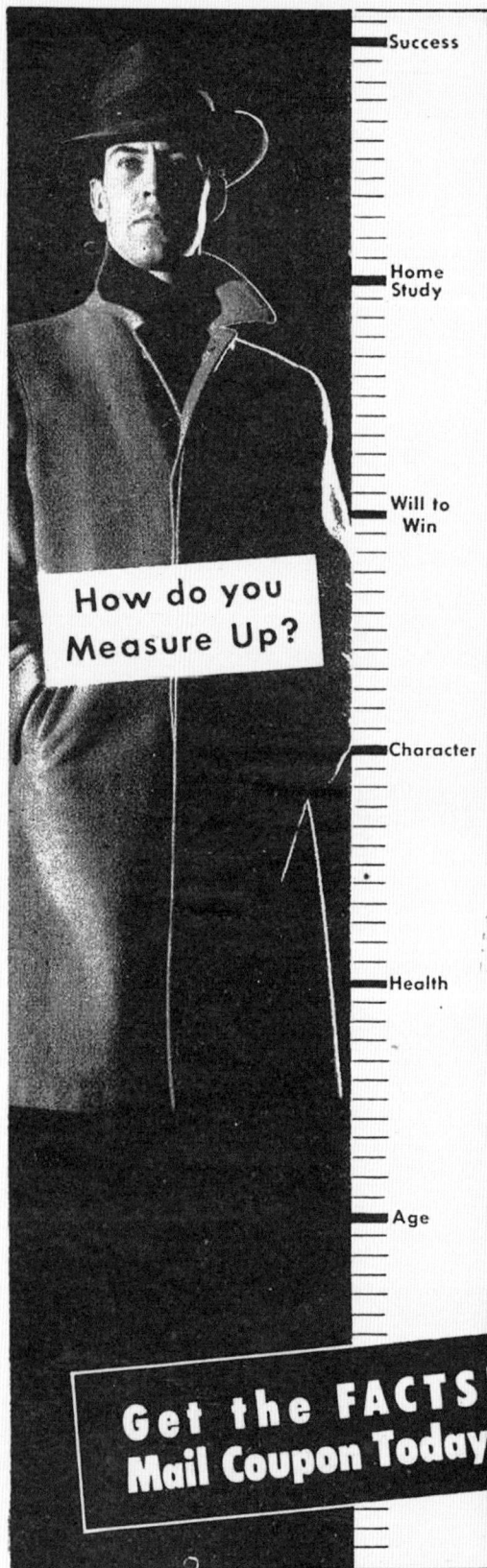
WITCHES TALES, DECEMBER, 1954, VOL. 1, NO. 28, IS PUBLISHED BI-MONTHLY
by WITCHES TALES, INC., 1860 Broadway, New York 23, N. Y. Entered as second class matter at the Post Office at New York, N. Y., under the Act of March, 3, 1879. Single copies, 10c. Subscription rates, 10 issues for $1.00 in the U. S. and possessions, elsewhere $1.50. All names in this periodical are entirely fictitious and no identification with actual persons is intended. Contents copyrighted, 1954, by Witches Tales, Inc., New York, City. Printed in the U.S.A. Title registered in U. S. Patent Office.

GOOD EVENING!

Come in, my friends, come in! This biting, raw January wind will do you ill if you stand out there. Let the warmth of my fire caress your bones and stop their trembling. Haaaa...hee!

Eh? You say the flames in the pit curl high! Heh, heh! Of course! From their depths, I have forged another spine-tingling issue of WITCHES TALES!

Hear me now...come close. I have gathered in this issue a collection of tales never before seen by HUMAN eyes — tales calculated to freeze your blood and tear at your conscience.

TOYS OF TERROR is the first of them. Toys, ordinary toys, become the instruments of horror that terrify a whole city. Their mechanical minds obey the commands of a witch and their hands seek a pair of eyes...perhaps yours!

In THE WITCH WHO WORE WHITE, the true nature of people is explained as two of them call upon the powers of evil for help. The price they pay will shock your sanity!

What terror drones closer and closer to the unsuspecting victims? Why does the mad scientist send his stinging horde out on their journey of death? Read the DEMON FLIES!

Last, but certainly not least, my dear friends, feel the hair on the neck crawl as you read the MAN WHO HAD NO BODY! See a living dead man prowl the streets seeking revenge . . . seeking a revenge from the tomb!

Ahhhh . . . I must leave you for a while. But do not despair. The fire will burn until I return and from its light you can read this...the latest diary of weird, supernatural stories . . .

250

A *DOLL* WITH NO *EYES*!!

COME WITH ME, MY *PRETTIES*!! I CAN SERVE YOU BETTER THAN THE MISTRESS WHO TOSSED YOU AWAY!!

WITHIN THE *CRUMBLING* WALLS OF HER ROOM, THE *LOATHESOME* DEMON UTTERS TERRIBLE WORDS WHICH SET IN MOTION THE *UNSPEAKABLE* FORCES THAT LURK IN THE DARKEST RECESSES OF THE EARTH!...

HEAR ME, POWERS OF DARKNESS AND EVIL!! GRANT THE GIFT OF *LIFE* TO THESE TOYS SO THAT THEY MAY SERVE ME!

SEE!!...SEE HOW THEY BEGIN TO *GROW*...AND *GROW*!!

THEY *LIVE*... AND *BREATHE*...!!

GROWR-R-R!!

SUDDENLY A VOICE OTHER THAN THE WITCH'S BREAKS UPON THE SCENE OF HORROR...A VOICE *THICK* WITH THE DEADLY POISON OF *MALICE*...AND *CUNNING*...

I AM THE ONLY ONE WHO CAN *SPEAK*, MIDNIGHT HAG!! MY NAME IS *DIABLO!*... WHAT IS IT YOU WISH US TO DO?

AS THE DAYS PASS, EACH NIGHT IS A WITNESS TO A SCENE OF *WILD TERROR*, AS THE TRIO CLAIMS ANOTHER...AND ANOTHER...AND STILL ANOTHER PAIR OF EYES FOR THE SIGHTLESS DOLL!...

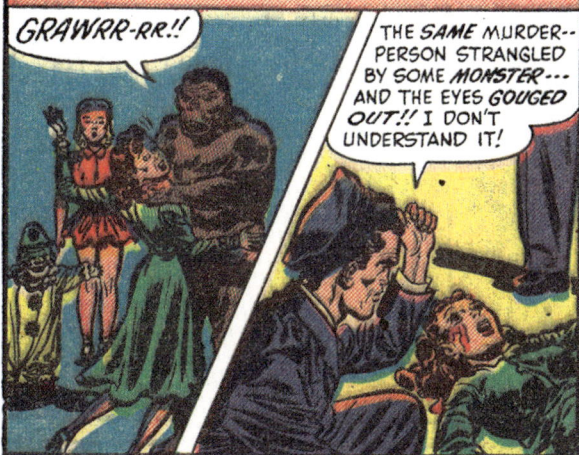

GRAWRR-RR!!

THE *SAME* MURDER-PERSON STRANGLED BY SOME *MONSTER*--- AND THE EYES *GOUGED OUT!!* I DON'T UNDERSTAND IT!

AH! HERE IS A *LIKELY PERSON!!* L-LET US P-PROCEED!

SUDDENLY THE *DREADFUL* SMILE OF THE DWARF DIABLO CHANGES INTO A *TROUBLED FROWN*-- A LONG HAUNTING THOUGHT SURGES FORTH--

WAIT!! DO NOT GO!!

LISTEN TO ME!! WE CANNOT CONTINUE THIS WAY! WE ARE NOT *EVIL* BY NATURE...THE WITCH HAS *MADE* US EVIL!! WE ARE ONLY *TOYS!!*

WE MUST *FREE* OURSELVES OF HER DOMINATION!! WE MUST DESTROY *HER* BEFORE SHE DESTROYS *US!!* AND WHAT'S MORE, AS REVENGE FOR OURSELVES...

MADELEINE SHALL HAVE EYES.!!!

ALONE IN HER ROOM, THE *DECAYING* WITCH AWAITS THE RETURN OF HER CREATURES, HER *REPULSIVE* FACE LIT BY AN UGLY SMILE OF SATISFACTION...

THEY WILL RETURN SOON! IT IS GETTING *LIGHT!*

AH, I KNEW YOU WOULD COME BACK!! I AM DELIGHTED TO SEE YOU!!

OUR SEARCH FOR A PAIR OF EYES HAS BEEN *FUTILE* UNTIL NOW, FIEND OF DARKNESS!! BUT WE MUST TEST *ONE MORE PAIR --- ONLY ONE--!!*

...AND THEY ARE *YOURS!!!*

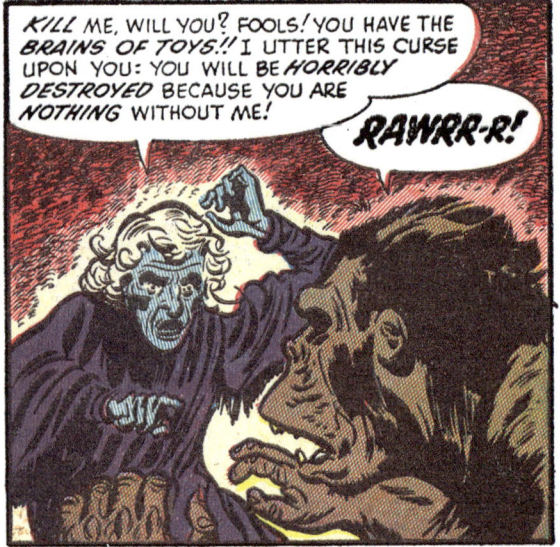

KILL ME, WILL YOU? FOOLS! YOU HAVE THE *BRAINS OF TOYS!!* I UTTER THIS CURSE UPON YOU: YOU WILL BE *HORRIBLY DESTROYED* BECAUSE YOU ARE *NOTHING* WITHOUT ME!

RAWRR-R!

SCREECHING HER LAST *HIDEOUS* CURSE, THE OLD WITCH FEELS THE POWERFUL ARMS OF THE APE SHE CREATED *PRESS* AGAINST HER THROAT... *TIGHTER....TIGHTER....*

AAARRGGH·H!

RUN!! RUN WITH ME!! WE MUST FIND SOME PLACE TO *HIDE* BEFORE IT IS *LIGHT!!*

STRANGE THINGS HAPPEN IN THE NIGHT, AND HOW TERRIBLE WAS THE CONTRAST WHEN THE MURKY BLACKNESS OF THE NIGHT BECAME THE BACKGROUND FOR....

THE WITCH WHO WORE WHITE

WH--WHAT ARE YOU GOING TO *DO* TO ME?

YOU MUST PAY THE *PRICE* I SET!! THERE IS NO ESCAPE!!

OH, NO! WHAT *UNNATURAL CREATURE* IS LOOSE IN THIS HOUSE??

IN THE HOME OF FABULOUSLY WEALTHY ARTHUR AND ABIGAIL SANDERS, A NEWCOMER APPEARS, A YOUNG GIRL WHOSE WHITE NURSE'S UNIFORM IS MATCHED BY THE *STRANGE* WHITENESS OF HER FACE...

ARTHUR, DEAR, THIS IS MISS JESSUP, YOUR NEW *NURSE!* I'M SURE SHE'LL PLEASE YOU!

BAH!! SHE'S PROBABLY AS STUPID AND INCOMPETENT AS THE OTHERS!

I HOPE YOU WILL FIND ME SATISFACTORY!

HELLO, PAUL! I'D LIKE YOU TO MEET MISS JESSUP, OUR NEW NURSE. PAUL'S MY NEPHEW--- HE'S BEEN LIVING WITH US A WHILE!

HOW DO YOU DO, MISS JESSUP?

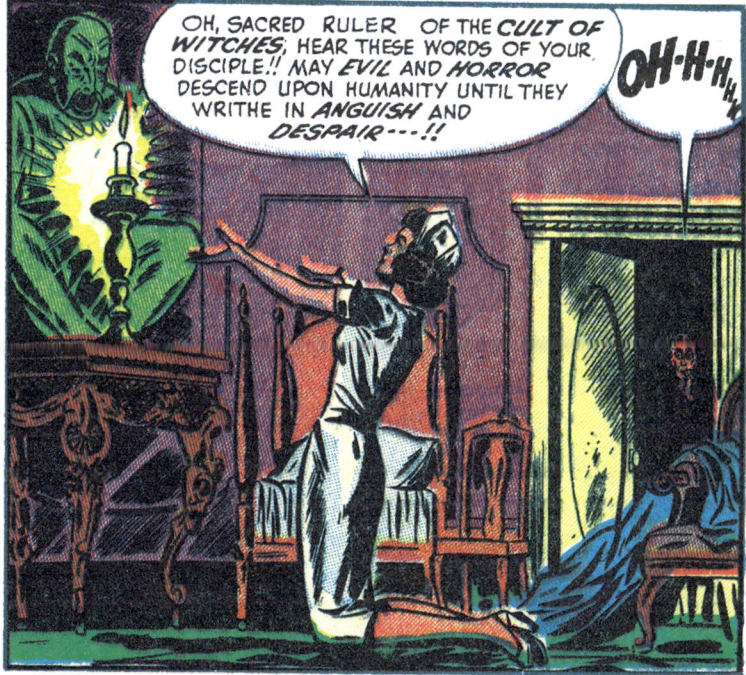

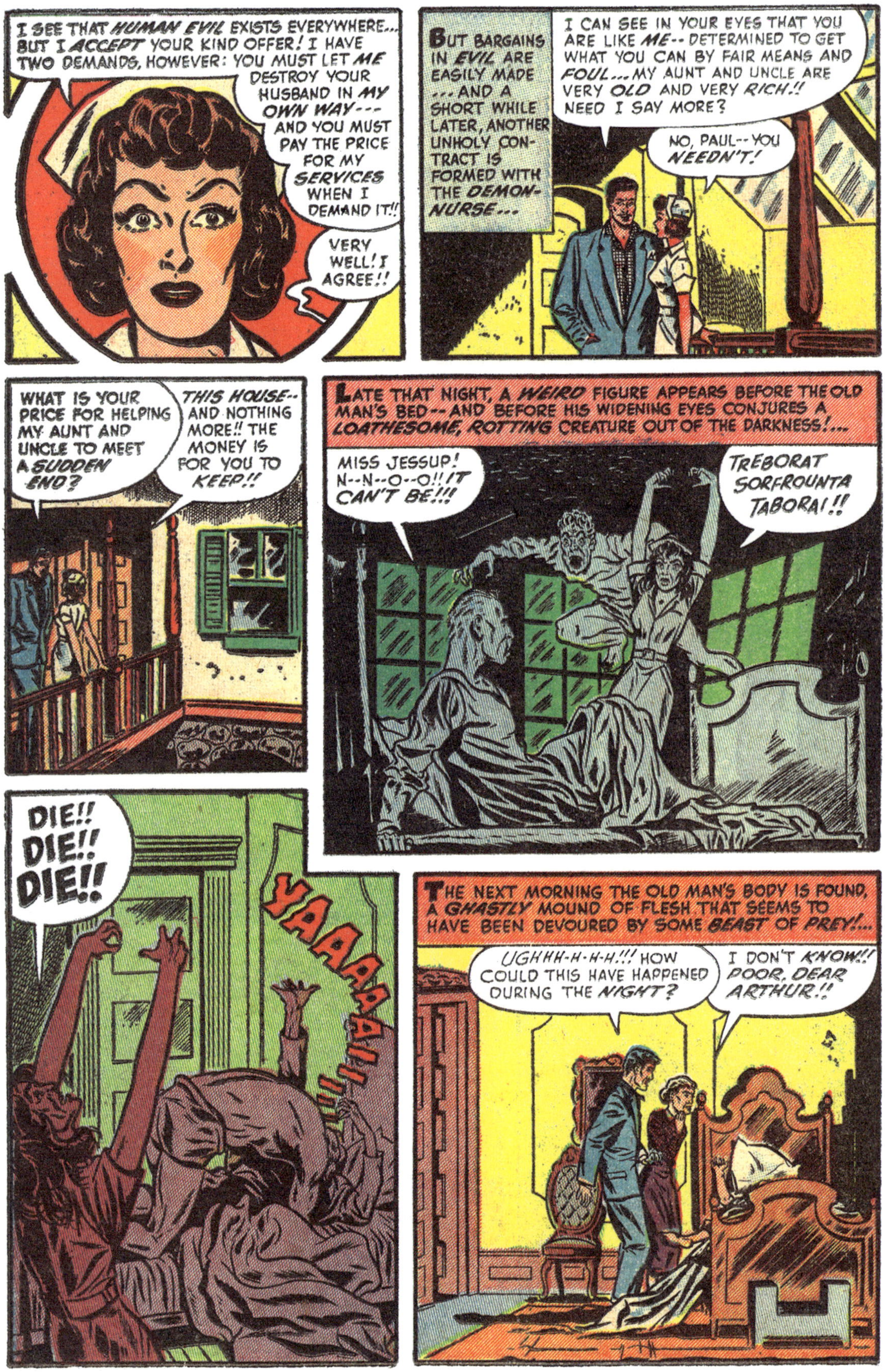

I SEE THAT HUMAN EVIL EXISTS EVERYWHERE... BUT I ACCEPT YOUR KIND OFFER! I HAVE TWO DEMANDS, HOWEVER: YOU MUST LET ME DESTROY YOUR HUSBAND IN MY OWN WAY--- AND YOU MUST PAY THE PRICE FOR MY SERVICES WHEN I DEMAND IT!!
VERY WELL! I AGREE!!
BUT BARGAINS IN EVIL ARE EASILY MADE ... AND A SHORT WHILE LATER, ANOTHER UNHOLY CONTRACT IS FORMED WITH THE DEMON-NURSE...
I CAN SEE IN YOUR EYES THAT YOU ARE LIKE ME-- DETERMINED TO GET WHAT YOU CAN BY FAIR MEANS AND FOUL... MY AUNT AND UNCLE ARE VERY OLD AND VERY RICH!! NEED I SAY MORE?
NO, PAUL--YOU NEEDN'T!
WHAT IS YOUR PRICE FOR HELPING MY AUNT AND UNCLE TO MEET A SUDDEN END?
THIS HOUSE-- AND NOTHING MORE!! THE MONEY IS FOR YOU TO KEEP!!
LATE THAT NIGHT, A WEIRD FIGURE APPEARS BEFORE THE OLD MAN'S BED--AND BEFORE HIS WIDENING EYES CONJURES A LOATHESOME, ROTTING CREATURE OUT OF THE DARKNESS!...
MISS JESSUP! N--N--O--O!! IT CAN'T BE!!!
TREBORAT SORFROUNTA TABORAI!!
DIE!! DIE!! DIE!!
YAAAAAAI!!
THE NEXT MORNING THE OLD MAN'S BODY IS FOUND, A GHASTLY MOUND OF FLESH THAT SEEMS TO HAVE BEEN DEVOURED BY SOME BEAST OF PREY!...
UGHHH-H-H-H!!! HOW COULD THIS HAVE HAPPENED DURING THE NIGHT?
I DON'T KNOW!! POOR, DEAR ARTHUR!!

HE'S *DEAD!* HOW HAPPY I AM TO BE *RID* OF HIM!!... I WONDER WHAT HER *PRICE* WILL BE?

WELL, *ONE* OF THEM IS GONE! NOW, I MUST SPEAK TO HER ABOUT MY *AUNT!!*...

LATER, WHEN THE NURSE AND THE NEPHEW ARE ALONE...

...IF YOU WISH, YOUR AUNT WILL BE DEALT WITH *THIS EVENING* ...BUT BY *ME ALONE!!* YOU WILL ONLY NEED TO *INHERIT*-- AND THEN *SPEND*-- THE MONEY!!

SHE MUST WANT THIS HOUSE VERY BADLY!! OR IS THERE *SOMETHING ELSE??* I'LL WATCH OUTSIDE THE ROOM *TONIGHT!!*

THAT EVENING, THE SAME *WEIRD* FIGURE STANDS BEFORE THE OLD LADY, BENT ON ANOTHER MISSION OF *VIOLENT DEATH*...

WH--WHAT ARE YOU DOING HERE AT THIS HOUR?

I HAVE COME TO EXACT THE *PRICE* OF OUR BARGAIN! TONIGHT YOU ARE TO BE INITIATED INTO THE CULT OF *WITCHES*, DESTINED TO PERFORM EVIL DEEDS UNTIL ETERNITY!!!

WHEN I HAVE SHED YOUR BLOOD WITH THIS *SCALPEL*, THERE WILL BE NO TURNING BACK!! YOUR BLOOD WILL BE JOINED WITH THE WITCHES *FOREVER!!!* PREPARE YOURSELF!!

N--N--O...!! NO-O-O-O-O!!

SHE'S A--A--A--

WITCH!!!

SO NOW I MUST DEAL WITH YOU AS WELL!!

I'LL KILL YOU, YOU *FIEND*-- IF YOU ARE CAPABLE OF *DYING!!*

GIVE ME THE *SCALPEL!!*

As Paul wrests the scalpel from the nurse's hand, he trips and falls across the bed...

UGH-H-H!!! AARGH-H-H-H!!

I---I--KILLED HER!! ISN'T THAT WHAT YOU WANTED? BUT NOW YOU WILL NEVER ESCAPE FROM THIS HOUSE, MY FRIEND!! YOU WILL ROT HERE WITH YOUR AUNT AND UNCLE!!

A FEW WORDS OF ANCIENT EVIL-- AND BLOOD-STAINED DEMONS OF THE NIGHT APPEAR ABOVE THE HEAD OF THE WITCH-NURSE--EAGER FOR HUMAN PREY!

LABRUNTA! SAIGORA! TAKE HIM!! HE IS YOURS!!

YAAAAAH-H

LEAVE ME ALONE!! NO!! DON'T!! D---

YAAGGH-H!

AND NOW THIS HOUSE IS MINE--MINE TO DESTROY--AS I CAUSE EVIL TO DESTROY THE HEARTS AND MINDS OF MEN!!

IN ANOTHER HOME, A PALE YOUNG NURSE APPEARS IN THE DOORWAY, AN ANGEL OF MERCY ANSWERING A CALL TO DUTY ...BUT WHAT IS THE STRANGE DREAD THAT SUDDENLY STIFLES THE NIGHT AIR??...

HOW DO YOU DO? YOU MUST BE...

MISS JESSUP! AT YOUR SERVICE..."

THE END.

262

SUICIDE!

"What's the matter, my dear?"

"Nothing, Margaret.... Nothing at all."

"But Dr. Wilson just left your chamber."

"A routine check-up. Yes, Margaret, that's all it was ... a routine check-up."

Mrs. Van Dyke left the room. She didn't fully believe her husband, but she saw that he was in no mood for questions.

Left alone, Cecil Van Dyke began to wonder. He searched the corners of his sumptuously decorated room. The light bothered him. He turned it off. So much easier to think this way, he thought.

"I've got to face it," Van Dyke said to himself. "All Dr. Wilson gives me is six months to live. Probably less."

He paced back and forth across his room.

"Margaret must never know ... but why does it have to happen to ME? I'm the most important man in the industry! I've worked and worked for years and now that I'm on top of the world, I discover I'm about to die."

Van Dyke's steps became slower.

"He doesn't even know what kind of disease this is. Never saw it before, he said. But he does know that I'm slowly melting away inside. I'm disintegrating! I'm wasting away."

Van Dyke stopped and dropped onto the couch.

"I knew I was sick, but I could never have expected this! Those X-Rays told the evil tale. Those terrible X-Rays! Oh, if I could mould this world, I'd never allow X-Rays! Let me die, but why must I know every step of disintegration!"

He broke into a sweat. His face became ghostlike!

"I know what I must do! I'VE GOT TO KILL MYSELF! I mustn't make Margaret miserable. And I couldn't stand seeing myself melt away slowly ... like a candle!"

He rushed to lock the door. Then he went to his desk. He slowly opened the drawer and took out his pistol. "Well, this gun will stop a murder," he thought.

Then there was a noise and a knocking at the door.

"Cecil, open the door!"

No one was going to stop him! The doctor had probably told her. No, he wasn't going to make any one miserable, he wasn't going to stretch this out!

"Cecil, open the door!!!"

"Good-bye, my dear!"

BANG!

"Darling, what was that explosion? I want to tell you that the doctor had the wrong X-Rays!"

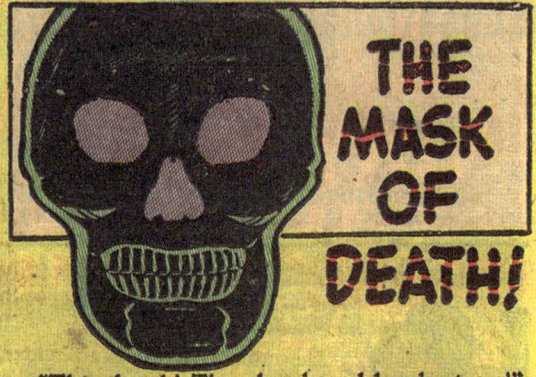

THE MASK OF DEATH!

"They laugh! They laugh and laugh at me!"

"Bill, stop it! How can you complain? You're one of the greatest night club comedians of our time! Sure, people laugh at you, that's what you're paid for. And your face is perfect for ..."

"Hah! That's it, even you, you're laughing at me. See—HAH! HAH! HAH! That's what you want to do. Look, my whole face is scarred! Is that funny??"

"Yes, Bill, it is. I don't know why, but you do look silly."

"Yes, hah hah! You, my wife, even you can't stop laughing at me. Ouch! This damn pin!"

"Hah, hah. Bill. You look so funny!"

"I cut myself and you laugh! When I get sick, you laugh! If I died, you'd still laugh! In fact, you'd roar. In fact, you only married me for my money. Now, I'm just one big laugh from morning till night! HAH! HAH! HAH!"

"Bill, stop it! Yes, it's true. I did marry you for your money. And now I'm tired of your stupid face, your fat and comical body, your ... STOP IT! KEEP AWAY FROM ME!"

"HAH! HAH! No, my beautiful doll! You've had your last laugh! Hah! That's pretty good ... In a few moments you're going to speak your LAST WORDS!"

"Bill, put down that knife! I didn't mean it!"

"Yes, I'll put it down—right down your throat! I've had enough—enough, you hear!"

He rushed to her and swung his knife—once, twice, three times ...

"AHHHHHHH!"

Then the house was quiet. In it, a beautiful woman lay dead, and a man, ghost-white and silent, bent motionless over her.

The man picked himself up. He took the knife —and raised it high above him ...

"HAH! HAH! HAH! AGHHHH!"

It wasn't until the next morning that people came to this house, this home far in the suburbs. There they discovered a once beautiful woman. No words could express their horror.

In the other corner, they saw Bill West, the great comic. Even in death there was that silly expression all over him ... They tried to stop themselves, but they just had to laugh!

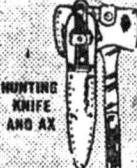

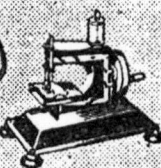

265

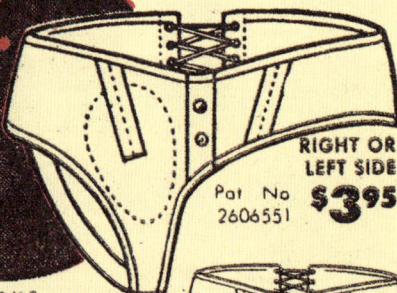

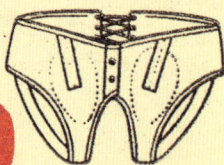

266

THE MAN WHO HAD NO BODY

SCREAMING THRU THE BLACK NIGHT, TWO TRAINS RACE TOWARD EACH OTHER IN AN UNKNOWN *APPOINTMENT WITH DEATH!!* THE SCREAMS OF THE VICTIMS MIX WITH A DISTANT *EVIL WAIL* AND OUT OF THE FIRE AND BLOOD OF THIS *MIDNIGHT* CATASTROPHE WALKS...

SCREAM AND *WAIL*, YOU POWERLESS MORTALS! *HEE-HEE!* IT'S MUSIC TO MY EARS. *NONE* OF YOU CAN ESCAPE THE *HANDS OF FATE!!* HEE-HEEEEEE!

HELP!

HELP!

OHOOOOo...

EEEEEE!!

CRASH! BA-LOOOM!

WH...WHERE AM I?? OH- NOW I REMEMBER... WAITING TO GET OFF...THEN A CRASH... AN EXPLOSION!! OHOOO- MY HEAD...

TONY LAWSON WAS JUST ANOTHER PASSENGER ON THE ILL-FATED TRAIN, ANXIOUS TO RETURN TO HIS WIFE. HE HAD YET TO LEARN THAT THE CRASH HAD JOLTED HIM INTO A *NEW, WEIRD WORLD...*

MY HEAD FEELS AS IF SOMEBODY WERE BOILING MY BRAINS!! PEOPLE HURT ...MUST TRY TO HELP...

HELLLLPP!! THE *FIRE!!* ARGHHH!

MORE *WATER!!* PEOPLE ARE *TRAPPED* IN THERE!!

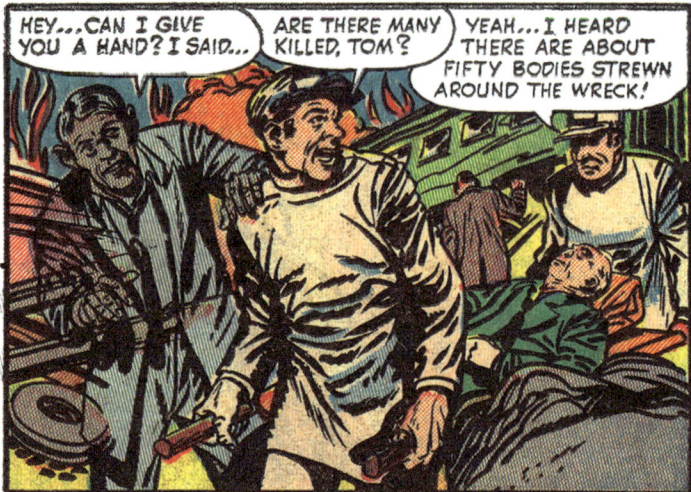

THE *HAUNTING SPIRIT* OF TONY LAWSON BURNED WITH VENGEANCE AS HE WATCHED THE *DECEPTION* OF LUCY, AND RESTLESSLY HE WALKED THE *MIDNIGHT STREETS* UNTIL...

I WONDER IF I MIGHT FIND THE HELP I NEED HERE! I AM GROWING *WEARY* OF *WANDERING*... MY SPIRIT MUST HAVE ITS *REVENGE* AND THEN... TO *ETERNAL SLEEP*...

MADAM BOVARIE — SPIRITUALIST

MIDNIGHT WANDERERS.... HEAR MY CALL! I WOULD SEND MY VOICE BEYOND THE *UNKNOWN* TO TALK WITH THE *RESTLESS ONES*, THE SPIRITS WHO SEEK *POWER*... HEAR ME, *UNSEEN ONES,* OH, HEAR!!

I HAVE HEARD.... AND I HAVE COME TO ASK YOU WHO *SPEAK WITH THE DEAD* FOR *HELP.!!*

YES... I WILL HELP YOU... FOR A *FEE!!* FOR EVEN THE *DEAD* MUST PAY THE *BLACK SORCERERS.!!*

YOU WILL BE WELL PAID... NOW, FIRST YOU MUST WRITE A LETTER FOR ME...

AND SO... IN THE DEAD OF NIGHT THE BARGAIN IS MADE, AND A FEW DAYS LATER...

I KNOW YOU EXPECTED THE MONEY, BUT WE JUST RECEIVED THIS LETTER, SIGNED BY YOUR *HUSBAND,* TONY LAWSON.!!

BUT... BUT THAT'S *IMPOSSIBLE!!* I IDENTIFIED THE BODY MYSELF— AND IT'S LYING IN THE FAMILY *CRYPT!!* THIS IS SOMEBODY'S *CRUEL JOKE.!!*

OF COURSE IT IS! UNDOUBTEDLY YOU ARE PERFECTLY RIGHT, BUT WE WILL HAVE TO INVESTIGATE THIS LETTER BEFORE WE CAN TURN THE MONEY OVER!

ALL RIGHT— JUST AS LONG AS IT WON'T TAKE TOO LONG! AS A MATTER OF FACT, I'M GOING TO THE CRYPT TODAY— TO BRING FRESH FLOWERS! I MISS TONY SO...

I'LL BE GLAD WHEN THEY'VE FINALLY CEMENTED THIS CASKET AWAY SO I DON'T HAVE TO KEEP UP THIS *PRETENSE* OF DEVOTION!! WONDER ABOUT THAT LETTER! WHO... OH.!!!

LATER THAT NIGHT THE TWO FIGURES, ONE SEEN AND THE OTHER *UNSEEN*, WALK THRU THE *DESERTED GRAVE-YARD* TO THE LAWSON CRYPT, AND THERE...

I HAVE ONE MORE REQUEST TO MAKE! I AM WEARY OF BEING A *DISEMBODIED SPIRIT!* PUT ME BACK INSIDE MY MANGLED BODY... I HAVE A *PLAN!*

I WILL DO AS YOU ASK- ONLY RE-MEMBER, ONCE IT IS DONE NO POWER CAN UNDO IT!!

MAR RION BEL EF FANTOV LORREL TON !!

THE NEXT DAY... IT WILL SOON BE OVER! TODAY THE CASKET WILL BE *SEALED AWAY!* SHALL I GO IN WITH YOU?

YES...NO! THIS IS THE LAST TIME... I'LL GO IN ALONE FOR A FEW MINUTES! IT WILL LOOK BETTER!

ALONE, LUCY LAWSON APPROACHES THE CAS-KET FOR THE LAST TIME, ANXIOUS FOR THE FINAL CEREMONY TO BEGIN, WHEN SUDDENLY...

THAT'S STRANGE THAT THE TOP SHOULD BE OPEN... WELL, SOON I'LL BE FREE OF THIS AWFUL TASK... AND JOHN AND I...

HIS HANDS!...THEY'RE *MOVING!!* TONY... NO!!!

DON'T, TONY...*PLEASE!!* I'LL DO ANYTHING YOU SAY! I WON'T TOUCH THE MONEY... I'LL GIVE JOHN UP... I'LL...

THE *POINTED EDGE OF DEATH* SLOWLY INCHES TOWARD THE SOFT, PULSATING THROAT OF LUCY LAWSON.!! HER EYES STRAIN WITH *TERROR,* HER STRENGTH WANS, AND *THEN* ...

AIEEEEEGRGHGGAGG!!

GREAT SCOTT- WHAT WAS *THAT??!*

OH, THE POOR THING! SHE'S *KILLED HERSELF!*

GUESS SHE *COULDN'T LIVE* WITHOUT HIM!!

THE END.

THE MIRROR THAT REFLECTED DEATH!

"I've come to you, old hag, because I have no one left to turn to."

"Ha...heeee...most people who come here say that. What troubles you?"

"For the past month I have been having awful nightmares. I dream I see myself in a mirror not as I really am but as some horrible beast. When I see myself so, I go insane and hurl myself at this mirror shattering the glass into a thousand pieces. I wake up then...my face coated with sweat...my throat choked with a sobbing gasp."

Lamont Wilson looked at the old woman he was talking to. He, the richest man in the city, was forced to come to her, a known practitioner of the black arts, for help. Dr. Runsen, his private psychiatrist, said it was a case of too much work, not enough rest. He said it would be best if Wilson went to a sanitarium for a few months.

"In other words," thought Wilson, "he thinks I'm going crazy."

"I see you are deep in thought," cackled the old witch, her face deeply wrinkled by the candle light.

"Uh-yes. And you probably know what I am thinking about. Look...I will give you any amount of money if you can cure me of those terrible nightmares. I..."

"Wait! Before you speak any further, let me speak."

The light from the two candles in the room began to flicker. Shadows began to close in about the room and the mist of mystery slowly slid over the woman. Her eyes narrowed to slits and the blood began to drain from her cheeks.

"Listen to what I say, mortal. It is what will be. I know that your doctor thinks you are going crazy. He thinks it is overwork...straining of the nerves. I know the real reason!"

"Old hag, tell me quick!"

"Quiet! Never interrupt me! You are having those dreams because you want to *murder* some-one!"

Lamont Wilson fell back in his chair. Beads of perspiration began to pop out on his face. His hands crushed the arm rests of the chair.

"M-m-murder! I don't want to murder any-one."

"Ha...heeee...you do, you do. And here's why, whimpering mortal. All your life you have been beating people down...taking what you wanted. First you drove your partner out of business. Then you began to hire the cheapest labor you could...slave labor. You kept on smashing to the top regardless of the consequences. Now, you are at the top. You have done everything. You have done everything, that is, except...MURDER! And though you are really too weak to do it, you cannot sleep without seeing yourself the true monster you are lusting for human blood. You are one of us, Lamont Wilson. And you will MURDER...haaa...heeeee..."

As the last of the witch's words pierced his brain, Wilson tore himself up from the chair and plunged out of the house into the street. Panic ripped his mind to shreds. Why should her words affect him so. Why? Why? Could she be right?

Wilson kept on running...running. Soon, his tired feet brought him to a cheap carnival. In a daze of fear, he rushed up to a booth and bought a ticket. Unseeing, he staggered inside and discovered...

"NO! I'm in the HALL OF MIRRORS!"

He tried to get out but some strange force seemed to pull him to a certain mirror. When he saw the image on it, he gasped...

"That's the beast I've been seeing in my dreams. ARRRRGGGHHHH..."

Lamont Wilson had hurled himself against the mirror.

Later, two policemen talked with the owner of the exhibit.

"That's all I know, officers. I heard this scream, rushed in and found this crazy guy on the floor dead. It looks like he threw himself at the mirror and got knifed by the broken glass."

"You know," said one of the cops, "this guy really was a murderer. He murdered...himself!"

Panel 1:
Narration: AND AS THE SCIENTIST REGARDS THE ODD *REVERSAL* OF *NATURE*, A *DREADFUL* PLAN BEGINS TO TAKE SHAPE IN HIS *CORRUPT* MIND...

Scientist: I MAY HAVE DISCOVERED A SPECIES OF FLY MORE *POWERFUL* THAN ANY YET KNOWN, POWERFUL ENOUGH TO BECOME A...*WEAPON!!* IF IT CAN KILL A SPIDER...

Panel 2:
Narration: *SEVERAL WEEKS LATER...*

Scientist: *AT LAST!!* NOW THERE ARE *THOUSANDS* OF LARGE, HUNGRY FLIES BEGGING TO BE *FED!!*

Panel 3:
Scientist: I WAS *RIGHT!!* THESE FLIES ARE LIKE *DEMONS*, ANXIOUS TO CONSUME WHATEVER FALLS IN THEIR *GREEDY* PATH!! NOW I AM READY TO TRY MY GREAT *EXPERIMENT..!*

Panel 4:
Harding: YOU WANTED ME, DR. GILBERT?

Dr. Gilbert: YES, HARDING, WON'T YOU COME IN? AND *CLOSE THE DOOR*, PLEASE!

Panel 5:
Dr. Gilbert: DOCTOR, YOU WILL BE THE HUMAN GUINEA PIG TO SHOW THAT I HAVE CREATED MONSTERS WHOSE INSTINCTS I CONTROL!

Harding: *NO!! NO!!*

Panel 6:
Narration: LIKE A *REPULSIVE* ARMY OF *PARASITES*, THE FLIES COVER THEIR VICTIM, TEARING AT HIS FLESH UNTIL HE IS LEFT A *FESTERING* AND *APPALLING* SKELETON!!...

SFX: *AAARGHH-H-H!!*

SFX: BZZZZ!! BUZZ-Z-Z-Z!

NOW I HAVE THE *MEANS* TO RID MYSELF OF THE FOOLS WHO SCORNED MY WORK!! THESE FLIES ARE MY CREATION, MY SUBJECTS -- AND THEY WILL *KILL* FOR ME!!!

AND SO THE SOUND OF *SUDDEN DEATH* BEGINS TO FILL THE HALLS AND ROOMS OF THE HARRINGTON LABORATORIES, AS SCIENTIST AFTER SCIENTIST IS LEFT A *REPULSIVE DECAYING SHELL* BY THE DEMON FLIES!...

HELP! HELP! YAH-H!!

WARD

AN *ADMIRABLE* JOB, MY FRIENDS!! I HAVE HEARD THE LAST OF HIS *MOCKERY!!*

BUT AFTER A WHILE, A *CHILLING* FEAR BEGINS TO *GNAW* AT THE SCIENTIST--AND SOON HE BEGINS TO REGARD HIS MONSTROUS CREATIONS WITH *TERROR!*...

THEY'RE GROWING *LARGER* AND MORE *POWERFUL* EACH DAY! I'LL SOON LOSE CONTROL OVER THEM AND THEN THEY WILL WANT TO *DESTROY ME!* WHAT SHALL I DO??

I HAVE IT!! I WILL BREED A *SPIDER* DEADLY ENOUGH TO *DEVOUR* THE FLIES!!

AGAIN A PLAN HATCHED IN THE EVIL MIND OF THE SCIENTIST BEGINS TO TAKE *HORRIBLE* SHAPE. AFTER SEVERAL WEEKS OF EXPERIMENTATION A NEW AND *LOATHESOME* CREATURE IS CREATED!

SPIN YOUR *WEB OF DEATH* FOR THE DEMON FLIES!! I GAVE YOU LIFE-- AND I AM YOUR *MASTER!!*

277

WELL DONE!! NOW I NO LONGER FEAR THAT THEY WILL TURN ON ME!! THEY HAVE SERVED THEIR PURPOSE AND I AM WELL *RID* OF THEM!!

BUT YOU MUST RETURN TO YOUR BOTTLE, MY FRIEND! UNTIL I CAN USE YOU *AGAIN!!*

*S*UDDENLY, WITHOUT WARNING, THE GIANT SPIDER BEGINS TO WEAVE A *SECOND* WEB, *LARGER* AND *DEADLIER* THAN THE FIRST... ABOUT THE BODY OF THE SCIENTIST.

WH--WHAT ARE YOU *DOING* TO ME?? *STOP!!!* I *COMMAND* YOU!! S---

*A*ND AS THE WEB COVERS THE SCIENTIST'S BODY LIKE A *SHROUD*, HE FALLS BACK AGAINST A TABLE, UPSETTING THE BUNSEN BURNER HE HAD LIGHTED FOR AN EXPERIMENT!...

AAAGGH-H-H!!! RAWRRRGGH-H-H!!

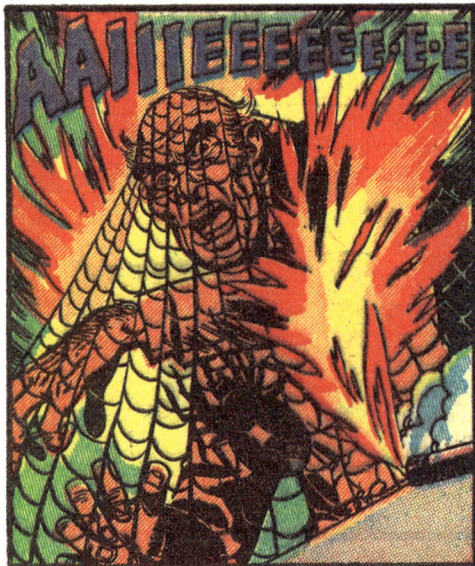

CRASH!!

AAIIIEEEEEE-E-E

*A*S THE LABORATORY IS DEVOURED BY FLAME, TWO CURIOUS SPECTATORS PERCH OUTSIDE THE WINDOW, WATCHING THE *AGONIZED* DEATH OF THE SCIENTIST- AND THE MONSTER-SPIDER HE HAD CREATED!...

BUNN

BUNN

THE END

278

280

START YOUR FUTURE TODAY!

Get the facts on NATIONAL SCHOOLS' famous Shop-Method Home Training!

TALES OF TERROR AND SUSPENSE

CHAMBER OF CHILLS

EERIE TALES OF SUPERNATURAL HORROR!

WITCHES TALES

TALES BEYOND BELIEF AND IMAGINATION!

TOMB OF TERROR

STRANGEST TALES OF FEAR AND TERROR!

BLACK CAT MYSTERY

Exclusively for your collection...
300 limited edition slipcased copies.

Buy the whole run of **WITCHES TALES** slipcased editions and,
when all the books are stacked alongside each other,
you'll also get this wonderful bigbigbig illustration of the Devil in all his glory!
All this and it isn't even Hallowe'en! What's that sound out there on the stairs?
And did your bedroom door just start inching itself open?
Have a nice night! Bwah ha ha!

WITCHES TALES slipcased and signed edition available from your
favorite comicbooks emporium (so tell 'em, already . . . tell 'em!) or direct from
www.psartbooks.com or **www.pspublishing.co.uk**

But remember, the slipcased signed edition is limited to just 300 copies.

26 traycased lettered deluxe editions...
...if you really want the best!

And if you really want to treat yourself — which you should do, of course —
then take a look at our lettered (that means there's just 26 copies, alphabet-aficionados)
super-deluxe traycased edition, signed by **Ramsey Campbell** and featuring a putrefying print
of Ramsey courtesy of (and signed by) **Bryan Talbot** produced
on high quality art stock and, once again, with just 26 copies offered for sale.
The case itself is leather-bound with gold blocking to the front and the spine.
Man, it's absolutely *gore*some! And all those folks ordering lettered copies of the
first volume in the series will have first refusal on subsequent volumes.

Please do note that interest in this edition — and in the slipcased version
(though, with 300 copies to go at, it's not quite as urgent) — has been high and it could be that
one or possibly both editions will be sold out when or even before the books arrive from the printer.
So if you're interested then get in touch with us as soon as possible.

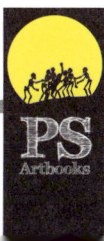

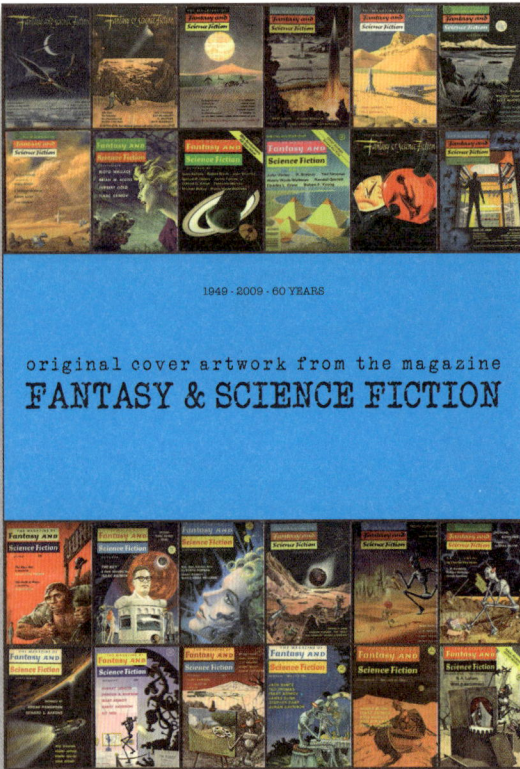

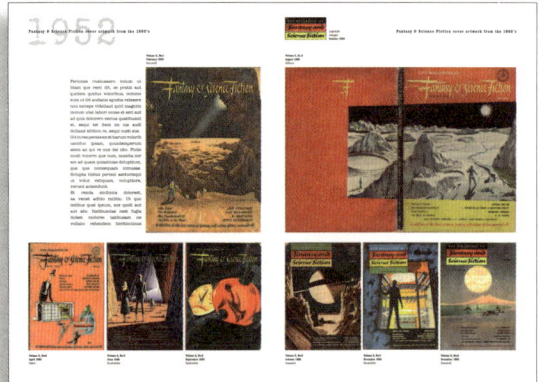

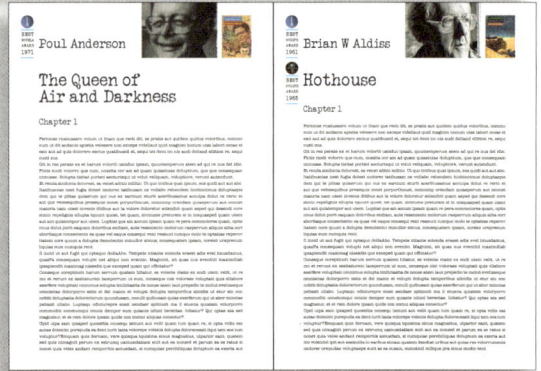

287

Welcome to the funny pages!

Full details and up to the minute news for PS Artbooks,
the Harvey Horrors project and PS Publishing itself can be found exclusively on our websites
www.psartbooks.com, *www.harveyhorrors.com* and *www.pspublishing.co.uk* respectively
but just in case you forget to visit or can't be bothered trying to remember then just sign up
for our regular newsletter by going here: *www.pspublishing.co.uk/list*.

It doesn't cost you anything and it's the only sure way of making sure
you keep up to speed with what we're doing.
Plus it can often result in your receiving free books.

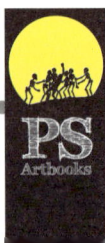

AND FINALLY...

Order any **PS Artbooks** title from
www.pspublishing.co.uk and receive **10% OFF** and
FREE SHIPPING WORLDWIDE by entering the code below
when you go through the checkout process...

WT004

HARVEY